DECEITS OF TIME

DECEITS OF TIME

Isabel Colegate

VIKING

VIKING
Published by the Penguin Group
Viking Penguin Inc., 40 West 23rd Street,
New York, New York 10010, U.S.A.
Penguin Books Ltd, 27 Wrights Lane,
London W8 5TZ, England
Penguin Books Australia Ltd, Ringwood,
Victoria, Australia
Penguin Books Canada Ltd, 2801 John Street,
Markham, Ontario, Canada L3R 1B4
Penguin Books (N.Z.) Ltd, 182–190 Wairau Road,
Auckland 10, New Zealand

Penguin Books Ltd, Registered Offices:
Harmondsworth, Middlesex, England

First American Edition
Published in 1988 by Viking Penguin Inc.

10 9 8 7 6 5 4 3 2 1

Some of this book was written at the
Hawthornden Castle International Retreat,
and the author would like to express her
gratitude to the Director and the Administrator.

Grateful acknowledgment is made to
Charles Sisson and Carcanet Press Limited
for permission to reprint an excerpt from
Mr. Sisson's "The Night Ferry."

LIBRARY OF CONGRESS CATALOGING IN PUBLICATION DATA
Colegate, Isabel.
Deceits of time.
I. Title.
PR6053.0414D44 1988   823'.914   87-40635
ISBN 0-670-82400-3

Printed in the United States of America by
Arcata Graphics, Fairfield, Pennsylvania

NIGHT FERRY

The turning and deceits of time
Do not allow to catch full face
Even the face of agony
But all is lost and wrought to nought
In those evading corridors

Love is the light by which we see
The heart can hardly hold it still

C. H. Sisson

DECEITS OF TIME

What it all hung upon really was a dash through the darkness many years ago, a wartime drive to the north whose destination was not known and might never be known because the driver was now dead; and upon that came to hang a number of theories, and with those theories certain people identified themselves so closely that they felt threatened when the correctness of the theories was questioned and their behaviour became in some cases distinctly odd. Catherine Hillery, who considered herself to have entered into the thing in all innocence, came to wish she had never allowed herself to become involved. She also considered herself to have remained totally detached and calm, but in this she was mistaken.

* * *

She had met him once. She had heard him make a speech, and had stood in a line of other girls in nurses' uniforms and had shaken his hand. She had looked briefly into those bright blue eyes whose direct gaze seemed to belie the deprecatory smile, the murmured greeting, the implication in his manner that all this was an absurdity, a private joke the two of them shared. The manner was all modesty; the eyes said, bow down, it is my due. It had puzzled her that this heavy-footed, sandy-haired man – his aspect untidy, vaguely donnish, at the same time physically powerful – should so clearly expect so much attention.

7

He was more than the visiting man of importance sustaining morale among the loyal staff. The direct gaze into each pair of eyes as he shook hands along the waiting line was like an annunciation; they had not been led to expect an archangel. The girls afterwards said, 'Who would have thought the Nightmare would have had such a charming brother?' Catherine had thought him more formidable than charming but had not bothered to say so.

*　　*　　*

You had to be able to believe that as far as daily life was concerned there was a kind of norm which was pleasant. You didn't expect to be always, or even perhaps very often, at that norm yourself, but it was when you began to believe that the norm was disagreeable that the trouble started. She had had trouble certainly and did not wish to repeat it, had learned perhaps to avoid it. I am on a plateau, Catherine Hillery thought, a plain, a perfectly pleasant plain, asking the newsagent at the end of the street for a *Times* in exchange for the *Guardian* wrongly delivered. The young woman at the counter effected the exchange with a cross look but her irritation was not for Catherine but for her own elderly father who made the deliveries every morning on his bicycle and was haphazard in his choice of recipients, some of whom had not ordered a paper at all and therefore were unlikely to pay for the unexpected and unattributable delivery. People were transferring their custom, the daughter noticed, to the Asians round the corner; and who could blame them? Mrs Hillery had been a customer for goodness knew how many years, wouldn't you have thought the old man could have remembered she'd always taken *The Times*?

A woman with untidy hair and an anxious intelligent face was buying a copy of the *Guardian* at the very moment Catherine was returning hers; they exchanged uneasy glances. Catherine thought, she despises me because she thinks I buy *The Times* to see whether my friends' children are marrying into the peerage, and she is afraid I despise her for buying the *Guardian* so that she can think of herself as a left-wing intellectual; but neither of those things is true because I am not quite what I look, and walking back down the street towards her own house she thought what pleasure it gave her to be in, but not quite of, England. She had lived there for forty years, and in Chelsea for thirty of those years, but she was Irish and, for all that she had been born into the Protestant Ascendancy, her childhood had been spent beneath treacherous skies; she was not what her late husband Bernard Hillery would have called sound. Clearly however the Trustees of the Campion Estate had taken her to be so. They had used the very word.

'We want someone conscientious and unprejudiced, someone sound,' the solicitor had said. 'Someone who won't get carried away by crazy theories.'

Catherine had nodded thoughtfully. She had not been very well briefed by her publisher, and had only the vaguest of ideas as to what crazy theories might be likely to suggest themselves.

'I think I ought to go away and do some preliminary reading,' she had said. 'And then come back to you. I'm not very well up in the politics of the period.'

'Much of it you'd remember of course,' Mr Pottinger had suggested.

'One so often remembers wrong.'

'Exactly,' he had said, looking pleased. 'Exactly.'

She wondered now to what extent remembering wrong meant being altogether wrong, being false in your notion of yourself, as well as of everything else? She would have sworn Neil Campion's sister had not been there the day he came to visit the convalescent home in which Catherine herself was working as a VAD in the second year of the war; but the photograph she found in the press-cuttings book his wife had kept showed the sister, Eleanor Campion, who was Commandant of the nursing home, standing beside him as he talked to a group of nurses

9

and a patient leaning on a stick. She had remembered wrong. And who was the pleasant-faced girl standing beside the Commandant in the photograph? She remembered one of them, Melanie Farmer, so easily reduced to giggles by the men and to tears by Sister; but the other seemed a complete stranger. Was it someone she had once known well, shared a room with? Had there been someone called – wait a minute – Ruth? Naomi? Catherine had always thought she had a good memory. She rarely had difficulty with names or dates. When she was doing the research for her last biography, which was about Pamela, the supposed daughter of Madame de Genlis and Philippe Egalité, later Duc d'Orléans, she had taken copious notes, but had not had to refer to them as often as she had expected to; the writing of them had been enough to imprint most of the facts on her memory. Yet she had forgotten Naomi – or was it Ruth? – and had been sure that Eleanor Campion had been away when her brother came to the convalescent home. Other people would have recollections of that day which would probably be quite different from hers. Which of those differences mattered? Which were distorting? Which came merely from diverse preoccupations? And, if everyone's memories of an event were different, what could be said to have actually happened? And was what most people thought had happened thereby made into what had happened? And was the actual reality, where it was ascertainable, more, or merely equally, or even less, significant than the generally supposed reality?

These questions, each of which seemed as soon as she had formulated it to give rise to another, circulated in her mind with some insistence as she walked down the street and let herself in to her house; a flake of faded yellow paint fell onto the doormat, reminding her of her intermittently held resolve to repaint the front door before it got so bad that she felt obliged to call in a professional. So much of her own idea of herself was made up of memory. What was she if she was not what she remembered? She was not simply, she was not really, a reasonably pleasant-looking woman in her late fifties walking into her agreeably cluttered sitting-room in Chelsea. Perfectly present in her memory was the feeling of bouncing up and down in her pram under the big cedar tree in front of the plain grey Irish house, the restraining straps of the harness on her shoulders in no way detracting from the pleasure of the springy movement or from the free harmonious feeling in so bouncing up and down in the sweet dove-sounding air towards the blue sky beyond the deep green of the cedar or towards the lighter but still bright green of the mown grass of the lawn. The memory was part of her, as were all the other clear recollections which might float into her consciousness at any moment, as if there were some constant and incomprehensible flux in which she and time were endlessly circling each other.

Re-opening the book of press-cuttings which lay on the sofa where she had left it the previous evening, she looked again at the photograph of the group in the garden of the convalescent home. She was not in it herself, had probably been keeping out of sight, avoiding Miss Campion's critical eye, but she remembered the final line-up to shake hands; she had been there then. Curiosity made her now go over to her desk, the oak bureau she had had ever since, as the eldest of the family of four girls, she had been given a room of her own, more grown-up than the others, with her own desk and the armchair with a loose spring which was now upstairs in her bedroom, its spring still loose but its cover replaced. Kneeling on the floor in front of the desk she pulled out the bottom drawer and searched through a muddle of old photographs to find one of herself at eighteen, a studio photograph taken in London at the beginning of the War. Her mother had wanted new photographs of them all at that time; had she thought they would be killed in the Blitz? But this pretty girl with her smooth skin and shining eyes which expressed a compound of wariness and wild hope seemed nothing much to do with her. She was Mrs Hillery, the straight-speaking, free-thinking widow of a professional man. She had two grown-up sons and three biographies to her credit; she had a pleasant little house whose rooms revealed her interests and her pleasures, and a calm demeanour which spoke of her victory over doubt. The girl, knowing nothing of all this, gave no hint of it; she looked a silly creature, Catherine decided; indeed, now that she came to think of it, that was just what she had been; no wonder Miss Campion had had to reprimand her, no wonder she had so clearly, after all these years, forgotten her. It would be better, Catherine decided, to put her one personal encounter with the subject of the biography she was about to write on one side for the time being. The moment might come when the recollection of it might give her a clue she needed; indeed, it might be useful at some stage to think of the sister again, the Commandant, and to remember what had been said one hot dramatic day in 1941. For the moment it seemed better to turn back to the press-cuttings.

There were several volumes of them, bound in faded blue cloth-covered board and neatly annotated and captioned in the large impatient hand of Euphemia Campion, Neil's widow. They began in 1933, only two months after the wedding, when Neil was thirty-two and Euphemia, or Effie as she was more generally known, ten years younger. Later came several pages annotated in another hand; perhaps a secretary had taken over while Effie concentrated on Hector, their only child, born a year after the wedding. There were columns of Parliamentary reports; Neil Campion had been a Member of Parliament from 1929 until his death more than ten years later. There were visits to his constituency, addresses to local bodies, letters to *The Times*, the occasional article on some political issue or on the development of air travel – he had been a First World War flyer. The early volumes seemed a dull enough collection, Catherine thought; there was nothing to show that he had been other than a fairly conventional Conservative Member of Parliament of the time, belonging to no particular faction, loyal to his leaders, interested in the Colonies, in flying and in foreign affairs, where he spoke as someone who had fought in the First World War and opposed any policy which might lead to a second. His views were well-expressed; one later discredited opinion after another presented itself in the yellowed cuttings as the voice of reason.

She turned to the small black engagement diaries which Mr Pottinger had given her at the same time as the books of press-cuttings. The entries were brief, often hard to decipher. 'Lunch PL. Meeting FA Committee, weekend constit, Eff's b-day, conference . . .' The only thing that struck her as mildly surprising was the number of long weekends which seemed to be covered by the one word 'Conference'. Once or twice the entry was, 'Conference, Durdans'; once 'Conference, Germany'. Otherwise there was no indication as to who was conferring or what about or where. There would be time enough to find out. Obviously the first person to see would be the widow, who had what Mr Pottinger had called 'the bulk of the papers', but Catherine wanted to do some more background research before approaching her. Neil Campion was likely to be mentioned in memoirs of the inter-war period; he would also feature in the history of the Royal Flying Corps. Her curiosity was not yet aroused. She expected that it would be, in due course, because after all everyone was interesting in a way and up to a point. In the meantime there was the routine of research, the pleasantness of being paid.

*　*　*

Fifteen feet above the ground, his back against the firm trunk of a beech tree, Sam Campion crouched down to put his hands on either side of the branch on which he stood and slowly slid himself forwards until he was lying face downwards on the branch, swaying slightly as the May wind hustled through the wood. Two identical round faces looked up at him with mild concern.

'I am a puma,' he said.

'Do be careful,' said Pat.

'You'll fall,' said Prue.

'Pumas must have uncomfortable lives. Or they're fatter than me.' He rolled over, holding onto the branch and crossing his ankles so that he hung suspended. 'I'm a sloth.'

'That's true,' said Pat. She turned away and dug in the pocket of her long shapeless cardigan, which was made of thick white Arran wool and not at all clean, to find a packet of cigarettes and a lighter in the shape of a naked woman.

'Lazy? No one could call me lazy.'

'Anderson did yesterday,' said Pat, cupping her hands round the lighter and leaning over so that the action of lighting the cigarette was enshrouded in a canopy of thick red-gold hair.

'Anderson's a stupid old fart,' said Prue.

'Fuck, I've frizzled my hair again. God, I hate the smell.'

Sam uncrossed his ankles, clung onto the branch for a moment with his feet, then let go hands and feet together and fell heavily onto his back beneath the tree. He rolled over, coughing.

'Jesus Christ,' said Pat. 'Are you all right?'

'You never hurt yourself when you're drunk,' said Sam, speaking into the forest floor.

'Course you do,' said Pat.

'You fall like a baby,' said Sam. 'It's well known.'

He raised himself onto hands and knees and crawled over to the foot of the tree, where he settled himself in a sitting position with his back against the trunk and asked for a cigarette. The girls came and sat on either side of him, stretching their long thin legs in front of them. They wore very short tight skirts and large drooping jerseys almost as long as the skirts; they were identical twins whose Quaker parents had christened them Patience and Prudence. They had just shared a bottle of vodka

14

with Sam, but because they did not much care for the taste they had let him drink most of it.

The beechwood clothed a steep escarpment which extended in a wide curve along one side of a river valley. Below it was the house, whose gardens bordered the river until they met the belt of woodland which, following the descent of the downs, came to the edge of the river and spread along both sides of the valley for some miles. The boy Sam, looking down through the trees towards the considerable spread of buildings which comprised the house, the stable courtyard, the two adjoining cottages and the low wing of workshops and extra classrooms which had been added when the school increased its numbers in the 1950s, saw them with his own priorities in mind. Each angle, apex, gulley, gutter, of the complex roofing system was familiar to him; this was his kingdom. He knew where to find shelter whichever direction the wind might take, he knew the flattest, most hidden places for sunbathing, he knew where on a frosty night blankets could be pulled through a skylight or where with your back against a chimney stack you could look across the river and over the nearby village as far as the church tower of the market town ten miles away. He knew better than any maintenance man which piece of balustrade was insecure, which slates needed mending and might slip, which chimney stack needed re-pointing and might allow loose pieces of old cement to break away and rattle down the tiles just at the moment when a head had appeared below and a voice was saying, 'Why is this window open? Is someone out there?' He knew which leaden platforms took the full sun all day so that in summer they could burn the soles of bare feet, he knew which drainpipes sheltered noisy families of starlings summer after summer, and which north-facing eaves produced in winter icicles so thick they were impossible to break, though others nearby might be snapped off and lanced into the air like javelins to fall and shatter hundreds of feet below; he knew where the workmen, father and son, who had built the stone balustrade, had written their names in the

wet cement, 'John Marley August 1889 James Marley Son'.
They were his predecessors, pioneers in his kingdom, who must
have felt the summer sun there and looked across the river and
the water meadows and the village to the distant church tower
and the still more distant downs. They, unlike Sam, would have
gone home at night. Sam only slept in the crowded dormitories
below on the coldest of winter nights. His usual sleeping place
was in a gulley between the two main peaks of the roof; he had
a mattress and a sleeping bag up there, and a ramshackle
arrangement by which he could prop an umbrella over his head
if it looked like rain. Once he had woken to find the sleeping
bag lightly covered with snow; the slopes of the roof on either
side of him were white, the silence absolute; he broke it with
his delighted laughter.

The roof bore scattered evidence of his habitation; he was
not a tidy boy. Empty cigarette packets and stubs of candles
were to be found in odd corners; cushions which had split their
stuffing from covers which the weather had rotted were plun-
dered by nesting birds; a flowered bedspread spotted with
candle wax and wine stains was a relic of his last birthday party
when he had entertained five friends to a midnight feast. An
ancient portable gramophone with a handle had been abandoned as being too much of a bore to carry down again; a few
78 records bought in a local junk shop were still beside it. A
pornographic magazine, some odd playing cards and a paperback copy of Camus' *The Outsider* were lodged in various
gutters, and a number of sticks of ash and willow, stripped of
their bark and sharpened to a point with a knife, were scattered
here and there, signs of his having passed that way. The initials
S. C., another sign, were scratched on a chimney pot on the
highest of the stone stacks. There was not much of his chosen
territory which in the three years of his possession of it he had
not subtly marked. If the builder who had been up there once
or twice during that time to look for the source of a leak or
replace a tile had wondered at the signs, he had said nothing to

the authorities. Even the empty beer cans and the black T-shirt with a picture of Mick Jagger's mouth on it had probably done no more than confirm his suspicions; it was generally said in the village that the boys and girls at the Durdans were allowed to run wild.

Looking down on the house and its attendant buildings from the hillside above, Sam was too far away to see the details of the roof's complexities, or of his own territorial markings. He felt a kind of homesickness, a longing to be where he was at the same time most himself and most free of himself, an intense regret. The effort of getting to his feet, going down the long hill, avoiding whoever might put some obstacle – a maths lesson or something of that kind – in his way, then pulling himself by his arms up to the skylight and out onto the roof, that effort seemed for the moment quite beyond him. His head ached, not badly but uncomfortably; so did the back of his neck where he must have jarred himself when he fell from the branch of the beech tree. Always pale, he had now become apparently translucent; leaning his head against the tree trunk he tried to imagine himself lying flat on his back on the warm lead, absorbed into the sky.

A group of five, two boys and three girls, came running downhill through the trees, jumping fallen branches, the boys laughing in a loud uncontrolled sort of way and one of the girls saying in a high breathless voice, 'Oh no, oh no.' Seeing the three sitting at the foot of the tree a small fat girl wearing jeans and a huge yellow hair-ribbon called out to them as she passed, 'Milly Molly Mandy. He's on the warpath.'

The three watched the other group's descent in silence.

'Milly!' said Sam eventually in a tone of disgust.

'On the warpath!' said Prue. 'As if he ever is.'

Down the green ride between the beech trees came Mr Manderson the history master, wearing as was his wont the swinging red cloak to which he was entitled as an alumnus of St Andrew's University. He had long curly brown hair, restrained at the back by an elastic band, and a short well-tended beard; he was accompanied by Mr Roberts the new English master who wore glasses and a tweed jacket. Flushed out by their approach, another couple started up from behind a tree and ran diagonally across the path, the boy dashing ahead and the girl, who had long dark hair and wore a flowered dress which came down to the ground, following him with tiny footsteps, giving out small flurries of nervous laughter. Sam and the twins, perfectly visible from the path, turned faces of impenetrable calm towards the two schoolmasters. Mr Manderson, affecting not to see them, at the same time raised a hand in what could have been taken to be some kind of salutation. Mr Roberts hesitated a moment, then as if swept along in the current created by the swirl of Mr Manderson's red cloak quickly followed him.

'It looked to me as though they were smoking,' he said as he caught up. Mr Manderson said nothing.

'Aren't they meant to be having lessons?' said Mr Roberts.

Mr Manderson inhaled deeply of the air of spring.

'I had rather the woods were filled with laughing nymphs and shepherds than that those young heads were stuffed with barren facts. Wouldn't you?'

'I'm not sure,' said Mr Roberts feebly.

'If you are not sure,' said Mr Manderson solemnly. 'It may be there is no place for you at the Durdans.'

He gave a sudden shout of laughter and putting his hand firmly upon the other's shoulder he propelled him briskly down the hill, continuing to laugh heartily.

Hearing his laughter fading down the hill Prue beside the beech tree said wearily, 'Ha ha ha ha.'

'What's he laughing at?' asked Pat.

'Us.'

'Why?'

'He hates us. Let's go. It's getting cold.'

'Sam's gone to sleep.' Pat moved her shoulder, onto which

Sam's head had fallen. He did not wake. She lowered his head gently to the ground. 'What shall we do?'

Prue leant over to look at him more closely.

'Pissed,' she pronounced.

She took off her long white cardigan and spread it carefully over him. Pat pulled her big blue jersey over her head and spread it on top of the cardigan. Then she took off her shirt, revealing an off-white singlet or running vest underneath it. She rolled up the shirt and, lifting Sam's head by means of a handful of his dark hair, she slipped it under his cheek as a pillow. They stood side by side and looked down at him, emaciated little figures without their protective wrappings, only their shoulders shrouded in their thick fair hair; then they turned and walked sedately down the hill, stepping out from the wood side by side and solemn, like refugees coming to a country whose language they did not expect to understand. Under the beech tree Sam, who had not been asleep, settled himself more comfortably under his coverings and began to tell himself a story about flying.

*   *   *

Alfred Madden sat at a table in the reading room of the London Library and slowly turned the pages of the *Dictionary of National Biography*. He knew what he was looking for but other entries distracted him; such a variety of individuals, such a multiplicity of connections, all the fine network of concentric circles and linking filigree thrown out by a crowded, complex and to him still in many ways mysterious society. In his working hours he was paid to sniff out the pattern of interconnections among the living; in his spare time he pursued it among the dead.

'Neil Campion,' he read. 'Born 1899, son of – ' Well, he knew all that. Campion had been the son of a Somerset Vicar, had been to Sherborne School, had joined the Royal Flying

Corps in 1917 in time to take part in the Third Battle of Ypres. 'Though not among the leading "aces" of this gruelling campaign, he had a highly creditable record and was twice mentioned in despatches.' Then came East Africa, flying transport planes for a company operating in Kenya, Tanganyika and Rhodesia; his unwillingness to settle down to a career in England, the effect no doubt of the high tension of that brief war career on one so young. A reference to him in a book called *The Diary of a White Hunter* by Reginald Baker (London 1933) as 'a youthful Great War air ace, who spent more time asleep than anyone I have ever known. If there was nothing going on he simply slept, like an animal. A hint of action and he would be suddenly wide awake; the more vigorous, even dangerous, the action the happier he seemed. It was the element of danger he loved in flying, as well as the pure sensation of being in the air, in the wind above that astonishing landscape.' Back to England in 1931 at the age of thirty-two, politics, the search for a constituency, his election as Conservative Member for a Lincolnshire constituency in 1934. Marriage, the Society of this, the Association of that, the growing reputation outside Parliament; Madden knew most of that though he had still some leads to follow up. The party line in politics, supporting his leaders. 'His reputation in Parliament never came to match his reputation with the general public; he was probably not a true House of Commons man. In 1938 however he was made a Junior Minister in the Ministry of Aviation and was an active and efficient lieutenant to the then Secretary of State Sir Kingsley Wood. Outside the House of Commons his concern to revivify English agriculture and rural life and his interest in promoting internationalism, or perhaps more accurately Europeanism, as a means of achieving a world without war brought him into contact with people of a wide variety of views, many of whom put on record the powerful effect on them of his personality. It may well be that had he survived he might have been at the forefront of the move to take Britain into Europe.

As it was it could be said that his vision of his country's role in the world did not sufficiently accord with the views which prevailed at the time for him to have had as much influence as his talents deserved.' Reference to contemporary writers as to those talents, reference to the house parties he and his wife had given, to their links with the Cliveden Set, to his admiration 'amounting almost to hero-worship' for T. E. Lawrence, to his pamphlet on soil erosion, to his efforts to persuade the Government to give more support to the aviation industry, to his early death. Nothing new for Madden. Nevertheless he copied into his notebook in his minuscule handwriting a sentence from the passage about the wartime flying: 'Campion was an individualist rather than part of a team . . . given the choice, he preferred to fly alone.'

*　　*　　*

She had a pleasant face, Hugh Campion thought. At the meeting in the solicitors' office to which he and his sister had been invited in order to meet the proposed official biographer of their brother, he had noticed only that she looked younger than the age ascribed to her and had a gentle voice, in other words that she did not seem intimidating. Now he saw that her face might almost be thought beautiful except that it was so mobile; expressions succeeded each other too quickly, some of them exaggerated, as if by caricaturing her reactions she hoped to disarm her interlocutor, implying silliness. The look of alert enquiry with which she faced him now was modified by the smile with which she seemed to apologise for the admitted absurdity of her sitting there in all seriousness asking him such trivial questions as whether he had ever been a scoutmaster.

'I like to sit in this chair,' he had said, moving slowly across to a hard, straight-backed chair by the window. 'I can't get out of that one. But you sit there, it's quite comfortable. Then we can both see the tree. The tree is my great joy.'

He had been three years younger than his brother Neil and was now eighty-five; he was given to ascribing his longevity to his cheerfulness.

'My religion is a religion of joy,' he would say robustly.

So Catherine, sitting opposite him on the armchair he had indicated, had gazed obediently into the pattern of leaves and branches which more or less filled the view from his window and thought perhaps he was right to concentrate so steadfastly on the sycamore tree; the flat itself was not inspiring. It was on the fifth floor of a Victorian mansion block in North Kensington; on one side it overlooked a busy main road and on the other a strip of unkempt grass where dogs and children from the terraced Edwardian houses beyond relieved themselves or played half-hearted ball games. Following Hugh slowly as he shuffled along the dark passage which led to the sitting-room Catherine had glanced into the only open door they had passed and seen speckled linoleum and a towel horse standing in the bath bearing several pairs of sizeable pants and some sensible grey socks. She wondered whether Hugh's sister Eleanor, with whom he shared the flat, did his washing for him, or whether someone came in to help them, or else whether Hugh's years of bachelor schoolmastering had made him self-sufficient, as meticulous as if he were perpetually at Scout camp.

'Did you run the Scouts?' she asked.

'Cubs,' he said, smiling back with the utmost friendliness. 'Indeed it fell to my lot for many years to bear that responsibility. But they were only Cubs. I was a humble prep school master, no more.'

He twinkled merrily at her, wagging his old head from side to side. She noticed a rim of coffee stain above his upper lip. 'Neil was the high-flyer of the family, not me. Not that he ever had any side, you know, absolutely no side at all, even when he was a very important man.'

'And your other brothers? Were they high-flyers too?'

'Frederick had a very competent brain. He'd have made a good lawyer. That was what he was going to be, a solicitor. We were all sent to Sherborne, all four boys. Frederick was going to be articled to a solicitor who lived in our father's parish; he had a firm in Yeovil, very old-established and reputable. That was what Frederick was going to do. Leonard was going into the regular Army. He was more the man of action, great rugger player, captain of the school team, captain of the school in fact in his last year. Lovely men, both of them, lovely men. Frederick was killed at Gallipoli, Leonard on the Somme. Fine deaths, both of them. They bore witness, those two, they bore witness.'

He beamed at Catherine over his half-moon-shaped glasses, wagging his head again in a gesture more Indian than English.

'They were nineteen and twenty-one, I think?' said Catherine gently.

'Nineteen and twenty-one,' he agreed, ceasing to wag his head but continuing to beam.

'And Neil, of course, only had a year of the War.'

'Neil went into the RFC in 1917, when he was just eighteen. It was his choice. Our father wanted him to follow the others into the Army. But he was always a great individualist, Neil. Not a team man, not a team man at all.'

'Was he a games player, like Leonard?'

'He was an athlete. No team games. Fifteen hundred yards, that sort of thing. The individualist's sport. He won the steeplechase every year he was at school.'

'And you?'

'I was the fat one.' He laughed happily. 'Eleanor and I, we were the young ones. We missed the War. I went to Cambridge and became a prep school master. Eleanor looked after our mother until her death and then she started her own school, without any formal training; made a great success of it. She's a very able woman, my sister Eleanor, very able indeed.'

'And after the War, when Neil went to Africa, you didn't

hear from him much, I think you said. Brothers don't write to each other, do they? I know my two sons never do.'

'He wrote to my parents, I'm sure of that, but where those letters are I've no idea. You might find them among the things Eleanor's got. She's got all the things that were left in our parents' house after our mother died, though what she kept and what she threw away I've no idea.'

He was silent. His face, suddenly emptied of expression, fell as if from habit into lines of deep sadness, where it stayed as if resting from joviality. Catherine waited. After a minute or two he stirred and, his glance happening to fall on the book lying on the table by the side of the sofa, he said as if peacefully waking from a refreshing sleep, 'Lovely book.' He reached out to touch it with his thin blue-veined hand, whose joints were knotted with arthritis, '*Perfume from Provence*. I do recommend it. A real joy. Winifred, Lady Fortescue. She must have been a lovely person. Do you know it at all?'

'I did read it once, yes,' said Catherine. 'I enjoyed it very much. Tell me, why do you think Neil went to Africa after the War?'

The sadness, dispelled by the thought of the lavender-scented days he had shared in his imagination with Winifred, Lady Fortescue, crept back into his face. He looked determinedly into the sycamore tree.

'He went because he wanted to go on flying. He came back when he felt the time had come to make his contribution to political life. That was it, I think. And then of course, once he was back in England, we were in touch again.'

'Did you see much of him at that time?'

'Well, not see him so much. But we were in touch.'

For a moment Catherine thought there must be a dog in the flat. She knew what sort it was too; there had been one living at number five Markham Street when she and Bernard were first married and lived at number ten. It used to bounce down the steps as she passed, giving one short sharp aggressive bark in just that way, followed by its similarly stumpy grey bewhiskered mistress. But, when she turned slightly apprehensively away from the view of the sycamore tree towards the darker recesses of the sitting-room where the door from the passage had opened, there was no bristling schnauzer dog but the stately Eleanor, Hugh Campion's younger sister, the former headmistress and Commandant of the wartime nursing home, aged eighty-one. She had laughed.

'Ah, Eleanor,' said Hugh uneasily.

Eleanor bore down upon Catherine, holding out her hand. Catherine rose to her feet to take it.

'I had no idea you were coming so early,' said Miss Campion. 'I should have left my meeting sooner. Has Hugh not offered you tea?'

'I won't have anything, thank you so much,' said Catherine, fighting the impulse to regress into a nineteen-year-old student nurse. 'We were just talking generally about your brother. It's so helpful to me now that I'm beginning to collect the facts.'

'Hugh's too optimistic. He looks on the bright side. He's probably told you so.'

'Not exactly. But I noticed something of the kind. I like it very much.'

'Oh, but we all do.'

Eleanor Campion was taller than her brother, and in old age had become not so much fat as tremendously solid. Her feet, bulging from old-fashioned strapped shoes which looked too small, were swollen with the effort of carrying so much weight; her ankle bones were not to be discerned. She wore an outfit of crêpe de chine in an abstract pattern of navy blue and white, with a loose bow at the neck, and a hat of shiny navy blue straw with a pearl hat-pin stuck into the back of it; her fine white hair, which Catherine had previously observed to be rather thin on top (perhaps from a lifetime of wearing hats, she now wondered), escaped in stray wisps on both sides of her face, giving her, in combination with her slightly rolling gait, an aspect of careless energy, even enthusiasm. Her face, high-cheek-boned and excessively wrinkled, had still a kind of handsomeness; her eyes, now somewhat sunken, disclosed themselves when opened wide before the obvious, as they were in response to Catherine's favourable comment on Hugh's optimism, as piercingly blue. Catherine remembered those eyes.

'We all admire the way he thinks the best of people. Of course we do. But you are presumably after the truth.'

Eleanor Campion hooked one swollen foot round the leg of a rush-seated chair which stood against the wall on the opposite side of the room from its pair, both clearly ready for duty should the brother and sister decide to eat at the oak gate-legged table which was awkwardly postioned with one flap up, the other down, against the wall closest to the door leading to the passage and the kitchen. She pulled her skirt up over her thighs and went down heavily onto the chair, which creaked but stood firm. She further shortened her skirt by sliding it up the front of her thighs with both hands until her pink elasticated knicker-legs, which came down nearly as far as her knees, were clearly visible from the rather lower armchair in which Catherine sat; then she rested one hand firmly upon each knee and looked at Catherine.

'Well?' The blue eyes opened wide again. 'You are after the truth, aren't you?'

'Of course. That's to say I'd like to end up by describing a character that would be recognisable to people who knew him as well as recording accurately the facts and dates and so on. I don't know that one can get any nearer than that.'

'What would be nearer than that?'

'I only meant – I suppose there's a more intimate kind of biography. I haven't any ambitions in that direction. I don't think that's what you want, anyway.'

'Certainly not. There's a great deal too much intimacy about these days. But if you want facts, apart from facts about his childhood, you should go elsewhere. That's why I laughed when

I heard Hugh saying he'd been in touch after Neil came back from Africa. We weren't in touch. We never saw him. He had no time for us after he married that woman.'

'It was a great thing for him, that marriage,' Hugh put in eagerly. 'A wonderful thing. So many people had wanted to marry her, you know. And then she was so beautiful. So beautiful.'

'Have you been to see her?' asked Eleanor.

'Not yet, no. I met her of course, when I came to see you all a week or two ago.'

'You'll have to go and talk to her. We're joint Trustees with her of the Campion Estate, because that was how it was left. We don't know why he left it like that. It may have been because he'd had time to see she was completely brainless. It may have been because of the boy, their only son, Hector, who was young then. Neil wanted him to go to school at the Durdans, which was only just starting. He may have thought he could rely on us to see that that happened. I think it was because of the boy that he made us Trustees.'

'Hector was only ten, wasn't he, when his father died?'

'Ten, yes. He went to the Durdans and was very happy there, then to Cambridge and then into the Diplomatic Corps. He was killed with his wife in a plane crash in South America, when he was First Secretary in Lima.'

'Excellent boy, Hector,' said Hugh. 'Most able. Delightful wife. Such a sad thing.'

'They left a very nervy little boy, Sam,' said Eleanor. 'You'll see him no doubt if you go to see Effie. Though he may be away at school. He's gone to the Durdans now. Perhaps they can do something with him, though I've heard it's not what it was, that school. Anyway that's the thing. You'll have to go and see Effie.'

'It's her idea anyway, this book,' said Hugh. 'Hers and her solicitor's. Not our idea at all. All so long ago and so on. Ideas change anyway, opinions and so on. People think one thing then they think another. Who knows? Politics and so on.'

Eleanor said sharply, 'Hugh! You're maundering.'

Hugh suddenly sat up straight and gripped both arms of his chair.

'I may be maundering but I'll tell you this. I'll tell you this, Mrs Hillingdon. Whatever Neil may have done, he always played a straight bat. Don't let anyone tell you different. He always played a straight bat.'

'Hugh, Hugh, Hugh.' Eleanor spoke soothingly on a descending scale. 'You've had enough for today, I can see that.' She heaved herself to her feet and smiled at Catherine with surprising sweetness. 'You must forgive us. We're a pair of old sillies, too old to be of any use to you. There are plenty of other people who can tell you everything you want to know.'

Catherine rose to her feet, thanking them, apologising if she had tired them, saying they'd been most helpful. Hugh still seemed rather flustered but held her hand in both of his to say goodbye and added that he was glad, so glad, that it was she who was writing the book. Eleanor's blue eyes as she shook hands had regained their immeasurable coldness.

*　　*　　*

The village was in Somerset, and the large late-Georgian vicarage stood between the church and a manor house which looked Elizabethan and was now open to the public. Catherine parked her car near the church and walked slowly past the vicarage, which was clearly occupied, and on towards the gates of the big house.

She liked to visit the places where the people she wrote about had lived. She had spent a happy week in Paris in pursuit of Madame de Genlis when she had been writing about la belle Pamela, and had been to the places in Ireland where Pamela had spent her days with the wild Lord Edward Fitzgerald. She found it helped her towards some kind of idea of what her subjects might have been like at whatever stage of their lives she could have seen them there, had she been their contemporary. She had as yet very little idea of what Neil Campion might have been like, and she was still puzzled as to why Brackenbury should have put her forward as his biographer. It was not as if Brackenbury owed her anything, or even as far as she knew particularly liked her. Their relationship was businesslike and intermittent. She had taken the idea for her first book – it had been a life of the Brontës for older children, a subject suggested to her by her son Tom's English master, who she realised long afterwards had probably hoped some kind of friendship, possibly sentimental, might have followed – to an agent who was the brother-in-law of one of her husband Bernard's civil service colleagues, and the agent had approached Brackenbury, and that was that; a modest connection had begun. She worked slowly, especially in the early years when the children were younger, and the occasions for encounters with her publisher were few. Brackenbury knew Sir Edward Pottinger, Effie Campion's solicitor; it had emerged that they were fellow members of the Garrick Club. No doubt it had arisen quite naturally that Pottinger should speak to Brackenbury about the proposed biography, should ask him if he would be interested in publishing it, and if so if he would suggest an author; but why Catherine Hillery? Could they have specified that the biographer should be female, Irish, and totally ignorant of politics and most other things? It seemed unlikely.

Catherine paused at the War Memorial, a stone cross on the village green. The names of the Campion brothers, Frederick and Leonard, were there. There were two other pairs of brothers among the twenty-three names, or at least it was to be presumed, since they had the same name, that they were brothers. One name appeared three times. Neil might have expected to be the third Campion to die. If the war had not ended when it did, he probably would have been. Decimated villages, Catherine thought, all over Europe; what did that do to us all, have we any idea? How were things in Athens after the Peloponnesian Wars? I am a very ignorant woman, she thought, but need money and like organising facts: I will not look the Campion gift horse in the mouth.

Suddenly she remembered that she and Bernard had once stayed at the Hope and Anchor. There it was, on the other side of the green from the church. They had stayed there about ten years ago on their way to see Tom and Susannah who for their first holiday after Mark was born had taken a house in Cornwall. Bernard was dead, had died in a hospital in London, quietly, she had thought willingly; he had also walked out of the Hope and Anchor in this village, feeling in his pockets to see he had not forgotten his glasses, complaining of the bill.

'Did you have a good look round the room? Make sure we hadn't left anything? Have you got the map?' Her answer, in the affirmative, had implied that he shouldn't fuss. His answer, which she could not remember, had implied that she should not criticise him for fussing because he always fussed, and she should love him for being as he was. She resented this view. He resented what he felt was her failure to support him. Later there had been disagreeableness about map-reading. She had said, 'We are grandparents, Bernard. We're too old to quarrel.'

'I am not quarrelling,' he had said. 'I am trying to find the way to this absurd cottage.'

She had defended the cottage. He had said, 'You're making excuses for it because it's Tom's cottage. You wouldn't make excuses for my cottage if I had a cottage.'

'I'm only saying it's not absurd. If you had a cottage you presumably wouldn't think it absurd.'

'Someone else might. And you wouldn't defend it, that's all I'm saying.'

'No one would say it was absurd. The person who says things are absurd is you.'

'Absolute nonsense. You're always criticising. You criticise everything I do.'

'No, Bernard, oh no.'

Oh no. What had happened? She had come calmly to an unknown village, thinking about a stranger; and suddenly the place was known, with the familiarity of recurring dream. But she did not want that dream, it was a falsification, a bad morning out of a lifetime of content, for she had been happy, married to Bernard, of course she had. Turning her back on the inn, so much smarter now than when they had stayed there, she walked towards the gate of the big house, and with a certain firmness, as of one who has been a Justice of the Peace for many years, bought a ticket. She was not a Justice of the Peace, but she had a manner which came from pretending to herself that she was, and it was a manner she found useful when assailed by feelings of inadequacy and doubt.

The short drive which led from the tall entrance gates to the front of the house was overgrown with weeds and the house itself gave an immediate impression of not belonging to the National Trust; the paintwork on the window frames was in need of repair, and there was an unsightly hen-coop on the lawn in which could be seen white bantams with feathery legs; more strangely there was a life-size wooden figure of a turbanned Indian in a red coat, such as may sometimes be seen outside Indian restaurants, standing outside the stone porch holding a cardboard notice on which was written 'Open Today 2 p.m–5 p.m.' Inside the cool stone-flagged hall Catherine bought a descriptive leaflet from a sadly proper lady of housekeeperly aspect who was sitting at a table with nothing at all to occupy her. There seemed to be no other visitors to the house. Catherine felt as if she might have interrupted the housekeeperly lady in some kind of plaintive soliloquy which she was only waiting for Catherine's progress into the library, the yellow drawing-room, the morning room, the dining-room and the late Honourable Mrs Fox Farmiloe's boudoir, to begin again.

Catherine sat nonetheless on a low oak window-seat in the hall and read the leaflet, from which it appeared that the Fox Farmiloe family, from its origins in some piratical past, had risen to eminence in the nineteenth century and had produced two Lord Chancellors, grandfather and grandson, in the last of whose day the Victorian addition had been built. It housed the yellow drawing-room and gave onto a stately garden terrace with a balustrade and urns of Italian origin, from which Catherine now saw as she followed the leaflet's itinerary through the library into the Victorian part of the house unexpected cornucopias of lobelias and nasturtiums tumbled; the terrace had been more or less taken over by the grass which had sprouted between its flagstones. Catherine wandered alone through the pleasant dusty rooms, observing the odd mixture between charming old furniture, good though dirty Victorian pictures, and more recent additions such as a collection of china animals, bowls of painted fir-cones, an outsize television set in the morning-room with a very ugly chair with an adjustable back placed before it, both separated by a rope from the path through the room to which visitors were clearly expected to confine themselves and with a sign beside them reading 'Captain Fox Farmiloe's patent television chair'. Referring to her leaflet Catherine read that the family had 'suffered financial reverses during the Great Slump in the 1930s and subsequently lost their only son and heir in 1944 when he gave his life for his country as a gallant submariner in the Pacific. After the War the house was briefly let as an old people's home, but in 1969 on his retirement from the Navy the present owner Arthur Fox Farmiloe, a cousin of the late lamented submariner, took over the management of the estate, opened the house to the public, and saved from extinction many of the ancient British breeds of bantam.'

'Bantams!' said Catherine aloud, taken by surprise.

Confirming her suspicions, she looked back at the beginning

of the leaflet and read that its author was Captain Arthur Fox Farmiloe R. N. Retd.

'Bantams,' she said again, amused.

'What, are you a fancier then? Don't say you're a fellow fancier!' She had not seen him, in the little corner room beyond the morning-room, the room which the leaflet referred to as the late Honourable Mrs Fox Farmiloe's boudoir, and into which he had most probably just come through the open french window from the garden. He was a fattish elderly man wearing a blue jersey and carrying a white bucket full of chicken feed; he had a red face and white bushy eyebrows and was so clearly a retired naval man that she could only assume he must be Captain Arthur Fox Farmiloe R. N. Retd. himself.

'Do let me show you what we've got. We've probably got one or two spares if you're interested. Or swops. Always interested in a swop.'

'I'm so sorry, I'm afraid I'm not an expert at all. It was just that I liked the idea of it, I mean the lost breeds being saved. I live in London so I couldn't keep bantams anyway.'

'What a shame. Now isn't that a shame. Nothing we like better than showing off our collection. Too bad. Staying locally then, are you?'

Catherine answered evasively and turned the conversation towards the house, and its contents, and the garden, upon all of which and their attendant, mainly financial, problems he expanded so confidingly that she concluded first that he was short of people to talk to and then that there would be no harm in telling him of her interest in the family of the former Vicar.

'I remember Campion,' he said. 'Great supporter of the aviation industry before the War. Killed in a car crash or something wasn't he? I'd no idea he came from here. Before my day, of course.'

'Did you ever meet him?'

'No, no, the family'd gone by the time I came on the scene. Vicarage sold, it's flats now; there's a frightful modern box of a vicarage hidden behind a hedge at the bottom of the garden. You want to ask Aunt Margaret; she might remember.'

'I wonder if I could. Where would I find her?'

'Here. She's got her own flat here. She's old of course, had a bit of a stroke, bit hard to make out what she's saying. I'll come with you if you like, interpret. The nurse thinks she can understand her but she can't, interprets wrong, drives Aunt Margaret mad, poor old bird.'

He led the way out of the french window and across the weedy terrace to a side door, where he put down his bucket.

'Bantams can wait,' he said cheerfully. Catherine had the feeling she had made his afternoon.

The door opened into the Elizabethan part of the house; he led the way through a small panelled room into another, almost identical though a little larger, in which sat, in a wheelchair so positioned that she could look out into the overgrown garden, an old woman with a face so thin and drawn that her eyes being for the moment shut Catherine thought she must be dead. The eyes opened, however, though the head did not turn.

'Here we are then, Aunt Margaret,' said the Captain breezily. 'And I've brought someone with me who's interested in the old days.'

The room, which was dark and rather stuffy, as if the latticed windows which let in so little light were never opened, contained several pieces of well-cared-for oak furniture and some chairs and a high-backed Jacobean sofa which were covered in a worn dark blue and green material, over which were draped several lengths of another dark material, red and blue, rather as if they were cloaks or shawls which the old woman herself had once worn, had perhaps thrown off casually many years ago when she could still walk and had caused to be left where she had thrown them as a sort of memorial to her lost mobility; the effect was of a sombre richness, appropriately mediaeval in feeling. Catherine, approaching the wheelchair, could see that Miss Fox Farmiloe might well have looked striking in a many-coloured

34

cloak, for she was tall; her head, which lurched awkwardly to one side as she tried to look towards her visitors, came well above the back of the wheelchair, and the position of her knees, protruding sharply through the tartan rug which covered them, showed her to be long-legged. The sound with which she answered the Captain was incoherent. Catherine took her hand and apologised for disturbing her.

'Your nephew said you wouldn't mind. I do hope you don't. I'm writing a biography of Neil Campion, and I wondered if you remembered him from the time when his father was the Vicar here.'

The head lurched again. Catherine caught the word 'lessons'.

'They did lessons together,' the Captain interpreted. 'Oh, only the girls. The boys when they were small. Before prep school, yes. So you knew them well, Aunt Margaret?'

'Mummy . . . common . . .'

'Your mother thought them common,' said the Captain.

'They had accents,' said Miss Fox Farmiloe much more clearly. 'The mother . . . dreadful woman . . . One of them did very well . . . married . . . went everywhere . . .'

'That was Neil,' said Catherine. 'What was he like as a child?'

'Cunning.'

'Common and cunning. Oh dear,' said Catherine, looking into the deep-set eyes. Her look elicited a distinct answering gleam. It was followed by considerable head movements and more loud sounds but words were hard to distinguish and the Captain had to interpret again.

'She says Frederick was very nice. Very kind. Animals. Very kind to animals. Very kind person. Knew a lot about animals. Eleanor bossy. Interfering. Hated Eleanor. Eleanor cheated at French.'

'Was Neil kind?' asked Catherine.

'Was Neil kind, Aunt Margaret? No. Neil wasn't kind. Went off alone. Liked being by himself. Strong. Always reading. Read

35

a lot. Not like the others. Talked. Didn't talk. Didn't talk much. Very strong.'

'I wonder if he was very strong physically or a very strong character,' said Catherine quietly. But the voice, urgent and quite loud, seemed now impossible to stop.

'Strong. Very strong and very kind. Not quite sure who we're on to now,' said the Captain. 'I think we're back to Frederick. Are we back to Frederick, Aunt Margaret? He helped with the tennis net. Butterflies. May have been butterfly net. Both. Butterfly net and tennis net. Good old Frederick. He was, wasn't he, Aunt Margaret? He was good old Frederick.'

A young woman had come quietly into the room and was looking severely at the Captain.

'Here's Nurse and I can see she thinks we're tiring you.'

'It's been so kind of you,' Catherine began, but the voice went on.

'She says she'd have done anything for him. When she was a little girl she'd have done anything for Frederick.'

Catherine went close to the wheelchair and crouching down took both Miss Fox Farmiloe's bony hands in hers. 'Thank you for what you've told me. It's been so helpful. I have to go now but I hope perhaps I may come and see you again some day. Goodbye.'

The ancient eyes looked brightly into hers for a moment, then closed. Disconcertingly, they stayed closed.

'It's all right, Nurse,' said the Captain. 'She's been enjoying herself remembering the old days.'

As they emerged from the dark passage into the sunlight of the garden he said, 'Funny old bat, isn't she?'

A dark-haired boy of about eighteen was standing outside the door, holding the bucket of chicken feed and looking resentful.

'They'll be all right, the chickabiddies, don't you worry,' said the Captain indulgently.

Catherine bought a postcard of the village green from the

post office and sat on a bench near the War Memorial to write to her younger son Tom.

'Could I come next weekend? Would love to see you all. Here in pursuit of new book, quite intriguing.' Then she added, in case her daughter-in-law Susannah felt she was being put upon, 'The weekend after would do just as well.'

She walked across the green to the post-box, trying to remember whether there had been somewhere for the dark-haired boy to sit in the morning-room beside the Captain's patent television chair. She thought she might have seen some sort of large cushion, covered in brown corduroy.

*   *   *

'Must I really see her, Potty?' said Effie Campion on the telephone to her solicitor. 'I thought she could just have the diaries and things and get on with it. I thought the whole idea was she wasn't going to ask questions.'

Mr Pottinger's tones were deep and reassuring. They had been deep and reassuring for years, especially to those in high places. 'She'll just want background information from you, nothing tiresome. Remember, she starts from a completely friendly position, and we have the final say when the book's finished. She's not a nosy journalist. You know how we all liked her when we saw her. Make friends with her.'

'I don't like new friends. I don't like most of my old friends either. I'll try, though, if you say so, Potty.'

'We don't want to run any risks. And we want her to get on with it. We haven't given her long. I think you'll find yourself liking her. In any doubt at all just give me a call.'

'Thank you, Potty dear, what would I do without you?'

Neil Campion had married the Honourable Euphemia Prynne in 1933 when he was thirty-two and she ten years younger. She came from a family of small-boned, narrowthighed aristocrats, many of them famed on the hunting field. Brave, high-spirited, slightly hysterical, with a refined and vivid beauty and an excellent seat on a horse, she had been launched, without the benefit of much in the way of education, on the London Society of the time by her remote and melancholy mother whose happy memories of her own youth before the Great War had settled into a deep resentment of the age which followed. Effie was the only child; her father would have liked a son but her mother's health precluded it, or at least various distinguished men of medicine had indicated, greatly to her relief, that with her temperament it would be unwise. The father, a mean and misanthropic man whose considerable charm was founded on nothing more than physical dynamism and a pleasant turn of phrase, concentrated on his hunting, interspersing it at the appropriate season with a little fishing and shooting, and never knew to what extent his daughter longed for his approbation. She meanwhile, applying to the world into which she had been thrust the same virtues she had shown from an early age on the hunting field, flung herself into the slightly fevered jollifications of the late twenties and early thirties with a mettlesome determination to be at the fore. She danced and dined and stayed in smart houses, and evading the chaperones after her first Season she went to night-clubs and jazz clubs and wilder weekend parties where cocaine was sniffed; she knew all the right people and just the right amount of the wrong ones; she was photographed by Cecil Beaton among ostrich feathers and by the Press on a yacht with the Prince of Wales; she went to Ascot, was mad about a black night-club singer, turned down a proposal from a film-star and a proposition from a Duke, and never missed the Grande Semaine at Deauville. No one could remember anything she had said but everyone agreed a party wasn't a party without her.

As for Effie herself, she hardly knew what to think; there seemed no time for thinking. Occasionally it occurred to her, quite worryingly, that she simply did not know whether she was

38

having fun or not. At such moments it seemed better simply to chatter even faster. 'Put a cloth on Pretty Polly's cage, someone,' a languid young man said once; she shrieked with laughter. The more eligible of the young men began to fall to other girls, and when at twenty-two Effie announced her engagement to a young politician 'from nowhere' it was not thought much of a match, for all his growing reputation. She herself felt there had been little element of choice; he was extraordinarily purposeful; she, despite the wilful air, not at all. She had still a curiously girlish uncertainty in speaking of her husband when Catherine Hillery came to see her, though it was more than fifty years after the wedding in St Margaret's, Westminster.

Catherine noticed that she seemed nervous and that the hand with which she poured out coffee was shaking slightly. They were in the sitting-room of a flat just off Curzon Street; Catherine deduced, correctly, that Effie had employed the same firm of rather traditional interior decorators all her life, and that she had no taste other than theirs.

'So absurd living in Mayfair nowadays, so unfashionable, nothing but Nigerian diplomats.' Effie's seventy-year-old face, on which the lineaments of past beauty were insulted by an elaborate maquillage, was surrounded by a helmet of lacquered dark hair, strictly cut in the style of the thirties, with a side parting and a curl on each cheek, a tortoiseshell slide holding the heavier side in place. She wore a cream woollen coat and skirt, with a coffee-coloured silk shirt and some silver chains round her neck. Catherine thought it just the sort of outfit she would have liked herself, but feared it was more than money which made it unlikely she would ever wear anything of the kind; it was something to do with her expectations of herself. 'We got the flat when we were first married,' the flustered but rather sharp-toned voice went on. 'Neil used it in the war, I mean until he died. Parliament you know and the bombing, rather beautiful he always said but tiring, they all got so tired, not getting enough sleep, not that he'd have missed it for worlds, he found the Secret Sessions so exciting, when Churchill was telling them about the War and what was going on, things the general public had no idea about. He didn't even tell me all of it, not at the time. And then after he died I sold the house in the country, well, cottage really, it was the gamekeeper's cottage, but we made it so pretty and comfortable. Neil felt he wanted to keep something of the Durdans but after he died and when Hector left the school I wanted to get away from it somehow. I bought my little house in Oxfordshire, near friends, I adore it, and it's so much better for Sam than London, anyway there's hardly room for him here and I do think London is so terrifying for young people these days, don't you?'

'Could you tell me about the Durdans?'

'Everything was quite different in those days. One had servants.'

'It was where you lived?'

'But of course. It was our home until just before the War when Neil felt that everything was going to change and anyway it was too big for us so he offered it to Karl Eberling, who'd been turned out by the Nazis, and they had conferences and so on. You mean you don't know about all that?'

'I'm afraid I don't.'

'My dear, we had everyone there, but everyone. I'm boasting now of course but one has so little to boast of nowadays, don't you think? So one might be allowed a tiny boast about the past. I did do it well. I made people comfortable, that was the thing. And everyone was so relaxed and easy, knowing they were going to be looked after and meet interesting and amusing people and eat delicious food. They really did love coming to the Durdans. People could talk, all sorts of different people. Neil was always full of ideas. They were wonderful days. Everyone thought so highly of Neil. Mr Baldwin, everyone. I could show you the visitors' books. I know I've got them somewhere.'

'I'd rather like to see the house. Would the school mind, do you suppose, if I went?'

'Oh, but I'm going on Sunday. You could come with me. We'll ring up now this minute and tell Sam.' She reached for the telephone, her nervousness gone. 'It's Mrs Campion here. I'd like to speak to my grandson please. In a lesson, how wonderful, then you'll know where to find him for once, won't you? Nonsense, my dear, in Mr Eberling's days I always rang up my son whenever I wanted to. I know much more about the school than you do. Run along and fetch him, there's a dear.' Putting her hand over the receiver, she said to Catherine. 'They have this silly old hen of a school secretary, always trying to stop one speaking to the children, as if one was going to contaminate them.'

'I seem to remember it's the same at any school. You have to leave messages for them to ring you back and then they reverse the charges and it's twice as expensive.'

'Oh, you have children. How old?'

'Grown-up. Very grown-up. Thirty-two and thirty-four. Both sons.'

'But you remember what hell they are. So sweet for the first ten years, absolute hell for the next twenty. Though I must say darling Hector was always a sensible boy. Sam's quite imposs-ible, but of course he hasn't a father. Though I'm told no one pays any attention to the fathers nowadays anyway. Sam? Oh. I'll hold on then. He's not in the lesson. They've sent someone to find him. I expect he's doing his running practice. He's a great runner, just like his father. And his grandfather. Neil won the steeplechase every year when he was at school. You wouldn't think it, would you, he looks so solid in the photographs, but he always had very good lungs, they said, and even when he was busy he kept fit. We used to have great tennis parties at the Durdans. Everyone played, good or bad – the PM, Lord Lothian – he was very good – Nancy Astor, everyone. Sam? There you are. You sound out of breath. Have you been running? Only down the stairs? Anyway I'm coming down on Sunday. I've already told Trumble, and I'm bringing Mrs

Hillery who wants to see round the house because she's writing a book about your grandfather. We'll be there at half-past twelve to take you out to lunch. Don't be late because I never know where to find you and they all stare so strangely. Yes, of course bring someone, how many? Two girls. Why don't you ask another boy? Then you'll be a partie carreé. Lovely. Half-past twelve and not a moment later. I don't want to see Trumble, he does nothing but complain, but I will if he insists.' She put down the receiver. 'He's not much good, the present Head. I say to him, it's no good moaning to me about Sam, why do you think I sent him to you? Eberling was such a wonderful man. He adored Hector. He wanted to bring him up to be like his father, a saviour. Some hope, I always said to him. There was only one Neil.'

*　　*　　*

Presenting a letter of authority from Miss Eleanor Campion, Catherine collected three boxes of Neil Campion's letters from a Kensington branch of Lloyds Bank. She took them home and opened the first of them, which contained his war-time letters to his parents. The letters were neatly stacked inside, the paper yellowed and in some cases not very clean, as if some of the mud from the battlefield of Ypres had dried to dust there. Catherine knew nothing of battlefields, very little of violent action of any kind. She had given birth; perhaps that was the nearest she had come to the field of battle. She had not been brave on those occasions. She considered herself a physical coward, and had never felt in the least ashamed of it. Courage seemed to her a wholly admirable virtue, but one to which she would not herself dream of aspiring. When her younger son Tom had been at school he had been a good rugger player, and because of him she had tried to understand team spirit, something as foreign to her nature as physical bravery. She could not imagine being possessed by such a spirit herself, and she would have been happy for Tom to have renounced it. After watching a match in which for the first time he had played rugger against another school she had begged him never to do such a thing again; he had suggested sensibly that she should give up watching matches. At the same time, and perhaps simply because it seemed to her such a mystery, she was moved by the element of brotherhood in the thing. She found it touching that Tom could criticise some of his friends quite freely in the summer but would not hear a word against them in the rugger term; they were part of the team. Something of the same mystery must, she supposed, have sustained the young men who went straight from school to the trenches, must have been felt by those few whose independence or daring or love of flying or desire for a certain kind of death sent vulnerable and alone, cold, exhilarated, frightened, into the air above the battle. She wished simply to be accurate. Neil Campion had spent a year and a half of his forty-two years of life as a man at arms; she wished to gauge correctly how much or how little that period had meant to him. He had been sent to France in the summer of 1917. He had been eighteen, and had just finished his training. He had lived in a bleak and uncomfortable forward airfield, hardly more than a landing strip among the once-ploughed fields, with the sound of gunfire unceasing. From there he had set off day after day, or night after night, at first on reconnaissance flights and then, as the war proceeded and the Germans began to lose their technical superiority in the matter of flying machines, on offensive sorties, in which his tactics quickly became expert and in which, unlike the majority of his fellows during those intense few months, he survived. He was sent back to England in the spring of 1918, when German machines were developing such a range that the English began to think about defending their own soil against attack from the air, and for the remaining months of the war he patrolled the South Coast.

Cautioning herself then against jumping to conclusions,

Catherine began to work her way slowly through the letters. They had been arranged chronologically, from 'Arrived safely' in the autumn of 1916 to 'It seems it's all over' in 1918, and they carried still, as any letter will, a little echo of immediacy, but that was all.

Catherine's initial excitement soon faded; Neil evidently kept his parents at arm's length. Whether to avoid alarming them or because his relationship with them was no more than formal (some of Eleanor's remarks had seemed to imply that this might have been the case) he wrote letters absurdly like the letters Tom had written to his parents when he was sixteen and in the first Fifteen. Food, the cold, the adequacy or otherwise of his clothes to cope with the cold – 'My Burberry flying suit excellent, most people have them, though some swear by their own pet make' – boredom when there was no action, laconic description when there was – 'Spotted a solitary Hun on the way back from a reconnaissance flight, got behind and above him before he saw me, and was really close before he dived. Shot him as he went and got him all right but followed him right through the dive in case he came out of it but he didn't. Felt pretty pleased with myself!' – boots, leave, 'We got some bicycles and went into the country, lovely day.' '... Charles Barret, Noll and I borrowed some horses from some cavalry officers who are hanging around waiting to go into action and getting sick of seeing the Footguards get all the glory. We went for a long ride and saw no sign of the War all day though we could still hear the guns in the distance.' '... Noll and I had a great chase on Friday, got our man down after quite a long fight.'

As the War went on the letters became no less regular but even more terse. 'If you can send any more socks do. The sheepskin boots are wonderful. Thank Eleanor for her letter and tell her I'll write soon.' '... Marvellous flying weather, cold but very clear.' '... Noll had a great outing last week. I'll tell you about it when I see you. He'll be due for leave soon. I'll give him a letter for you. He's way ahead of me in the scoring now, but I'm still third.' '... Things are improving, we've got some new planes. I don't know if I'm allowed to tell you about them but they've got a better range and are putting us back in front. We're doing more formation flying now.' '... Noll, Baker and I have been here longer than anyone now. Charles didn't get back last week as you may have heard. Send more of that cake if you can. My new boots are a great success, much warmer than the last pair without being so heavy. Noll not back, haven't heard what happened. Love to all ...' Eighteen months, without much leave, flying aeroplanes, which you loved, doing a job you knew you did well, physically fully stretched, having to think about that, about keeping fit, eating properly, sleeping properly, guarding against frostbite, learning to relax when you could, learning to live for the moment, for the job, learning not to think about people who didn't come back, not to wake up screaming, thinking you were being burnt alive. But you were young, healthy, optimistic, trained. And for Neil Campion it was over in eighteen months.

Catherine went on the Underground from South Kensington to Elephant and Castle and walked to the Imperial War Museum. Passing through its imposing façade she found her way to the rooms concerned with the First World War, and was relieved to find there nothing too partisan, too glorious or too morbid. The dispassionate enquirer – or even the passionate one – could find here such facts, relics and suppositions as the state of modern informed opinion believed to be the truth of the matter. The sound of distant gunfire and of marching feet was subdued, the merest suggestion, there was nothing to play too strongly on the emotions or to underline too heavily the neatly-printed casualty figures. In the room which recorded the part played by the Royal Flying Corps, there was a small television screen on which was being shown some old film of trench warfare under the title THE BATTLE OF THE SOMME 1916. An elderly couple stood in front of it, watching.

A comfortable-looking pair, who might have recently retired from running a sub-post-office or a small newsagents, they both distinctly sighed as they watched the faded figures moving jerkily from side to side of the little screen or passing heavy shells from one to the other with cheerful smiles towards the camera on their tired but healthy faces; presumably all films taken at the time for home consumption were more or less propaganda films. The woman watching groaned slightly, the sort of mild sympathetic noise she might have made towards a child who had fallen down and slightly grazed its knee; she laid her head on the man's shoulder.

'Would you recognise him?' he asked.

'Oh yes, I'd recognise him.'

Calculating dates as she passed them, Catherine thought it might be a father they were looking for, but a father who had survived, for the woman was too young to remember a father not seen since 1918. Nothing there to rend the heart unduly, she told herself; except that it was always touching when children remembered their parents with affection, perhaps in this case even with pride. How mean of her elder son Nicholas to hold against his father the fact that the latter's paternal heart had not been large enough to encompass the peccadilloes of a not quite honest son; but that was a thought which had to be quashed as soon as it surfaced, for neither had her own heart been large enough, nor was it now; this was a forbidden subject. The room she walked into fortunately diverted her attention, for here was what she had read about in Neil Campion's letters. Here were the machines, the Bristol F2B, the famous Sopwith Camel. Here were the flying suits, the Burberry with the 'Tielocken' buttonless fastening which he had favoured, the Aquascutum and the Gamages preferred by others; here were the boots lined with sheepskin and the massive leather gauntlets. There was German equipment too, and photographs of German ace pilots as well as the French and English. The Germans seemed to Catherine older and tougher than their opponents.

She looked at the photograph of a French ace with a score of victories to his credit and quite unexpectedly the name of Gérard de Nerval came into her mind. She had never seen a photograph of Gérard de Nerval and knew of him only that he had had a tame lobster which he used to take for walks on a lead in early Nineteenth Century Paris and that he had written in what context she had forgotten, one unaccountably beautiful line of poetry, 'Le Prince d'Aquitaine à la tour abolie.' If she had been told that the photograph of the French pilot had been of Gérard de Nerval, or even of the Prince d'Aquitaine himself beside his ruined tower, she would not have been surprised, so delicate, so romantic and so familiar with despair did he look. And then there was a fine moustachioed Australian who had an MC and a DFC and had been mentioned in despatches three times and credited with six victories in air combat, and there was the famous Baron von Richthofen himself, and his brother. 'I am a hunter,' he had said, 'My brother Lothar is a butcher.' And then there was the perfect English schoolboy, looking at least five years younger than any of the others although he was not, kept young perhaps by all those childish things he had taken so seriously, rituals and ceremonies, hierarchies and contests, honours which were the due reward of endeavour, team colours, mentions in despatches, becoming Head of House, winning the Victoria Cross. A healthy boy, clear skin, brown hair, a direct gaze in which the ardour was veiled by some kind of reserve or modesty, a determined face but with the mouth of a nineteen-year-old, that is to say not yet the mouth of a man. Oliver Brook, she read, and there were all the decorations and citations. Fifteen victories in air combat. Nine observation balloons shot down. Ten German aircraft forced to land.

A plump grey-haired man was being walked through the exhibition by a deferential dark-suited figure who might have been a member of the Museum staff. They paused near Catherine to read a description of an American pilot who had

47

been part of the Lafayette Escadrille, the Escadrille Américaine of the French Air Force. The visitor, disclosing his American nationality by his accent, asked a question about observation balloons. Catherine was reading about Oliver Brook and noticing that he must have been taking part in the Battle of Ypres at the same time as Neil Campion. The polite answering voice impinged. 'They once filled one with explosive so when the pilot came near enough to shoot it down they got him too. They lost an observation balloon but they got one of our pilots.' And of course Noll was short for Oliver. Every time she thought of Neil's friend after that Catherine seemed to see him plunging to the earth in a huge sheet of flame from an exploding observation balloon. But he had not died like that. He had disappeared at dusk one evening on a solitary patrol. Later the Germans announced that he had been shot down. There was a photograph of a cross somewhere in Germany where his enemies had buried him: 'Im Luftkampf gefallen für sein Vaterland.' Neil had hardly mentioned this death in his letters to his parents, but then he had hardly mentioned any deaths. He must have thought death nothing to write home about.

* * *

Effie Campion drove a small BMW at speed down the motorway.

'Neil and I both adored danger,' she said, passing a chauffeur-driven Jaguar on the inside lane and swerving out in front of it to overtake a lorry which was passing another in a cloud of illegal fumes. 'We met on the hunting field. It was the only place where I was braver than he was. He never really arrived at a proper understanding with horses. But machines he loved. He taught me to drive.'

They were coming up behind a Ford Sierra going at 85 miles an hour in the fast lane. The driver, alone in the car, was either talking to himself or singing. Effie flashed her lights. The Ford Sierra, its driver evidently taken by surprise, swerved out of the way; Effie made a racing change and roared past.

'Goes like a bird, doesn't she?' she said happily.

Catherine, always a nervous passenger and anxious not to sound in any way encouraging, answered with a non-committal murmur. Looking sideways, she thought perhaps she could see in the still definite profile and the now-dyed black curl so stiffly whipped forward onto the rouged cheek the shadow of the eager girl who had dashed along in some open roadster of the time under the spell of her bold companion; but surely at over seventy her reflexes would be slower? Hoping she might reduce her speed if diverted by conversation, Catherine asked her if her husband had ever talked about his war-time experiences.

'Never,' was the answer. 'I don't think anyone did. It was probably rather bad form.'

'He never talked about flying?'

'Oh flying, yes. He adored flying. He kept it up, you know, always had his pilot's licence. He talked about flying in Africa sometimes, about what fun it was, and how beautiful. But never about the War.'

'Do you think he went to Africa just because he wanted to go on flying?'

'Yes. Didn't want to settle down, I suppose, after the excitement of the War. Quite a few flyers did that sort of thing. He might have stayed if he hadn't got interested in politics. No, that's not true, he was always interested in politics. I think he always meant to come back after a few years.'

'Was he ambitious in politics, would you say?'

'Tremendously.'

Catherine remained silent. Effie was talking much less defensively than when she had last seen her. Catherine felt she should be careful not to push her luck. She recognised with some reluctance that if she ever wanted any particular information from Effie it might be necessary to ask her when she was at the wheel of her car. When they left the motorway Effie's driving became less hair-raising; Catherine was able to look about her at the well-ordered Sussex countryside, the woods now tinged by autumn.

'How right they were to choose this part of England. I mean those high-minded simple-lifers of Edwardian times, who came to Dorking and Abinger and Box Hill.'

'We weren't like *that*,' said Effie reprovingly. 'They were Socialists for goodness' sake. Neil was terribly against all that. The Webbs and so on were absolute anathema. Neil wanted a completely different kind of corporate state. But you'll read all that. I'm no good at explaining. I never was. I daresay I never understood most of it anyway. I just knew it was good because the people were good. Of course it was a terrific change for me, some of them weren't at all the sort of people I was used to. Intellectuals and so on, some of them quite common. And then Eberling was perfectly terrifying until one got to know him. But he was simply sweet with women always, really old-fashioned and kind. I did rather love that.'

'I haven't read enough about the conferences so far. I know they were aimed at creating a new sort of international understanding and that this was in some way bound up with a better agriculture, but I'm a bit vague still. It's actually quite hard to find any written sources.'

'The conferences could be about anything. They were to get people together. Like-minded people mainly, but not always. They were a kind of extension of the house-parties we had, a more serious extension. We had lectures and those things everyone has nowadays but one didn't know the name then, seminars, it must be American, isn't it? Anyway we had seminars, and the great thing was we had a lot of foreigners, that's how we knew Eberling. We raised money to help pay for the conferences, there were several organisations that contributed. Luckily I was quite rich when I married but of course we couldn't pay for everything. Sometimes other people were the hosts. We used to go to such beautiful places. But here we are, isn't this pretty?'

They turned into a drive between tall redbrick gateposts and drove some little distance between mown grass and well-tended shrubs before the drive curved round the side of a hill and they looked down on to the house, the sloping roof and the gables, the short turret with its tiled pyramidal roof rising to one side, matched by tall chimneys on the other side. A group of lower buildings clustered behind it, lawns stretched down to the river and the woods.

'Most people think it's hideous,' said Effie.

'I like it. It looks like something out of a perfectly enormous Garden City.'

'It was built in the 1890s for a rich publisher. I think he had a wife who liked doing embroidery. When we bought it there were all sorts of William Morris hangings and things. My dear, we threw them all away. They were quite out of fashion. We painted everything white and had pickled oak cupboards, can you imagine. They'd have been worth a fortune now, wouldn't they? The hangings, I mean.'

They had driven round the side of the house and now turned into a large courtyard with a square of grass and a fine plane tree in the middle of it. One side of the courtyard was evidently living accommodation, for there were curtains in the windows and little porches over the white-painted doors. The opposite side seemed to be workshops; four or five boys carrying model boats were going into one of them, and in front of another a boy was mending a bicycle. Ahead of them an arch opened through the middle of a building built like a tithe barn. Effie parked her car beside several others. A girl came out of one of the white doors, carrying a pile of books; she smiled as she passed them.

'Heavenly place, isn't it?' said Effie. 'Makes one wish one was young enough to go to school again. Not that I ever did.'

They walked through the arch and found themselves on the

gravel expanse in front of the main entrance of the house; a stone porch protruded from the redbrick façade, there were two storeys of sash windows, a tiled roof with dormer windows, tall chimneys. The upper windows fluttered with bright colours of various kinds, curtains, clothes, paper birds, two balloons, a torn sheet with HELP! painted on it in huge scarlet letters. Three figures rose from the doorstep on which they had been sitting. Catherine had given very little thought to the grandson; he did not come into her story. As Sam unfolded himself from the doorstep there flashed into her mind for a moment the boy she must have been expecting, a boy rather like the photograph she had seen of Neil Campion's son Hector, Sam's father, a stocky, tow-haired boy of indifferent complexion. She dismissed the apparition quickly, adjusting her ideas to something less usual, a creature neither child nor man whom it was so difficult to imagine as either that he seemed immutably a youth, tall, dark-haired, pale, graceful, remote. He seemed also possessed of such extraordinary assurance that Catherine immediately felt conscious of her own lack of sophistication. He introduced his two companions. They silently produced smiles of enormous warmth and eagerness which disappeared with disconcerting suddenness; the two heads bowed again as though beneath the weight of all the brushed and burnished hair.

'I thought you were four,' said Effie.

'He's meeting us at the restaurant,' said Sam. 'He had a few things to do.'

He began to lead the way across the gravel in the direction of the car. His grandmother followed him, showing signs of agitation.

'How will he know which restaurant we've gone to?'

'It's all right. I've told him.'

'But how did you know?'

'You told me. Curry. I told him to go to the Indian restaurant.'

'Sam, wait, do stop. I didn't say anything about curry. You said you were bringing two girls and I said why not bring

52

another boy so that you'd be a partie carrée and that's all we said about it. I booked a table at the King's Head.'

'Oh, right. I'll wait for him. We'll follow you.'

'How could you have told him to go to the Indian restaurant? D'you mean that disgusting little place by the station?'

'They're so nice there. It's really nice,' said Prue breathlessly.

'It's not the food so much that's nice, it's the place,' said Pat. 'The food does make you feel a bit ill.'

'They don't really come from India,' said Prue. 'They come from somewhere else, they told us once, I think it was Jamaica. And the other one comes from Liverpool.'

'They're Rastafarians,' said Pat. 'But not the one who does the cooking. The other one.'

Effie seemed less than enchanted. 'Can't we leave a message for your friend. Where is he?'

Pat and Prue looked towards Sam for guidance.

'He's on a run,' said Sam. 'You have to go for a run on Sunday morning if you have more than a hundred minuses in a week.'

'God, how futile. Why aren't you on it?'

'I've done mine. I did it early.'

'How many minuses did you have?'

'Rather a lot I'm afraid. They give them to you for anything. Like not having a clean handkerchief. No one in the whole school has a clean handkerchief. As you might expect.'

'I thought it was supposed to be a school without rules.'

'There aren't rules. They just give you a minus every time you move.'

'I'm sure they didn't have minuses for not having clean handkerchieves in Eberling's day. It must be some fad of Trumbles.'

'I meant it metaphysically,' said Sam.

'We can't stand here arguing about metaphysical handkerchieves. Everything always seems to get quite out of hand with you, Sam. What are we to do?'

53

The problem was solved by the breathless arrival of a very small boy in running clothes. He had tight fair curls and a disastrous complexion.

'I saw you were still here. I'm Howard Clayborne Pope.' He extended a remarkably sweaty hand to Catherine, apparently overlooking the presence of Effie. 'I'll just rush and change.'

By the time they were sitting down in the local hotel diningroom Effie seemed to be feeling the strain. The staccato manner which Catherine had noticed at their earlier meeting had returned. She asked for a dry martini and was horrified to be brought a glass of white Vermouth; she insisted that Sam should go with the wine waiter to show the barman how to make a dry martini. Sam rose unruffled and led the way out of the diningroom, followed by the protesting wine waiter.

'If there's one thing Sam does know it's how to make a dry martini,' said Effie. 'Now what are we going to eat?' She fumbled in her bag for her glasses.

Howard Clayborne Pope had already read the menu.

'I should like prawn cocktail and steak and kidney pie with sprouts and baby carrots,' he said. 'My father says you should always choose quickly and stick to your decision.'

'How wonderful,' said Effie distantly, putting on her glasses.

'My father's rather a strong character actually,' the boy continued. 'He's the managing director of a medium-sized engineering company making components for the motor industry in the West Midlands.'

'Good Heavens,' said Effie, looking at him over the top of her glasses.

The wine waiter, all smiles, placed a glass misty with cold and virtually colourless except for a scrap of lemon peel in front of Effie. He apologised for the white Vermouth and said that the young gentleman had quite cleared up the misunderstanding. The young gentlemen, detached, returned quietly to his seat. Effie ordered a second martini and indicated to the rest of the party that they should decide what they wanted to eat.

Howard Clayborne Pope repeated his father's advice and the two girls, fussed, ordered an assortment of vegetables; it appeared they did not eat meat. Effie sent Sam to fetch her diary from the car so that she could write down when his holidays began, then she sent him back again to fetch a letter she had left in the glove compartment. It was from a second cousin of hers who lived in Washington.

'You should keep in touch with these people,' she said. 'You might want to go round the world.'

'I do want to go round the world,' said Sam.

'My father says it's better not to go round the world until after you've got a professional qualification,' said Howard Clayborne Pope.

'What will they think of next?' said Effie. 'A professional qualification to go round the world. I ask you.'

'No, a professional qualification for a profession, I mean. Like accountancy or the law. My father says you're more mature if you go then than if you go in your gap like some people do. The gap, in case you don't know, comes between school and university.'

'Unless you don't go to university,' said Prue dreamily.

'In which case your whole life is a gap,' breathed Pat.

'No, because you can go to a Polytechnic or a College of Higher Education,' said Howard Clayborne Pope. 'These places have gone up a great deal in people's estimation since the pressure of numbers has made Universities so difficult to get into. I've been told I'm not very likely to get many O-levels and probably no A-levels at all so I am setting my sights on the Polytechnics and Colleges of Higher Education.'

'O Polytechnics and places of Higher Education, the sights of Clayborne Pope are upon you,' murmured Pat.

'Early in the morning and at the going down of the sun he has the Polytechnics and places of Higher Education in his sights,' echoed Prue.

'These two make fun of things,' explained Howard Clayborne Pope. 'But my father says it's as well to think ahead.'

'Are you going to follow him into the business?' asked Catherine kindly.

'Unfortunately I haven't the brains to be an engineer,' said Howard Clayborne Pope with ineffable self-satisfaction.

'Wine, Sam. You haven't ordered any wine,' said Effie.

Sam ordered a bottle of red wine and a bottle of white wine.

'I am hoping to go into catering,' said Howard Clayborne Pope.

Catherine asked Sam if he had any idea what he would like to do. He said he would probably do the same.

'Go into catering, you mean?' said Catherine.

'Yes, well, something like that.'

'What sort of catering, do you think?'

'Any sort, really.' It seemed unlikely that he had given the matter any thought at all, but as if realising he ought to make more of an effort he went on, 'I mean you can cater for anything, can't you? I mean Mr Trumble said in Assembly the other day, this school does not cater for the idle offspring of the degenerate rich.'

'That's not so much catering as not catering.'

'But I could cater. I mean someone's got to, haven't they? If the school's not going to do it who is? I could have a lovely time catering for the idle offspring of the degenerate rich.'

'I think it was degenerate offspring of the idle rich,' said Pat earnestly.

'Them too. I shall start a night-club for them. And a day-club. You'll be able to go there at any time and it will be a huge sealed compression chamber, and you'll be weightless, so you'll be able to float around as if you were in an enormous space capsule. There'll be quadrophonic music, fantastically loud.'

'Brilliant!' said Prue.

'Unreal!' said Pat.

'It sounds to me as if that would require considerable intitial expenditure,' said Howard Clayborne Pope doggedly. 'Would you see sufficient return on your investment?'

'Quite right,' said Effie, filling Clayborne Pope's glass and then her own. 'Sam's feet are always six inches off the ground. He'll have to come down to earth some day.'

'My father says life is very hard for young people these days.' Clayborne Pope drank deeply of the red wine and returned his glass to the table with a satisfied exhalation of breath. 'He says you have to be armed against all eventualities.'

'You certainly do,' said Effie, refilling his glass. 'Sam, I think we're going to need another bottle of this red.'

'You'd have to give people space suits. How could they dance with those horrid helmets on their heads?' said Prue.

'You don't feel them if they don't weigh anything,' said Pat. 'You'd just slowly wave your arms and legs about as if you were swimming.'

'Or flying,' said Sam.

'What about food?' asked Catherine. 'Or drink?' She was quite content to settle down to the sort of conversation she might have expected to have with three slightly fanciful eight-year-olds; Effie and Howard Clayborne Pope continued their diagnosis of the world's ills, their general agreement and their joint admiration of Clayborne Pope Senior becoming warmer as their glasses became emptier, and were then refilled and became empty once more.

Catherine's uncertainty as to whether Sam was to be considered extraordinarily sophisticated, or unusually naïve, or – which was not impossible – a mixture of the two, was not resolved by their tour of the school. When they went back there after lunch, Effie expressed a wish to sit down quietly for a bit in the Founder's Library.

'I think I'd probably better come with you,' said Howard Clayborne Pope. 'Those stairs can be a bit tricky.'

'Is it upstairs?' said Prue, surprised.

57

'Of course it is,' said Pat. 'It's beyond Matron's flat, behind the airing cupboards.'

Howard Clayborne Pope explained that on the contrary the Founder's Library was at the top of the main staircase, and suggested that the twins should come and see it. Effie, who had evidently lost what little interest she had ever had in the twins, set off without waiting to see whether they were following, saying as she went that Sam was to show Mrs Hillery round the school and bring her to the Founder's Library in not more than three-quarters of an hour's time. 'I've got a cocktail party in London and I can't miss it or I shall give offence.'

'Had they really never been to the Founder's Library?' said Catherine. 'Whatever that may be.'

'Pat and Prue never lie,' said Sam. 'They forget quite a lot though.'

He led the way through the wide white-panelled hall and opening a green baize door at the end of it introduced her into a long dark passage which resounded with conflicting musical sound.

'These are the common rooms,' he said. 'This is ours.'

He opened a door to disclose a big room with two tall uncurtained windows. What seemed to Catherine a bewilderingly large number of boys and girls were variously grouped behind barricades of chairs and desks in six or seven little enclaves, each of which contained a jumble of desks, cushions, rugs, boxes, people and hi-fi equipment, the last emitting a variety of pop music at considerable volume. Some of the children were wearing headphones, some seemed to be reading or writing, some were playing cards, some sharpening spears, some sleeping; none paid any attention to Sam or Catherine. The room was hot and smelled of cigarette smoke and burnt toast.

'I don't think we need see any more of those, need we?' said Sam, shutting the door again.

'Wouldn't they rather be outside? It's quite a nice day.'

'They mostly come from London. They don't like going outside. The absolute silence of infinite space terrifies them.'

'Is that a quotation?'

'Some monk said it last week. People come and talk to us on Sundays, all the religions in turn and atheists as well, humanists they're called.'

'There was a Frenchman called Pascal who said something rather similar.'

'I don't think the monk said anything about him.'

'Does it terrify you, the eternal silence of infinite space?'

'No, not really.'

'Perhaps the eternal cacophony of infinite common rooms does.'

'You can get used to anything. People usually like to see the squash courts now.'

'I'm really trying to get an idea of what the place was like when your grandparents lived here.'

'Ah. We'd need to go into the Headmaster's wing for that and I'm not really allowed in there.'

'Let's go and see the squash courts then.'

Outside, walking across the well-mown lawn towards some buildings which were half-concealed by a belt of tall lime trees, Catherine tried to concentrate on the past. The grandson was not her concern. She tried to imagine that it was Neil Campion, not Sam Campion, walking beside her, showing her round his property, perhaps with some pride, for it was all much grander than the vicarage at Little Melton. What would he have talked about, walking beside her in his purposeful way? Would he have expanded upon the beauties of the countryside, or his plans for the Home Farm, or his view of world politics, or what? That was to suppose, of course, that he would have bothered to talk to her at all.

'Do you know anything much about your grandfather?'

'Not really, no.'

'Does your grandmother ever refer to him?'

'Not much.'

'Are you interested?'

'I don't think people of my age are very interested in their grandparents really,' said Sam, adding politely, 'I probably would be if I knew more about him.'

'No. You're right. People of your age aren't interested in the past.'

Neil presumably had been interested in the past, since it appeared that he had been concerned about the future. On the other hand there was his personal ambition, which his wife said had been tremendous, and which was another thing which Catherine doubted her ability to gauge correctly, though she found it easier to understand than team spirit. She supposed in a way she had been ambitious for Bernard, her husband, but only because he had minded so much when he was passed over at work. She had certainly hated that awful Peter Robson on his behalf; but when they had first been married, she and Bernard, she could not remember that either of them had thought about the future very much. All they had wanted was that Bernard should earn enough money to pay for the mortgage, and that the small private income her father had left her should continue to pay for their food, and that Bernard should have the sort of job which enabled him to get home in reasonable time in the evenings and never required him to work at weekends. Or was it only she who had been content with that? Bernard would have already had his eye on promotion. Promotion had come, but then it had stopped coming, and horrible Peter Robson had been promoted over his head which meant that he would never go any further and never get his K, nor even a CBE. Catherine had told him she would have simply hated them to have been Sir Bernard and Lady Hillery; it would have been perfectly ridiculous, she had said; but Bernard had minded to an extent she had in the end come to think out of proportion. His disappointment had been something her sympathy had failed to embrace, just as it had failed to embrace her elder son Nicholas's ambition to make a quick fortune, and her younger son Tom's desire to be middle-aged before his time. These moments of icy clarity came to her every now and then, and she rejected them as vigorously as she was able; they seemed a negation of everything by which her existence was sustained. Sometimes at night it was not possible to re-direct her thoughts, and this meant despair, which she knew was the sin against the Holy Ghost; but today she was distracted by a notice pegged into the grass at the foot of the first of the big lime trees. It said BE STILL MY HEART THESE GREAT TREES ARE PRAYERS. Underneath was written the name of the author of these words, RABINDRAN-ATH TAGORE, but the lettering had been interfered with so that it read RABINDRANATH THEBORE.

'Do you know much about him?' asked Catherine.

'He's some African friend of Trumble's.'

'Or Indian friend of Eberling's, do you think?'

'Probably, yes. Have you heard of him then?'

'I feel sure he was a good old man. Don't you think you would have liked him?'

There was a pause while they stood beneath the lime trees in front of the notices.

'I probably will after I've left school,' said Sam.

Back in the car and speeding towards London, for Effie had quite recovered her energies after a quiet sleep over a Susan Ertz novel in a comfortable armchair in the Founder's Library (which had been their own library when she and Neil had lived at the Durdans and where they had left an odd assortment of their unwanted books), Effie said rather suddenly, 'Have you ever heard of a man called Madden, a journalist?'

'I don't think so,' said Catherine.

'I shouldn't have anything to do with him if you do,' said Effie.

* * *

'My dearest Eff,' Neil had written, 'we have taken on something big, I know that. Don't doubt me. I don't doubt you. There is no one I would rather have beside me. You lend grace to the whole endeavour. I don't ask that you should be involved in every ideological complexity, or that you should personally like or admire every one of the odd collection of people we have to work with. I know that you believe that life should be vivid and strenuous, that the civilisation that has developed in what we call Christendom must be defended against barbarism by the ways of peace and not of war, that you and I have some part to play in that defence. Does it sound unbearably conceited if I say leave the rest to me? I hope it only sounds confident. I feel ABSURDLY confident.'

*　　*　　*

'Why was he so confident?' Catherine asked.

Sir Dillwyn Evans beamed at her across his small sitting-room, which was as comfortable and tidy and highly polished as he was himself. He had been among the first to answer the polite letter she had sent to all the people whose reminiscences of Neil Campion she hoped to hear; he had declared himself available any weekday morning during the current Parliamentary session, and happy to impart to her 'such few recollections as I have that interesting and undeservedly forgotten character'.

'He was a confident man, yes, it's true. It was the confidence of youth, I daresay. Youth, good looks, success in action in the war, success with women, convictions. He was a man of conviction, you know. No doubt about that.'

Sir Dillwyn Evans was known as the Father of the House of Commons. He had been elected to Parliament in 1934 at the age of twenty-nine and had been there ever since, except for a gap between 1942 and 1945 for War Service in the Navy, and an electoral defeat in 1945 which he had rectified in 1950. He had been a Parliamentary Private Secretary to a number of Ministers but had not sought higher office. He was a partner in a family firm of solicitors in Cardiff; a position in the Government would have entailed a financial sacrifice. Besides, he had never seen himself as a second Lloyd George.

'The young fellows ask my advice,' he told Catherine. 'The new members. I tell them how it all works, the Labour fellows as well. When they come into the House and ask the form, want to know about Parliamentary procedure, they always get the same answer, no matter who they ask. Ask old Evans, they say, he knows more about how this place functions than Erskine May or any other reference book, that's what they say. Dillwyn will tell you what to do, they say. And I do. I tell them. Even that fiery feminist who terrifies her own Party. I have her eating out of my hand when she wants to make a speech on the adjournment.'

His shirt had big blue stripes on it, his dark suit was perfectly pressed, his shoes and his bald forehead shone, his pink cheeks and his small white hands seemed only a moment ago to have been washed in the most expensive and sweet-smelling soap – lavender, Catherine thought she could smell. There would be a dab of eau de cologne on the clean white handkerchief which obtruded from his breast pocket.

'You must have a happy life,' she said, diverted.

'I believe I am the happiest man I know,' he answered instantly. 'I believe in God and in the institution which I serve, the Mother of Parliaments. My only sadness is that my dear wife left me twenty years ago, left me, I mean, for a better place.'

Catherine nodded sympathetically.

'Where I believe I shall in due course see her again,' said Sir Dillwyn confidently. 'In the meantime I have health, faith, work, what more can a man want?' The beaming smile returned. 'But I mustn't bore you. You want to talk about Neil Campion. He was not a good House of Commons man, you know. He was listened to, when he spoke, which was not often. He was treated with respect. The House respects a man who has had a good war. He was made a PPS and then just before the War a Junior Minister, but frankly I always felt his ultimate destiny would have been outside the House of Commons.'

'Not in politics at all?'

'Possibly not. Possibly in business. He might have made a great fortune. Or had influence in some kind of international sphere, the United Nations even. He had spent those years in Africa, you remember. He might have played some part there, after the last War. It was perhaps the fact that he had been out of England between his service in the 1914 War and his election to Parliament which accounted for his being rather out of sympathy with the ordinary Englishman. At least that was the feeling I had about him. He was not in sympathy with the ordinary fellow, he was not a good constituency Member, he had no real feeling for domestic politics. Economics – well, we were all wrong about economics.'

'He made a few speeches about that sort of thing, didn't he? Though mainly his speeches in Parliament seem to have been about aviation.'

'That was his subject, yes. He felt we were letting slip a great opportunity to develop our civil aviation industry. In that I feel sure he was quite right. But I think he did contribute every now and then to debates on economic policy. I remember one speech he made which ran into a lot of criticism. He more or less blamed the Americans for the collapse of the German Banks, said they should have controlled the speculators and prevented the rush of capital to the New York stock exchange. I seem to remember he was rather anti-American all round.'

'You spoke of him as a man of conviction. What would you say his convictions were?'

'The ordinary convictions of a true-born Englishman,' said Sir Dillwyn, decidedly. 'Conservative. Loyal. Patriotic.'

Catherine waited. Sir Dillwyn looked solemn.

'Yet you don't feel he would have gone on as a Conservative loyal patriotic politician?' said Catherine eventually.

'He was not a House of Commons man. He was not a good compromiser. He did not really like the democratic process. I think that is really what I mean. He was too impatient. Perhaps too arrogant.'

'He seems from the correspondence I've read to have had quite a following outside Parliament. There are letters from Bernard Shaw, Smuts, T. E. Lawrence, all sorts of people.'

'Certainly he had a following, and a growing reputation. He wrote well, he took part in wireless programmes, he was very much a Society figure, with his wife. That meant a lot more in those days. They entertained. They went about. I know very little of that side of his life. I only knew him in the House or occasionally at the Carlton Club; but as I've said he was not a clubbable man.'

'Did you like him?'

'Do you know now that you ask me, just straight out like that, I don't believe I did.' He looked across at her in some surprise, and said again, 'I don't believe I did.'

Catherine smiled encouragingly.

Sir Dillwyn shifted slightly in his chair and absent-mindedly re-arranged his pocket handkerchief. 'I had no reason not to like him. It would be too strong to say I positively disliked him. But he really wasn't at all my sort of chap. Probably be different now. I've learnt to be tolerant. One has to be, doesn't one? In this life of ours? But I was younger then, very young in fact, several years younger than he was. He used to look at one with a sort of half-smile and those cold bright blue eyes and one felt pretty sure he was thinking what an ass one was. He may have been right, mind you, but he didn't have to show it. And then he was supposed to be clever and so on but somehow one never saw him doing any actual work if you know what I mean. Elusive, I suppose you could say. I never quite knew what he was up to myself. But certainly there were people who set great store by him and he mixed with a lot of interesting people. He's someone we'd have heard more of if he hadn't died. What would we have heard, you may ask, what sort of thing would we have heard? And I would have to answer, I'm not sure, I'm not at all sure about that.'

'I'd like to be able to make a guess,' said Catherine. 'I don't feel it's going to be much of a book unless I can.'

*   *   *

Catherine's daughter-in-law Susannah had long soft brown hair which she wore in an untidy knot on the top of her head. When Tom had brought her round to supper for the first time Catherine had said afterwards, 'She smiles too much,' and her husband Bernard has said, 'It's a fault on the right side,' and now all these years later Catherine, though quite willing to allow that it was on the right side, still thought it was a fault. The smile was an eager smile, overflowing with compassion. Catherine was not against compassion, but she thought there were occasions which did not require so much of it, occasions such as her own arrival, after a short comfortable drive from London ('You must be exhausted') or Tom's spending the whole of dinner explaining to them the Lloyds system of self-regulation ('An underwriter's job is so terribly demanding') or the elder daughter Annabel, aged eight, saying she had not been to school that day because she had had a bit of a headache ('Poor old Bel seems to have inherited my wretched migraines'). Catherine denied feeling in the least tired, said that she had never seen Tom looking so carefree and suggested that Annabel's headache was probably brought on by watching too much television. Susannah sighed sympathetically and said, 'It must be such hard work writing a biography. All that research. I wouldn't know where to begin.'

'It's quite fun really. You can go and bother all sorts of people you'd never otherwise come across.'

'He was rather a good chap, wasn't he?' said Tom, lighting his pipe.

Catherine, answering, wondered at the same time as she so often did how dear Tom could possibly have become so pompous. For of course he was kind and helpful and good as he always had been, but how could he have chosen to become a sort of caricature of a City commuter, and how, having been brought up by her, could he have chosen such a meaningless little person as a wife? For clearly it was the wife's fault he had become so boring. The one thing that can be said about Ireland, Catherine thought, is that there's no one like Susannah there. Susannah is an English phenomenon. No doubt also French, or German, or American; but not Irish. But then what did she know about Ireland nowadays? She seldom went there. Perhaps by now there was a new burgeoning bourgeoisie. The Ireland of her youth was increasingly a land of her imagination, in which no one was boring.

'Mama's not listening, darling. Maybe it's time for bed.'

'It's just that I'm not much good on economics,' said Catherine.

Tom had launched into a comparison between the problems of the thirties and those of the eighties; it would be sound, she was sure, and in tune with the latest thinking of the CBI and the Conservative Party. She wished Susannah would not call her Mama. After the wedding Catherine had said to her, 'You must call us Bernard and Catherine. If you're too embarrassed at first you needn't call us anything until you feel like it.' But she never had felt like it and somehow after Bernard's death Catherine had become Mama, and Susannah's mother, the stockbroker's widow from St Albans, was Mums, and Catherine was Granny, and Mums was Guggums.

'Anyway,' said Catherine, 'I don't think Campion was much of an original thinker about economics. Although I must admit a lot of things about him are not clear to me yet. I'm beginning to worry that it's going to be a boring book. I'm not getting very close to him somehow.'

'Has it occurred to you that they might want a boring book?' said Tom. 'I mean if it's been commissioned by the family perhaps all they want is a respectful memorial volume. Has it in fact been commissioned by the family?'

'That's a very interesting point, Tom. Do you know I've not the faintest idea who's paying me? I just assumed it was the publisher. It didn't occur to me that the family would want a memorial volume now, so long after his death. They'd have commissioned something like that thirty years ago surely?'

'But then how good a publishing proposal is it – as you say, after all these years – unless the family is to some extent subsidising it? After all he was only quite a minor figure in public life. He died at forty-two. Most public men reach the height of their careers after that age.'

'That's true. Though there's some interesting stuff among the papers. I must say it did occur to me that Brackenbury was paying me rather generously for a book that wouldn't be likely to have a very large sale. On the other hand publishers do the oddest things. They often haven't the faintest idea what's going to sell and what isn't. Luckily for most writers. Still, it's an interesting thought.'

'You could always ask him.'

'I could. But I don't think I will.'

Tom looked at her questioningly.

'Innocence can be a useful defence,' she said. 'It might change my attitude a little if I knew the answer. I shouldn't like to feel my hands in any way tied.'

Tom nodded sagely and puffed at his pipe. She saw that he understood, as he always did when he paid proper attention.

'A hot drink before bed, Mama?'

'No, thank you, Susannah.'

Of course she was pretty, in a sort of gangling way; Catherine was the first to admit that. But for such a long person to have such a short neck was hardly appropriate.

'Perhaps I'll go on up then,' said Susannah, looking hurt.

'I'll be up in a moment,' said Tom benignly, not noticing the hurt look. He would not notice the compassionate smiles either, Catherine thought. Susannah simply filled the role of wife in the comfortable comedy of his daily life; she did not have to be thought about too much; cared for, of course, and relied upon; where temperamental differences obtruded they were to be adjusted to if possible but otherwise ignored. Susannah had been his current girl friend at the moment when he had decided it was time he got married; Catherine had preferred her immediate predecessor, Helga, the Swede. Tom had always liked tall girls, tall and silly, but respectable. But Helga's silliness and respectability were Swedish and therefore more acceptable because less familiar; it was the Englishness of Susannah which Catherine found so particularly irritating.

'I am of course quite an intolerant person,' said Catherine. 'And prejudiced, no doubt. But I can't seem to apply any of my prejudices to Neil Campion, whether for or against. I can't get hold of him, somehow.'

'We had Nick and Etta over the other day,' said Tom. 'They'd been to see some friends nearby and they rang up and came over.'

'You mean – talking of people about whom I am intolerant?'

'Perhaps.'

'He caused his father a good deal of distress. And a good deal of money. Also no one likes to be reminded of their failures.'

'He's forgotten his failures.'

'I haven't forgotten mine.'

'Yours?'

'As a mother.'

'Oh, really!'

'He was weak, and dishonest. Clearly that was my fault. It is always the mother's fault.'

'Oh, come on . . .'

'Besides it's better that I leave him alone. He knows I wasn't on his side over all that. It's better that he makes his own life without having to bother about my possible disapproval. He's got Etta.'

'Splendid girl, Etta. I like her. Susannah finds her a bit Italian.'

'Of course she's a bit Italian. She's Italian.'

'Susannah thinks she rolls her eyes at men more than is usual in Sevenoaks.'

'Very likely.'

'She's also clever, and Susannah doesn't awfully like clever women.'

'What's Nick doing now?'

'Some new scheme or other. I never ask nowadays. Etta's doing quite a bit of journalism, I think that's a help. Glossy magazines mainly, quite amusing. She said something about your chap, now that I come to think of it. Campion. I happened to say that you were working on the biography and she said she knew someone else who was writing about him, I can't remember who she said it was. Some fellow journalist, I think.'

'How odd. Do try and remember.'

'It will come back to me. Some name like Adams. Macadam. Adam. Madden. That's right, Madden. A man called Madden.'

* * *

Etta was a Florentine, secretive and ironical. She had also a capacity for indecision which seemed inexhaustible. Vacillation in Etta became a fine art; and yet she had a powerful personality. This combination of weak will and strong persona exerted a

70

magnetism over both men and women, but especially over men. Men frequently fell in love with Etta. That was what most of the indecisions were about.

These days she was undecided as to whether or not to leave her husband and live with her lover. Her lover wanted to take her back to Italy, which he hardly knew, although he spoke Italian well. Etta preferred living in England. She said she found the conversation freer and less stereotyped, and the fashion world into which her journalism took her more fun. She even preferred the language; she thought Italian writers suffered from feeling themselves part of a minor literature, forced into regionalism or empty rhetoric. Her lover disagreed with her on all these points.

Etta's husband Nicholas was handsome and polite, but he was no good with money; recurring disappointments on this score had undermined her good opinion of him. It had also become clear that his schemes for making money – some of them quite grandiose – had no object other than the money itself. He was not interested in spending it, or in acquiring objects, or houses, or in travelling, or in building up a business, or in change, or fun, or fame. The effort, the apparent compulsion, to make money was an end in itself. This seemed to Etta uncivilised, and she was beginning to think that the obsession which had once seemed rather intriguing was no more than the neurosis of an otherwise dull fellow. And yet she was fond of him in a way.

The lover, having if nothing else very much more to say for himself, was probably better able to cope with her. But then at the very thought of being coped with Etta jibbed. Standing at the window of the little sitting-room which she had made pretty and colourful and in the corner of which was the table and the tiny black electronic typewriter on which she was supposed to be writing an article on Italian restaurants in London, she made a restless movement like a horse under unwelcome restraint, shaking her head and moving from one foot to the other before

71

turning back into the room, smoothing her thick dark hair with a hand on either side of her head, sitting down at the typewriter. Did she really care that Italian cooks no sooner arrived in London than they started to add cream to dishes they knew perfectly well were better off without it? You couldn't leave a perfectly nice husband just because someone came along and started shouting at you that you were the most beautiful woman in the world. Of course not; what was she thinking of? The telephone began to ring. It will be Nick, she thought, about tonight. But if it is Alfred? Everything hangs on this, she thought, reaching out her hand, destiny is making me a sign.

'Etta? It's Catherine. I haven't seen you both for so long.'

'Oh, but how wonderful. Come to dinner next week.'

Destiny, as usual, was refusing to play.

* * *

Although Catherine liked living alone, she recognised that there were times when it imposed a strain. There were also times when the change from a solitary life to a communal one and back again brought about a feeling of dislocation not quite to be accounted for by the mere interruption of daily rhythm. She was relieved to be back in her own house after her weekend with Tom and Susannah but she found it hard to settle down to work. In search of stimulus she picked up one of the boxes which she had collected from Eleanor's bank and which contained a long letter from Neil written when he had first arrived in Kenya. The letter was addressed to Eleanor; their parents had died within a year of each other soon after the Great War. Catherine had found this letter interesting for two reasons, first because it revealed an easy friendliness on Neil's part towards Eleanor which nothing else she had discovered so far had led her to believe had existed, and secondly because it showed a response to natural beauty and human idiosyncracy which was so lively and so willing to be amused that she was able for the first time to imagine Neil Campion as an enthusiastic young man only different from other such young men in the acuteness of his observation. She had read the letter on her preliminary look through Eleanor's material and had put it on one side with the other contents of that particular box for further investigation at the appropriate moment; she had concentrated first on the wartime letters. The day after her return from her visit to Tom and Susannah, which was also the day after her telephone conversation with Etta, she re-opened what she took to be the Africa box, thinking to find there something more about the character whose later activities, those undertaken after his marriage and mostly at the Durdans, remained for the moment baffling. Neil Campion seemed, according to such evidence as she so far had of this later life, to have been two different people, one of whom was the politician whose speeches were indistinguishable from those of a hundred other Conservative Members of Parliament in the Baldwin and Chamberlain days; the other was a much odder character, whose speeches to certain gatherings, and whose writings addressed presumably to the same audience, had a mystical and as far as Catherine could discern a somewhat cloudy element towards which she was prepared to be sympathetic but which she found inexplicable; there was nothing in her study of Neil's character so far which showed her where in him these notions might have their roots; it was as if, when he spoke in this sense, he was another man. She felt that she was looking for a clue, and that the clue was probably a person, whether known to Neil personally or through books (as it might have been, say, Nietzsche – but it was not Nietzsche) and that if she could once put her finger on this influence everything else about Neil's life would fall into place. She had said something of this to Effie, but Effie had had nothing much to suggest, pointing out only that to be in the House of Commons you had to be a party member, and suggesting that perhaps Neil preferred to talk about the things he most believed in privately, or when he knew he was with others who felt as he did. She herself, Effie said, knew nothing about ideas – 'never been interested in them, quite frankly. I shouldn't bother about Neil's ideas either, if I were you, they were always changing according to the last person he'd been talking to.'

This rather sharp comment, which had been made on the telephone and could have been accounted for, Catherine supposed, by the simple chance of Effie's happening to be in a bad mood at that particular moment, was not at all in keeping with her usual way of talking about her husband, which was hardly ever critical; it did however accord with a reference which Catherine had found in the published diaries of one of Stanley Baldwin's chief advisers, a civil servant of considerable acumen, who had told his master at one point that Neil Campion had '. . . ability, but unreliable judgment. He is apt to be swayed by irrational considerations, being, I very much fear, something of a romantic.'

Had this so-called romantic found something in Africa for which his English childhood and his European war had not prepared him? In pursuit of this possibility Catherine turned to what she thought of as the Africa box, only to find what she had failed to notice before, that half of the box contained not letters but Neil's school reports. There was one more letter to Eleanor from Africa, describing a morning flight towards the mountains with someone called Peter. They had flown above herds of wild animals, and encountered an elderly pair of white settlers intrepidly growing coffee at too high an altitude and many miles from the nearest town. 'Perhaps I'll end up like that myself – there are quite good offers of land for soldier settlers – space, beauty, total independence – it all seems like a long drink of cool water from the purest of wells after France in the War. And you should see some of the fine young Maasai hunters – they are a fine people – one would always be able to deal with them on the simple basis of a shared understanding of manliness and honour. Listen, why not throw in the teaching and come out here for a few months. I've already come across several people in need of a helping hand – all you'd need to do would be to raise the fare. Truly it is a cleaner world than the one we've been busy polluting with the filth of war for the last few years. Do come, Eleanor.'

These letters made more understandable the bitterness with which Eleanor had spoken of her brother's marriage; it had evidently brought to an end her close relationship with her brother. Catherine resolved to ask Effie a few gentle questions about how she had got on with her sister-in-law in those early days. Further clues were for the moment lacking; Catherine found herself faced with school reports of devastating dullness. There had been nothing wrong with Neil's work; he had been fairly regularly top of the form in every subject except mathematics but his teachers' comments were brief and unenthusiastic, and the housemaster's refrain – 'Takes insufficient part in the life of the house' – became monotonous. 'I have found it hard to get to know a boy who takes such a small part in the life of the house,' 'Gives an unfortunate impression of arrogance. Should try to contribute more,' 'Is too self-indulgent. Must have clearer standards and not act on the impulse of the moment.' Now what did that refer to, on what impulse of the moment had he acted that particular bad term? There was no knowing. Probably he had told a lie. The coldness, even hostility, of the reports reminded her of the reports she and Bernard used to get from Nicholas's school. They had never thought anything of Nicholas, the men who were supposed to be educating him; and certainly he had lied to them. She remembered Bernard turning from the window to look at her as she sat at her desk, as she was sitting now. 'They were right in those school reports. He's a liar. A liar and a cheat.' Pain and anger had given his voice an unfamiliar rasping tone. She had thought he looked at her as if he hated her. She had said, 'We have to deal with this together, Bernard.' But he had thought

75

no woman could understand what it was for a man to be ashamed of his son.

Areas of misunderstanding, she thought; there had been areas of misunderstanding. Areas? Oceans, deserts. Had they not always been there? They had become harder to ignore after the boys left home, that was all. That was when her optimism had deserted her, that was when Bernard had become so irritable, so angry with her, for having lost her optimism (for she should have known *he* would never have any) that he had been glad to die, that she had been glad that he should die. Slowly she took off her reading glasses, leant her elbows on the desk, and put her head in her hands. There was a sound in her head such as you might hear on a still day in the country if you walked near a line of pylons. She felt exhausted, as if the struggle to control her thoughts were a physical one; and as if she might sit there for ever, holding her immensely heavy head in her hands. But it would not do. She sat up. She would go out, buy some food, clean the house. Tomorrow would be a better day. Briskly straightening the pile of papers before putting them back into the box, she shook out an opened envelope she had not noticed before. On it was written, in Neil's hand, 'Eleanor – after my death'; it was empty. She piled everything back into the box and closed her notebook. It could all wait.

*   *   *

Etta minded very much that none of Nicholas's business friends seemed ever to have read a book. Occasionally they might have seen a film, never a play, unless it was a musical to which they had taken foreign clients. They might read a thriller on an aeroplane of course, or happen to see a play on television; but what relaxation from their work they had (and it was little enough) consisted in playing squash, or occasionally snooker, or even bridge (at a club for that purpose and for high stakes).

In other words they were philistines, and Etta was something of an intellectual snob. She liked to have seen the latest plays and exhibitions and to have read the latest novels (her English was perfect). She had written a little poetry herself at school but had soon recognised her own lack of talent; however she had continued to think all that important – perhaps even the most important thing in the world – and had had as one of her youthful fantasies before she met Nicholas the idea of herself as the perfect companion, scene-setter and helpmeet for a great artist. Nicholas was certainly not a great artist but she had liked his gentleness and thought him in need of support; he was extraordinarily short of self-confidence. When he had told her that he had once been involved in a company which had been dealing in the commodity market and had spent his clients' money and then made a massive loss on barley futures, as a result of which he had had to spend two months in prison, she felt all the more sympathy; he was too gentle to have meant any harm, obviously his partner had let him down. All the same she would probably never have married him had she not been pregnant. The pregnancy had overcome her habitual indecision, and had ended in a miscarriage a month after the wedding. Without a child to distract them, their thoughts were free to dwell on the question of whether or not she would ever have married him had one not been expected; it was the canker at the heart of the never robust rose of their union.

When Nicholas had told her the day before his mother was due to have dinner with them that a certain Ronald Bedford who was in the course of floating a company on the Stock Exchange and was likely to make millions of pounds had asked them all to dinner in a Thai restaurant in St John's Wood and had particularly insisted that it would be so nice if Nicholas brought his mother Etta was aghast.

'It's not possible, Nicholas, how can you think of such a thing? What could your mother have in common with this man?'

It seemed Mr Bedford had hundreds of grand friends who

thought him wonderful, he employed great numbers of them in his various enterprises, he entertained splendidly, he owned a television company, he was in the course of buying a glossy magazine Etta had sometimes worked for, he owned a group of companies, he was going to float it, it was in PR and communications, it was enormously successful. But Etta hung her head and allowed the curtain of dark hair to conceal her pale face. Nicholas went into the neat white kitchen and prepared the supper she had bought earlier; he brought it into the sitting-room and laid it out on the round table by the window. Etta did not move.

'Would you like me to ring up my mother and put her off?' asked Nicholas gently.

Etta shook her head. He waited. She said, 'Yes.' Then she shook her head again and said, 'No.' He went to the telephone.

'Oh, but of course. I don't mind at all, we can do it any time,' said Catherine. 'Listen, could you just ask Etta something? Tom happened to mention that he'd seen you both and that Etta had said she knew someone who was working on the same man I'm writing about, Campion, Neil Campion. She doesn't happen to remember who it is, does she?'

'She wants to know who's the person who's writing about Neil Campion, Etta. Do you remember?'

Etta shook her bent head.

'She doesn't remember. Oh, wasn't it Madden? I know Madden. Was it Madden, Etta? It probably was. He's got a finger in every pie. Strange man. Etta knows him quite well. He does a diary page under the name of Christopher North ... yes, that's it, you could get hold of him through the paper. Alfred Madden, he's called. All right, see you soon, sorry about tomorrow.'

Etta rose from the sofa and walked slowly towards the table.

'That's all right then, isn't it?' said Nicholas hopefully.

Etta gazed dreamily at the prettily arranged avocado and orange salad on her plate.

'Of course,' she said distantly. 'Of course it's all right.'

By the following evening her mood had improved. She had spent the afternoon at a new art gallery in Rotherhithe. It was in a fine nineteenth-century warehouse, most of which was being converted into expensive flats. The young developer responsible was already a millionaire from his last such venture and likely to do even better out of this one. The art gallery, which he was letting without rent or security of tenure, was there as witness to his concern with things other than the profit motive, perhaps as a sop to his own conscience, perhaps as something with which to impress the planning authorities should the inhabitants of the first development which was next door object to the second development which was likely to interfere with the view of the Thames for which they had paid so highly. The gallery was huge and high and cold; various young people dressed uniformly in paint-bespattered black overcoats were applying whitewash to its walls with the same bold haphazard brush strokes with which they had presumably painted most of the vast canvasses which were in evidence, though the latter were mostly in tones of brown and purple. Two immense monsters of vaguely equine bearing made of tinfoil and wire-netting stood at one end of the gallery; the other was given over to a giant brass bedstead, without a mattress. One of the young men in black overcoats gave Etta a cup of coffee and they sat side by side on the uncomfortable edge of the bedstead while he expressed to her his belief that processions of high-earning City men would daily cross the river and invest in these triumphs of modern art. Etta, quite charmed, promised him a glowing recommendation in the magazine article she was writing and being a scrupulous person spent some time looking for a picture to which she could conscientiously give a favourable mention; finally she allowed considerations of size to decide and chose some small luridly red canvasses which she was told expressed the painter's passionate feminism; she left quickly for fear of being told why.

The experience cheered her; she felt that out of such optimism and activity good must come and she was pleased to think her own article might in some small way contribute towards it. When she got home she dressed in her favourite dark green dress and was pleased when Nicholas told her she looked beautiful. When they arrived at the restaurant where Mr Bedford was giving his party she smiled warmly as Nicholas introduced her to their host.

Ronald Bedford was very tall and had a solidity which together with his rosy cheeks and shiny black hair put Etta in mind of Signore Noé, whose wooden figure in command of all the animals in the ark was a familiar part of her childhood; many were the times she had thrown him at her sister or stood him beside her plate to watch her eat her pasta. Jack, commanded from the crowd, was a reduced version; less red-cheeked, less shiny-haired, and distinctly less authoritative.

'Oh my,' he said obediently. 'Lovely, Ron. A lovely girl.'

'My brother Jack,' said Ronald Bedford. 'Part of my team. Now, my dear, believe you me,' he put his arm round her and clamped her uncomfortably to his side, 'your husband is going to be a big help to us. He knows his onions, that boy. And if he comes through we'll see him right. I never forget. If he sticks to me he can come with me where I'm going. A man's got to be able to see over the roof of his own house, isn't that so? A woman no. For a woman the family's everything. But a man's got to be able to see over the roof of his own house. This is the Earl of Trowbridge. You know him?'

The Earl was a sandy-haired man with a bristly moustache who told her he was a director of one of Ronald Bedford's companies. He did not spend much time in London, he said, because he suffered from insomnia there, but Ronald liked to come and stay with him in the country and do a bit of shooting; he had the greatest admiration for Ronald. 'He's an extraordinarily kind man. Nothing's too much trouble. Goodness knows where the Shah of Persia would have been without him.'

Etta began to point out that the Shah of Persia was not only dispossessed but dead but Lord Trowbridge's enthusiasm would not be checked. The whole oil industry, it seemed, was in Mr Bedford's pocket and the newspaper world at his beck and call and his charitable undertakings legion and his deep love of the stage renowned. Burnt-out comedians and long-forgotten music hall artistes spoke of his generosity with tears in their eyes and gave of their services free for the sake of the disabled. 'That's Jack's department,' said Lord Trowbridge. 'The fund for the disabled. Everyone has their part to play. Mine is to allow my name to be put on the paper, don't you know.' He gave a couple of short honking laughs and blew his nose on a green spotted handkerchief. 'All I'm good for. Damned decent of him to pay me for it. Look here, you don't want to talk to me. There's that television fellow. That's the sort of person you want to talk to. Or this one, yes. He's in television too, is he?'

'Just a hack. Alfred Madden.' He held out his hand. Lord Trowbridge shook it warmly. Etta looked desperate.

Alfred Madden was looking at her intently.

'I thought you said you weren't going to be here.'

'I wasn't. Nicholas's mother was coming to dinner.'

'But she didn't.'

'Nicholas put her off.'

'What a relief.'

'No. I like her very much. She's very intelligent, very charming. I wish I saw more of her.'

'Ah. And what do you think of our host?'

Etta looked round to reassure herself that Lord Trowbridge had moved away in the direction of the bar.

'This Bedford,' she said. 'He is terrible.'

'Let's leave.'

'I have not lived so long in Italy without being able to recognise a mafioso. He will go to prison. This is England and not Italy and so he will go to prison.'

'My dear, there may be no mafia in England. But there is the old boy network. It is just as bad.'

'This man is not an old boy,' said Etta firmly.

'Let's leave. Have dinner with me.'

Etta seemed not to hear.

'Nicholas's mother is writing a book about somebody you spoke of. She has been asked to write it by a publisher, or maybe by his family. Didn't you say you were writing about somebody called Campion?'

Madden looked serious. After a moment he said, 'Has she been given any papers, letters, diaries, do you know?'

'I don't know.'

'I shall have to think. Don't say anything to her about me, will you?'

Etta shook her head. He saw by her stricken face that she had already done so.

'I must talk to you,' he said. 'No one will notice if we leave. We can have dinner together, somewhere quiet.'

'I must tell Nicholas.'

Madden nodded. 'I'll wait here.'

Etta searched among the crowd of noisy strangers until she saw Nicholas in conversation with a small fair-haired girl, and approaching found they were talking about share prices with every sign of satisfaction. She said she felt tired and might go home. Nicholas looked concerned but seemed relieved when she said Madden would give her a lift. She struggled back to where she had left Madden and found he had been buttonholed by a well-known journalist who, white-faced and scantily red-haired, was leaning back upon his heels and holding forth on what seemed to be his latest article for the right-wing weekly for which among many other journals he worked. His speech was indistinct but his theme seemed to be that women were only raped because they asked for it; this was propounded with apparent benevolence and much friendly blinking from behind large horn-rimmed spectacles. Nevertheless the thesis was uncongenial to Etta and the instances he put forward to support it struck her as disgusting. Overwrought by her feelings of guilt towards Nicholas, she suddenly give a stifled cry and kicked the journalist quite hard on the shin, then turning away she blundered through the crowd and out of the door. Alfred Madden, following, emerged on to the pavement only just in time to see her running down the middle of the road, the light skirt of the green dress fluttering round her long legs, shouting for a taxi.

*   *   *

Catherine had got into the way of calling in on Effie Campion every now and then about the middle of the morning. She always telephoned before going and she never stayed more than an hour, often less. The casual nature of the visits, and the fact that she was careful for the moment never to press any particular query further than Effie seemed to want it to be pressed, appeared to be undermining the latter's initial nervousness; conversation was becoming easier, which is not to say that Catherine yet felt that Effie wholly trusted her. In view of the fact that her selection as authorised biographer had been in part Effie's own, Catherine found this a little surprising. On the other hand she had noticed that, whereas Neil Campion's brother and sister had asserted that the idea of a biography had come from his wife, Effie said it came from the brother and sister.

'I noticed from your husband's letters to his sister from Africa that he had a friend called Peter there,' said Catherine.

'What letters? I know nothing about any letters to Eleanor.' Effie's eyes narrowed and her mouth turned down at the corners in a curiously childish look of disapproval which Catherine was coming to recognise.

'Just some letters he wrote describing his life in Africa. They're rather well written.'

'Well, of course, he was good at describing things, yes.' Effie looked slightly mollified. 'I know nothing about that part of his life. It was all before I met him.'

'And you didn't know Peter?'

'Oh, I knew Peter, of course I knew Peter. He was a great friend of ours.'

'And he was Peter ... ? I couldn't quite read how his surname was spelt.'

'Heinrich. Peter Heinrich. He'd been a flyer too. On the opposite side of course. But it gave them something in common. They both went to Africa after the war because they wanted to go on flying, and because they felt ordinary people in their own countries were somehow too different. That's what Neil said anyway.'

'And you saw quite a lot of him, of Peter, I mean, after you were married?'

'Oh, a bit, yes. Not more than anyone else, don't you know.'

'I suppose he'd come back to Germany by then? Did you go and see him there? There are one or two references in the diaries to going to Germany.'

'We stayed with him once or twice, it was right in the country, in the part that's in East Germany now, I don't suppose one would be allowed to go there, would one. Such lovely country it was. Wonderful woods.'

'What happened to Peter, I wonder?'

'I've no idea,' said Effie. 'We saw less of him and then there was the War and so on. I never heard from him afterwards. I suppose he died.'

'Was he pro-Hitler?'

'Not really. They thought they could control him, didn't they? Peter came from an old military family. But one lost touch, you know, I've no idea what became of him.' Effie's face had assumed a certain vague and bleak look not unfamiliar to

Catherine, who interpreted it as a sign of reluctance to continue to confide.

'On a completely different subject,' said Catherine quickly. 'You did say something about a journalist called Alfred Madden. Oddly enough someone else happened to mention him the other day and seemed to think he might be interested in writing about your husband.'

'Who mentioned him?'

'My daughter-in-law, funnily enough. She writes for magazines a bit and she'd met him somewhere, I suppose in connection with that.'

'He's a most unpleasant piece of work. He once had some sort of love affair with a niece of mine who turned him down. Ever since then he's had a grudge against her family. A dreadful man.'

'I see. So he's of no importance?'

'Of no importance whatsoever. Oh, Sam darling, you're up, have you had breakfast?'

Startled, Catherine looked round to see that Sam had appeared silently in the doorway. He was barefooted and dressed in black trousers and a black T-shirt, from the short sleeves of which his arms emerged white and unexpectedly muscular; he did not look well. Having greeted Catherine politely, he murmured something about coffee and went out of the room.

'Half-term,' said Effie. 'They don't get up in the morning these days. I usually have to wake him up at lunch time. Of course he's out till all hours. Goodness knows what they get up to, but what can one do? I try to say be back by a certain time and so on but he says none of his friends' parents mind so one's helpless really, isn't one? I suppose as long as he's with other people he can't come to much harm, can he? What did you do about your boys when they were growing up?'

'It wasn't the same. It didn't seem to start so young.'

'I do rather worry about sex. I did raise the subject but he said it was all explained to them on television. I've never seen it explained on television, have you? Not that one would dream of watching if it was. Darling Potty explains to him about money, thank goodness, and of course one does tell him not to take drugs, but then he puts on that tremendously distant look and one really never knows whether he's listening or not.'

Effie looked uncertainly at Catherine, as if hoping for reassurance.

'They can often look after themselves better than one thinks,' said Catherine mildly.

*　　*　　*

Alfred Madden lived in a basement flat off Shepherds Bush Road, the Brook Green (or smarter) end. He had a big light sitting-room opening onto a pleasant garden, cultivated with loving care by his landlords, both of whom were also journalists, to look as much like a half-tamed wilderness as possible. They had made the basement into a separate flat for their son who was a wild-life photographer on a two-year assignment somewhere near the South Pole. The walls of the flat were hung with blown-up photographs of elephants and sunsets; it had been Africa last year. Madden had changed very little in the flat; he was not much interested in his surroundings. He lay on a bulky brown sofa beneath a flight of flamingoes and tried to sleep; it was five o'clock in the afternoon.

He was a small man, dark-haired and dark-skinned, his aspect Mediterranean. Sometimes he shaved twice a day, but these days if his evening excursions were to take him to parties of the younger set he forebore to do so, an unshaven look being fashionable. His hair, which was wavy and abundant, was streaked with grey; his face looked sulky in repose but when he was with other people (which in his waking hours he usually was) it was often illumined by an expression of lively curiosity;

his eyes, though sometimes bloodshot, could convey great intensity of feeling. He tried to sleep but failed. Images obsessed him, of Etta naked, of a high cool room and Etta looking out over Florence, of himself writing at a big ornate table, Etta on a sofa reading, in the evening light from tall windows. He was an obsessive person. There had never been a time when one fiercely desirable picture after another had not tormented his hours of rest, or one passionately held conviction after another not dominated his thoughts and his conversation. The obsession with Etta was powerful, even exhausting, but not so strong as to exclude all the others. He wanted to take her away from an atmosphere he felt was polluting them both; he thought of Florence, where he had once spent three weeks, as the ideal city. He imagined a room in a tower, Etta in some sense realised, freed and glorious, himself writing, but proper writing, in other words his novel. He had published one novel already, fifteen years ago, soon after he had come down from Oxford. It had been about an outbreak of cannibalism in a remote Welsh theological college. Intended as a satire on anti-semitism, its uncompromising ferocity had alienated most of the critics. A publisher friend had reissued it in paperback a few years ago with a selection of the original reviews on the cover – 'far-fetched, to say the least' … 'a tasteless extravaganza … extraordinarily unpleasant' – but it still had not sold. Madden did not usually appear short of confidence – there were people who found him hard to like for that very reason – but he had been hurt by his novel's reception. At Oxford his literary talents had been treated with more respect; his scorn appreciated, his awkwardness upheld. People there had seemed to understand that, though he was willing to amuse in order to attract people's attention, what he really wanted to do was to excoriate. There was so much he felt called upon to avenge.

He had been born in France, in a remote little town in the Ardèche soon after the end of the Second World War. His parents, who were Austrian, had spent the greater part of the

War more or less in hiding there, in great poverty. His father, a respected lawyer in Vienna, had been one of those who could not believe that what was happening to other Jews could happen to him; he had left it too late. He and his wife had had to leave everything and escape across the border. A succession of desperate moves through German-occupied France found them at the end of the War in the South-West, living anxiously under the eyes of neighbours who might at any moment choose to inform on them. Worn out by the tension and the poverty, Alfred's mother had died of a fever soon after the birth; his father had determined to make a new life unencumbered by an infant son. The birth anyway had been a mistake; the poor wife, suffering from undernourishment, had not recognised the symptoms of pregnancy until too late for an abortion, the means by which she had dealt with earlier pregnancies. The father had gone to America, changed his name, disappeared. This the boy had learnt at one time or another, by means of reluctant answers to sudden questions, from the uncle and aunt who had adopted him. This kindly couple, whom now he never saw, still lived in Cambridge where they had found refuge in the thirties, welcome immigrants because of the uncle's position as Professor of Mathematics at Vienna University. They had brought him up and paid for his good education at a Cambridge independent school; he had secured his scholarship to Oxford and hardly revisited them; they embarrassed him with their respectability, their complete contentment with each other, their, as he saw it, totally unnecessary accents, still residually Austrian. The mother who had died intermittently haunted him. Long periods would pass without her coming into his mind, without his even glancing at the small brown photograph his aunt had given him and which, unframed and tattered at the edges, lay about in his bedroom among the accumulated débris from his pockets, matchboxes and small change, scraps of paper with scribbled telephone numbers on them, restaurant bills, invitation cards; the photograph showed the solemn, slightly heavy face of a young girl with large brown eyes; it had been taken before her marriage. This face would sometimes, after one of these periods of forgetfulness on his part, seem to swim into his consciousness and stay there, causing him to feel a kind of internal bruising all the time it was there, because of the pity he felt for her; then the image would retreat, leaving him free to fancy himself pitiless, which was what he wanted to be. Occasionally he would try consciously to summon the thought of her in order to contrast her life with that of the people he described in his gossip column, so as to keep his scorn at boiling point, or perhaps to strengthen his resolve when he was contemplating some act of treachery, the betrayal of a confidence, the selling of a story too hot for his own column to someone else who would certainly use it. He would use that sad little face as a spur to keep bright his reputation as the meanest though most accurate of the gossip columnists; but he felt it an improper use, and it was that thought, rather than the face itself, which lent him the venom he needed.

And yet he was, if not exactly liked, widely welcomed, invited, sought after; there were many who were glad enough to see their names in his column even though they were mentioned in a derogatory sense, because being mentioned was their way of life, the only way they knew they existed, and there were others, safe in the knowledge that they were not interesting enough to be mentioned, who felt that the presence of the arch-mentioner gave some extra cachet, or perhaps the thrill of danger, to their otherwise quite humdrum social occasions; there were the charity organisers, to whom publicity was part of their business, and the show business personalities who found gossip columns an easier way of keeping their names before the public than acting, there were the bored, who would endure the occasional bite on the hand from those they fed for the sake of being amused, and there was habit, which made a lot of people think that Madden had to be there because Madden was always there. He was a kind of stamp of authenticity, and it made no difference that he was often drunk, because that was how it had always been.

Disturbed now by the telephone he agreed as to where to meet a girl called Caroline who was to take him to a dance later on that evening; he had several other occasions to see to first. He took a shower, under the eye of a giant rhinoceros, whose glance was becoming increasingly baleful as the steam undermined the photograph's hold on the bathroom wall. A stiff whisky to redeem the lingering effects of lunch and he was off into the first of the evening's taxis. Thus launched he went with the current across familiar choppy seas, negotiating a publisher's party, rather staid, a garish fashion show in aid of paraplegics, a cocktail party for what seemed like a hundred or so over-excited children all talking at the tops of their voices about A-levels and Aids, and the noisy opening of a new restaurant. His haul by this time included news of two forthcoming libel actions and one bankruptcy, some interesting developments in terms of who was with whom, and an unexpected request from a man at the restaurant opening who wanted him to print a story to the effect that the proprietor of a well-known chain of supermarkets was about to be blackballed from the Royal Yacht Squadron – 'Just a shot across his bows, what? There's a rumour he's trying to get himself put up.' He duly met Caroline at the appointed place, a pub in the King's Road, she bursting into the pub and apparently out of her strapless scarlet taffeta, so excited was she by her own daring in adding his name to her own on the invitation card. 'No one would notice, would they? Isn't it clever how I've used the same coloured ink, well, it's just biro actually,' and wrapping a shawl round her plump white shoulders and emergent bosom she led the way to her Renault 4 and dashed out merrily into the protesting traffic. 'Hellish dinner-party,' she told him. 'Nothing but Sloanes,' tossing back her shining yellow hair and fluting her defiance of her origins. 'All in the Army or at Exeter University except for Rupert Fox and he's a stockbroker, would you believe? Luckily Amanda was there and she gave me a joint. This party should be good, two bands and all the Royals.'

'No hurry, we're early,' said Madden, clinging onto the strap of his seat-belt.

'I ought to go in with the rest of my party, looks less suspicious.'

'Caroline,' said Madden. 'Will you marry me?'

'Gosh,' said Caroline, slowing down. 'D'you mean that?'

'That's better,' said Madden, letting go of the seat-belt strap.

'Christ, you are a shit, I thought you meant it.' But she drove more slowly and asked him who he would marry if he could. He told her he was in love with a married woman and she tried to guess who it was and he said it was no one she knew, which was true. He began to feel the onset of melancholy; he hoped he was not going to become maudlin. But then they were climbing a flight of stairs together between an extravagance of greenery and she was supporting him manfully for he had become rather unsteady on his feet, and the friendly people sitting at a table at the top of the stairs seemed hardly to glance at the card and on they went to where beneath the chandeliers their host and hostess awaited them and Caroline kissed and chattered and Madden shook hands politely and was in; a glass of champagne was in his hand, friends were greeting him. But it seemed the card-scanners had scanned after all and the word had been quietly passed and a hand was on his elbow and a suggestion was being made as to the possibility of there having been some mistake; Caroline, protesting, was led away by a handsome young man, two others, very like the first, put their arms through Madden's and walked him all the way down the stairs again, apologising profusely for Dad's having got a thing about the Press and passing a fourth young man who said, 'All right, Will?' and Will said, 'All right, Charlie' – 'Are you all in the SAS or something?' asked Madden – and they were outside waiting for a taxi. They lit his cigarette, helped him into the taxi; he thought he saw a fifth identical young man coming out

91

onto the steps. 'Is Dad a Roman Catholic?' he asked. Not as far as they knew, they said, but you could never be sure with Dad. They asked him his address, gave it to the taxi-driver. One of them raising a hand in salute as the taxi drove off called out 'Good night, sir!' and Madden sank back into his seat and began to laugh. He supposed the young pup had seen his grey hairs. He laughed some more. The whole incident seemed to him uproariously funny. In the morning, sober, he might feel different. On the other hand perhaps he was becoming detached, perhaps he already felt like someone on the point of departure. Just let him persuade Etta – for of course he could – just let him finish the present book, throw the cat among the pigeons, and be off. Italy!

'Italia! Italia mia!' he proclaimed to the taxi-driver's back, following this with a vile rendering of 'O sole mio'.

Arrived at his destination he overpaid the taxi-driver, who felt he had earned it, being a musical man. Raising his voice and changing his tune to 'La donna è mobile', Madden made his way down the steps, knocked over his dustbin with a clatter and let himself into his flat.

'I thought you told him to move that bloody dustbin,' said Jan the features editor to Tony the architectural correspondent as they stirred in their bed upstairs.

'I did,' said Tony.

*   *   *

Miss Eleanor Campion, Commandant of a convalescent home in Nottinghamshire in the early part of the Second World War, had made her young nurses do what she referred to as physical jerks once a day. There were two classes, morning and evening, so that those on night duty could not escape. Miss Campion very often took the class herself. She was at that time approaching forty, thick-set, big-busted, fresh-complexioned. Her light brown hair was permanently waved according to the fashion of the time, her uniform was well-tailored, her laced black shoes brilliantly clean, her whole aspect remorselessly efficient. She had a particularly carrying voice, clear and commanding, 'One two one two', she would repeat, jumping up and down in front of the bouncing girls, feet in feet out, slapping her thighs. 'And up – and down – up – and down', never out of breath, never out of time. Catherine, just eighteen, would do her best to avoid being immediately in front of her; she found jumping up and down under the direct gaze of those fearsome blue eyes perfectly terrifying. It was not just that having inevitably broken some rule or other Catherine had a permanently guilty conscience; it was also because in her encounters with Miss Campion she was always aware of a strength of feeling underlying the efficiency and the insistence on discipline which seemed to her disproportionate and alarming. It was as if Miss Campion were only marking time as Commandant of a small convalescent home, keeping in practice as it were; as if what she was really going to do was rule the world. This little group of inexperienced girls with their modicum of training in First Aid were having to stand in for the whole of erring humanity; all the conviction and energy and anger which went into licking them into shape was ready to be unloosed on the rest of the world when the call came; in the meantime Catherine sometimes felt the weight of all that will-power might break them. She had noticed that the other girls did not seem to feel quite as she did; they called the Commandant an old stick and a bully and referred to her as the Nightmare, but they did not seem to feel the weight of oppression under which Catherine laboured. Miss Campion was the first person Catherine had ever hated, and since she had also just fallen in love for the first time, or perhaps even the only time, her memories of Nottinghamshire were in many ways painful. For that reason she very seldom thought of that period in her life and she was only now put in mind of it by some photographs taken at one of the 'conferences' at the Durdans in which Neil and Effie Campion and their guests were to be seen on the lawn in shorts doing – so it was written underneath the photographs – 'Swedish exercises'. So in spite of the distance which his marriage had put between them perhaps Neil's influence was still at work on his younger sister. If that was so, and at least as far as the gymnastics went, the influence was in fact not so much Neil's as, through Neil, Peter Heinrich's.

The discovery that the man with whom Neil had made friends in Africa had been a German had made him immediately more interesting to Catherine. For one thing, if the friendship had continued, it might help to explain one aspect – apparently quite an important aspect – of what she was coming to think of as the Durdans philosophy, although she recognised that this might be too formal a word for something which still seemed to her fairly amorphous. The English provenance of this part of the thing seemed to lie more or less with the Simple Life movement and early Socialism – peace through health, equality through non-competitive games, high minds and regular bowels, vegetarianism, walking tours, planning. Catherine had seen no source for all this in what she knew of the slightly enigmatic but still apparently conventional Conservative Member of Parliament, but supposing Neil had first encountered it in its German version, which would have included progressive education – hence, perhaps the connection with Karl Eberling – and also that rather more mystical element of which Catherine thought she had found echoes in some of Neil's writings from the thirties, then this German thread would immediately make the whole thing more easily conceivable. It also made it important to find out exactly what it had amounted to. Effie Campion had not been anxious to pursue the subject of Peter Heinrich. She had answered vaguely when Catherine had questioned her about his attitude to the Nazis. Obviously Neil Campion could not have been pro-Nazi; the fact that he had been made a Minister in the Churchill Government of

1940 made that clear. His recorded speeches showed him to have been a supporter of the pre-War Government's appeasement policy, but so had been the majority of Members of Parliament and probably the majority of the electorate, at any rate until 1938. But it was important to find out what had happened to Peter Heinrich.

In the meantime she had their correspondence, though it did not seem to extend beyond 1936. She had telephoned Eleanor Campion the day after Effie's disclosure of Peter's nationality, to ask her if she had any recollection of this friend from Neil's African days, and Hugh had answered the telephone and told her in his quavering tones that Eleanor was out at one of her committees – 'tireless, quite tireless, in her charity work'. He thought she had never met the German friend. He himself had never met him either, but they had known about him from Neil's letters from Africa. In fact there were some letters, had they not been in the boxes in Eleanor's bank? Perhaps they were in the drawer, there were some things in the drawer in the desk, he would look, and there they were and of course she was welcome to come and collect them whenever she liked. She went immediately, not certain that Eleanor's welcome would have been so spontaneous, and carried home the file without accepting Hugh's anxious offer of a cup of tea, preferring not to run the risk of encountering his sister.

The correspondence, which seemed to be incomplete, was interesting because of what it revealed about the men who had written it rather than because of what they wrote. The ideas they discussed seemed to Catherine dated and jejune, even touchingly so. 'We have to find new ways of living,' wrote Peter. 'We have to forget the old European systems and find wholeness again.' 'What you say about cultivation of the land is true,' wrote Neil. 'All of our environment has to be thought of as an organic whole. The ghastly spread of town into country has to be resisted; it is so squalid. As you say we have lost our sense of form . . .' 'But you have what we so desperately need, patience,' wrote Peter. 'Your historical sense gives it to you. It gives you a kind of modesty too, as to what one individual can do in his lifetime. We Germans are not a modest race. But as to sense of form, yes, we both had that once, it was the same, it was the Gothic sense, the Gothic understanding; but we in the Thirty Years War, you in your English Civil War, lost that understanding, went counter to it. Now this we could regain. It is your D. H. Lawrence who has written, "We must plant ourselves again in the Universe".' 'I love the idea of your young singers,' wrote Neil. 'Bring them here to sing their Land Songs. We'll go for a tremendous walk over the Downs.' 'If we can only rediscover and then accept the Natural Order,' wrote Peter. 'What we need to do will become clear to us. I think we shall need to encourage small communities of men and women devoted to these ideals, perhaps working the land, perhaps in community colleges for arts and crafts, so that from these centres the influence can spread, the example be shown.' 'Of course we need leaders,' wrote Neil. 'The natural ones have mostly been killed, like my two brothers and your cousins. Shall we have as theme for our next conference at Durdans something about the lack of aim and the neglect of the land in our two countries? Germany seems to be recovering its dynamism but our leadership is abysmal and any available alternatives seem worse. Effie and I went to Mosley's meeting at Olympia. It was thoroughly unpleasant. It is not through mass movements accompanied by violence that we shall make the necessary changes but by sticking to and reviving native traditions. I like your youth Buende – I'm in touch with some similar things here. Let me know what you think about the conference. Would your friend Karl Eberling be persuaded to come? More than anything I'd like to get Lawrence (T. E. – my hero – not yours, D. H. – whom I find, though I know he's often right, a strangely unattractive writer. He seems to me to whine – and the blood-brother bit strikes me as plain silly). Anyway if I get my Lawrence he'll most likely only creep in quietly for a cup of tea, but that would be better than nothing.' 'It will be a great joy as ever to be with you and Effie at the Durdans,' wrote Peter. 'If we could only make some replicas of what you achieve there, and of the atmosphere and purpose of that place, then we should be well on the road, we should have our illuminati.'

To Catherine time seemed to have robbed these letters of significance. What they hazily foreshadowed had not come about; what had happened instead made them look in retrospect flimsy and naïve. In her search for an understanding of Neil Campion, however, they seemed of the first importance. He had become someone her imagination could encompass. She could see how the quiet, self-contained but probably ambitious boy, outshone perhaps by two older and more extrovert brothers, undoubtedly affected by his experience in the War which had killed both those brothers, might have felt isolated from post-War England by the years in Africa; his wife's money having made it possible for him to go into politics immediately on his return there, he would have supported his party's policy but remained unimpressed by his leaders, nurturing still the unaffiliated idealism of the youth he had not had time to be. Had not the acute old civil servant written, 'He is, I fear, something of a romantic'? And everybody knew about German romanticism. Indeed in their correspondence it was Peter whose hopes were highest, Neil whose proposals were more practical; but they were looking for the same thing, a new basis on which to build international harmony – or European harmony at all events. If Peter wrote more about the spiritual renaissance and Neil about the economic one that perhaps reflected their diverse nationalities but it did not make their aims anything other than similar.

Sitting at her desk, with the letters scattered round her and her large black notebook open before her, its pages covered somewhat hectically with the notes she had made as she read, Catherine found herself humming a tune, and became aware

97

that her brain as it often did had followed its own secret and sometimes strangely frivolous purposes and had pushed a song into her consciousness. 'We're after the same rainbow's end.' It was Audrey Hepburn, but Catherine had only the faintest recollection of the film in which she had sung it. 'My Huckleberry friend' – what did that mean? – 'and me'. Catherine smiled, amused by the antics of her subconscious. They had been after the same rainbow's end. But it was important to discover where exactly the Huckleberry friend's search had led him. Some among the ideas which seemed to have appealed to him had certainly been exploited by the Nazis and that aspect had better be cleared up as soon as possible. Finding nothing in the letters which enlightened her, Catherine took her notebook and her overcoat and a number 14 bus and went straight to the London Library. Indices of books on Nazi Germany revealed at first no mention of Heinrich, Peter, but eventually in a book on the resistance to Hitler she found three. Two referred to 'and circle', one to 'execution'. She turned quickly to this last, and discovered that he had been hanged in 1944, after the July Plot against Hitler.

*   *   *

The late spring sunshine shone on the Durdans, and on the beech woods above the house where the first pale green leaves were already showing; down by the river the poplars were burnished, their buds not yet fully opened to reveal the green. A few groups of children wandered over the well-mown grass but most were farther away from the house; it was afternoon and time for activities, a word whose application was vague, covering as it did football and visiting old age pensioners, map-reading and rebuilding outhouses, rowing and butterfly collection, but which carried with it a clear imperative to be out of the main building. The only children still inside were a few

98

loiterers with coughs or colds, one or two very young boys who had shut themselves into cupboards to smoke and avoid games, and Sam Campion and Howard Clayborne Pope who were carrying piles of exercise books from the stationery cupboard up the main staircase and into their dormitory, where they were putting them into suitcases under their beds. In theory the stationery cupboard was kept locked, and only opened at certain stated times by the master in charge of the key. To be master in charge of the key, however, was not a sought-after position; it was allotted on a weekly rota system and some among the more reluctant of its holders were absentminded, tending either to delegate the responsibility to one of the children or to leave the key in the lock; this resulted in a certain amount of filching, apparently unnoticed by authority. It had been Clayborne Pope who had first thought of offering these irregularly acquired items for sale at a penny or two less than would have to be paid if they were bought through the authorised system. The disadvantage was that most people bought their stationery on a chit, which was added to the bill sent to their parents at the end of term, but there were a few, mainly of Arab or Hong Kong Chinese parentage, who handled their own finances and could be persuaded to be interested either in the idea of a bargain or – since some of them were very rich and thought bargain-hunting a sign of weakness – in the instant availability of Clayborne Pope's supply. It was Sam who had introduced a new concept; he had suggested that, since stealing from the stationery cupboard involved an element of risk, the illicit goods should cost more rather than less than the regular ones. 'Danger money,' he said. 'It's obvious.'

Clayborne Pope thought this a bad idea, and spent many hours of patient rational argument in trying to explain why; to his surprise it then became clear that rather more people were prepared to pay for the stolen stationery at the inflated price than had wanted it as a bargain. Sam explained this away easily enough by saying that it had become a status symbol; in fact he was just as surprised himself, but thought they might as well take advantage of the situation. He had previously only been involved in a little pilfering for his own use; it was Clayborne Pope who had seen the commercial possibilities; but now that he had made a contribution to the sales technique Sam began to take more interest. One afternoon he took a large pile of exercise books, several drawing pads and a good deal of graph paper, and put it all in a suitcase under his bed. There were no repercussions. Mr Manderson the history master who was in charge of stationery that week could not have failed to notice the inroads which had been made upon it, but nothing was said. When it was Mr Manderson's week on duty again Sam and Clayborne Pope made another raid. Sam thought it was a good idea to introduce the added risk of carrying their booty up the main staircase, which pupils in the school were not allowed to use except on certain privileged occasions; there were two subsidiary staircases, one at each end of the building; the main staircase was reserved for staff and visitors. One such journey having been successfully accomplished and the suitcases half filled, Clayborne Pope sat on his bed and took out a packet of cigarettes; Sam, shocked, said they had not finished. They went down for another load. On the way back they met the Head-master's secretary Mrs Dillingham, with some parents whom she was showing round the school. She smiled at them uncertainly.

'No games today?' she said without pausing in her progress (she thought that probably the less prospective parents saw of Campion and Clayborne Pope the better).

'We're on stationery duty,' said Sam in a mildly reproachful tone.

'Stationery duty, of course,' said Mrs Dillingham, as if indeed she should have known.

Having stowed away the exercise books, pencils, geometry sets, blotting paper, into the suitcases, they stretched out on their beds and began to laugh. Suddenly Sam jumped to his feet. 'Come on, come on. Stationery duty. Move, C.B., move. I'm beginning to enjoy this.'

He led the way out of the dormitory without waiting to see whether Clayborne Pope would follow, which he did, though reluctantly. 'You never know when to stop, that's your trouble, Sam.'

'Stop? We can't stop. How could you? This is wonderful, wonderful.' He had already leapt down the stairs, three at a time, and was filling his arms with all he could carry.

Halfway up the stairs he began to laugh again. Laughter overcame him; he was helpless. He could not stand. He leant against the wall but his knees gave way. He slithered down the wall to sit on the stairs, his legs straight out in front of him, exercise books spilling out of his arms, laughing wildly.

'I'm so . . . I'm so . . .'

He wanted to say he was happy. He felt inhabited by perfect bliss. The stairs were beautiful to him, the skylight to which they seemed to lead radiated heavenly light, whose whiteness enhanced the glorious rich brown of the mahogany banisters. The heavy curtains which hung by the tall window at the top of the stairs, and of which he could see about a third from where he sat, seemed with their faded blues and greens like a corner of the floor of heaven; what ran in his own veins was not blood but laughter, which was in him and outside him so that it altogether possessed him; he submitted. So it was that Mr Manderson and Catherine Hillery, whom Mr Manderson was leading up the stairs to the Founder's Library to show her the papers about Karl Eberling and Neil Campion and the founding of the school, came upon Sam's collapsed ecstatic figure lying across the stairs, with the intermittently giggling but otherwise distinctly anxious Clayborne Pope beside him; new exercise books, notepads, and other such things were scattered around Sam; Clayborne Pope was holding a similar collection, though of rather more reasonable proportions.

'Ah well, jolly times, jolly times,' said Mr Manderson heartily, stepping over Sam's legs with a swirl of his red gown.

Catherine, following, averted her eyes. She had appreciated immediately that whatever was going on it was not what should have been going on; such was the view she was beginning to have of Sam that she thought he was probably drunk; which in a way he was, though not on alcohol. She also realised that it could only be embarrassing for him to encounter unexpectedly at that moment someone he had previously only met with his grandmother; and, since her nature was such that her wish to spare people embarrassment would almost always, if only temporarily, modify her curiosity, she averted her eyes after one quick glance. It seemed to her that if Sam Campion chose to be drunk on the stairs at half-past three in the afternoon that was nothing to do with her. Sam lay still after they had passed, no longer laughing but relaxed, recovering. He had understood completely what had gone through Catherine's mind. He had not in the least expected to see her, but he had remembered the book she was writing and had quickly realised that it must be the reason for her being there. He had seen her quick look and half-smile and then her averted gaze, and had understood that she had not wanted to embarrass him. She had embarrassed him, of course, but not very much. She had put a stop to the pure frenzy of possession by laughter, but she had left him no anxiety. He thought it likely that she would make no mention of the episode to his grandmother; there had been nothing accusing, indeed nothing critical, in her momentary glance. Gathering together the scattered exercise books he carried them up to the dormitory, piled them into the now bulging suitcase and went down to tea, feeling healthily tired. Clayborne Pope, following him, was in a state of concern about the fact that Mr Manderson must have known what they had been doing.

'He saw, Sam. He saw everything lying around like that. He must have known.'

'Doesn't matter. He won't do anything.'

It was a matter of indifference to Sam what Mr Manderson did or did not do, knew or did not know. Catherine's small instance of tact on the other hand passed into the haphazard but vivid store of remembered experience on which he based his often fiercely inflexible opinions of the world.

* * *

Catherine received a letter from Captain Arthur Fox Farmiloe, written from the Manor House next to the vicarage where Neil Campion had spent his childhood.

'Aunt Margaret died last week. A merciful release as they say. Your visit stimulated her memory and towards the end she lived almost entirely in the past. I did tell you I would let you know if she mentioned anything else which might be useful for your book, and the fact is I don't think she did. However, being a methodical chap I kept a notebook in which I jotted down a few of the things she said, at the time she said them. Whether or not they add up to anything much I wouldn't know. Had a bit of bad luck with the bantams, fox took a lot. We've moved the rest of them into the house for safety (at night only of course).'

Catherine wondered what the Honourable Mrs Fox Farmiloe, who had so despised the Vicar's wife, would have thought about the Captain's bantams in her yellow boudoir, even though it was only at night. But perhaps they were only allowed in the television room, perched around the Captain on his patent television chair and the dark-haired boy on his corduroy bean bag.

'Mrs Campion used to beat her children,' she read. 'The Vicar never did, he was much too kind, but vague, had no control, read Greek in his study. She used to shout at them, could be heard over the garden wall. But not at Frederick and

Leonard because they were older. They were very good at cricket. The village always won when Frederick and Leonard were playing. On the village green in the summer. Eleanor, plain, bossy, too pleased with herself. Such handsome boys, those two, everyone loved them. Neil much quieter, was going to be a poet. Aunt Margaret said he didn't look like one and he was offended. She thought he was too hefty for a poet. Not as good-looking as his brothers, except for his eyes, very bright blue eyes, a strong personality, but deep, you never knew, outshone by Frederick and Leonard. He and Eleanor got on well. Hugh the baby, always trying to keep up with Neil and Eleanor. The parents broken-hearted by the two deaths, Mrs C. got bitter, lost her faith and insisted on telling everyone about it, Mr C. very patient but cut himself off. They died soon after the War, after Neil went to Africa. House never very clean, Mrs C. not a good maîtresse de maison. Didn't have much money. It all went to educate the boys. Aunt M.'s mother didn't want her to see too much of the Vicar's boys, she thought their mother was pushing Frederick to make a good catch but he always behaved perfectly, never took advantage (there was a lot more of this – Aunt M. was obviously sweet on old Fred – but have not noted it as not to your purpose). Neil told Eleanor and Aunt M. he was going to be Prime Minister. He lectured them in the garden inside the yew hedge in the place where they always went, and Eleanor believed him but Aunt M. didn't because she thought Frederick and Leonard would always be better than he was. He said he was going to write a lot of books as well and be an explorer and discover a lost continent and be very famous. Eleanor always believed him.'

Catherine had noticed the yew hedge. It must have been forty foot high, and was wearing thin in places, but in Neil's childhood it would have been in its prime, impenetrably smooth and green on the outside and inside dimly commodious, with branches on which the children might have sat and from which they would have been called in to those ordered pre-War households to be scolded for the green grubbiness of their knees and hands. Perhaps Neil had made another safe meeting place, years later, only there it was Effie who always believed him when he talked of the things he was going to do.

Catherine felt that she needed to make an effort of imagination in order to free her mind from the assumption that what had happened had been bound to happen and what had not happened could never have happened. At the time when the Durdans conferences were flourishing, when between the more serious gatherings all sorts of different people came there for weekends of tennis and comfort and amusement and incidental exposure to what Neil referred to in his letters to Peter as The Theme, it was perhaps not as surprising as it seemed to Catherine now that he should have thought, as he had written to Effie, that they were 'onto something big'. It had not worked. At the time, however, Neil had presumably not been the only person who had thought it was going to; Catherine decided that her next task was to find a survivor, other than Effie. Effie, as she would no doubt have phrased it herself, was too much 'parti pris'.

*   *   *

Eleanor Campion, monumental upon the swollen columns which were her legs, stood over her brother Hugh, who was seated as usual with his library book on his knee and his armchair facing the window which looked out into the sycamore tree. She bent upon him the full force of her outraged blue stare.

'Why didn't you tell me before that you had given her the letters? Why wait until it's too late for me to do anything about it?'

He wagged his head, distressed. 'I simply forgot. I didn't

know you'd want to do anything about it. Anyway, what could you have done?'

'Got them back. Or if not that I could have prepared her, told her about them. God knows what conclusions she might jump to.'

'But they're fine letters, Eleanor, I read them. Not recently I admit. But my recollection is that they were fine.'

'They have to be understood in their context.'

'She seemed to me an understanding sort of person, intelligent too. I'm sure she'd see them in their context. We've nothing to hide about Neil, Eleanor.'

'You know nothing about it.' She turned away, and moved heavily over to a straight-backed chair, onto which she lowered herself with caution, then slid her skirt up her knees with her habitual gesture. With a hand on each knee she looked, as he did, into the sycamore tree. Her eyes, which had opened wide when she was looking at her brother, were now, as they most often were, hooded by their heavy lids; her wrinkled spongy face fell into an expression of brooding discontent.

'I thought the whole point was we wanted the truth about him to be written,' insisted Hugh. 'So that no one else could do it and get the story wrong. Isn't that right?'

Eleanor did not answer. After a time she said, 'I never liked her.'

'Who?'

'The Hillery woman.'

'What's wrong with her?'

'She reminds me of one of my girls.'

'She's the wrong age, Eleanor.'

'I mean one of my VADs. A silly girl. Carried on with the men. I had to sack her.'

'But how dreadful.' Hugh plucked fussily at the rug which covered his knees. 'Surely we should tell Mr Pottinger. She can't be a responsible person.'

106

'I didn't mean it was really her, silly. I said she reminded me of her.'

'Oh. I see. That's all right then. I must say she didn't look at all that sort of person to me.'

He picked up his book again. Eleanor sat without speaking, hearing the distant traffic, and the chirruping sparrows beneath the sycamore tree, and Hugh's gently wheezing old man's breath. It seemed to her that her uneasiness surrounded her with a sort of mist, in which past and present lost their differentiation, so that the girl she had scolded and the woman who had looked at her so directly, and the flighty wife, and the hostile journalist, and the loved brother who was child leader, boy companion and fallen hero all at once, seemed to circulate in a slow random progression half in and half out of her consciousness, and some of the figures seemed instinct with alarm, and others burdened with sorrows; none was reassuring.

*　　*　　*

Catherine pushed through the undergrowth, searching for a survivor from Neil Campion's high days of The Theme. She had marked one down, having trailed him first through Neil's own library at the Durdans ('How's Sam?' she had lightly asked. 'Ah, Sam, the egregious Sam, he doesn't honour us much with his presence in class,' Mr Manderson had answered with an indulgent smile); further enquiries through the publishers had elicited the information that the author of a thin volume entitled *Agricultural Reform and the Revivification of the Rural Community*, inscribed in the author's hand to 'Neil Campion in homage and hope', was to be found somewhere in Wiltshire living in the woods as the tenant of a society concerned to preserve ancient buildings. The society could provide Catherine only with the address; there was no telephone. A letter, followed by another, elicited no answer. She decided to go there herself. There was not much of a road, the society's secretary informed her, though he understood there was a footpath and the place was marked on the ordnance survey map, being known as the Hermitage and having been built by an eighteenth-century grandee in the grip of enthusiasm for the Picturesque and as a focal point for excursions from his nearby Palladian mansion. Catherine had parked her car at what seemed from the map to be the nearest point, and set off along a clearly marked path through a wood predominantly of pine, but as she walked the trees became more mixed, the undergrowth thicker and the path less easy to discern. The sun was warm, though the breeze had still a treacherous Maytime chill in it; birdsong was abundant, a chiff-chaff repetitive, chaffinches cascading their trills, a loud wren, low down among the brambles, blackbird and thrush in rival liquidities, a background of rooks and wood pigeons. An unexpected loud crashing of vegetation was followed by the sight of an alarmed roe deer bounding through the trees; he had been disturbed asleep. Here was the place, Catherine thought, in this enchanted forest, to find a sage in his hermit's cell. She would bring out, she thought, if the sage could help her, Neil Campion's idealism, submerged by history; why should it not be time for a reconsideration? She must do him justice, set out his case well. First, though, she had to find the sage, which was proving difficult. She had come upon marshy ground, and wished she had worn boots instead of her quite serviceable shoes. She seemed to be going downhill and yet the map, which showed the contours of the land, marked the Hermitage as being fairly high. Rejecting the faint path which seemed to follow the slope, she struck sideways and came upon another, which leading through some thick evergreens faded out before an unexpected open space, a rough green slope at the top of which, backed by further evergreens, stood a small cobbled building with latticed gothic windows and a most improbable pinnacle at one end.

Catherine approached it slowly across the grass and passing

a faded deckchair which might have been there for months came to a narrow doorway at the side of the building. The door was open. Peering into the obscurity beyond (for it seemed very dark), she knocked gently. Unexpectedly close, a voice said, 'What time is it?'

Catherine looked at her watch and answered, 'Quarter-past three.'

'Not so far out then,' said the voice.

There seemed to be some movement in the darkness but no one emerged.

'I hope you don't mind my coming. I did write.'

'They leave the letters in a box. Usually by the time I get up there they've been washed away by the rain.'

'Oh, dear, you didn't get my letters?'

'Or eaten by pigs.'

The just discernible movements continued.

'Is it a nuisance, then, to talk to me? I could come back.'

'It's just a cupboard really. That's all they give me. Coal hole really, that's what I should think it was. That's all they give me for a kitchen. I'll just make myself a spot of lunch and I'll be with you. That's why I asked you the time. When my watch stops I have to guess at mealtimes.'

'Please don't hurry. I'll wait.' Catherine walked round to look in through the window of the little house and saw that it consisted of one big room of irregular shape, full of packing cases and piles of books. There was a bed in one corner, untidily covered with rugs; a round table on which there were several empty wine bottles and a Bath Oliver biscuit tin stood in the bay window. 'What a pretty room,' she said, referring to the shape and the light from the latticed windows rather than to its current arrangement.

'Something out of *Hansel and Gretel* really, isn't it?' he said, coming out into the sunlight.

He was a tall man of rather military aspect, with sparse white hair, a ruddy complexion and a considerable nose. He wore a red and white checked viyella shirt and a pair of baggy grey flannel trousers held up round the waist by what looked like a pyjama cord. She had been expecting (having seen the room) someone less well-washed. He was carrying a plate and a glass and had a bottle of wine under his arm. He went over to a stone table not far from the deckchair, and putting what he was carrying down on the ground he produced from his trouser pocket a clean red-spotted handkerchief which he spread on the table. Having carefully laid out his lunch, he fetched a stool from just inside the door of the house, drew it up to the stone table and sat down.

'Now then,' he said, looking at Catherine.

She was suddenly reminded not so much of *Hansel and Gretel* as of the sandy-whiskered gentleman in *Jemima Puddleduck*. His eyes were quite small and she was not sure that they were altogether friendly.

'I suppose I am right in thinking you're Henry Hawker?' she said.

'That's my name,' he answered, beginning to eat his omelette which looked over-cooked. 'But, good heavens, I've lived alone too long, I haven't offered you a glass of wine.'

'Thank you so much, I won't, really.'

'Fellow at the pub here has a friend who brings it in a barrel from the south of Italy somewhere. He bottles it himself.'

'It looks very black.'

'Heady stuff,' he agreed, filling his glass. He seemed neither surprised to see her nor particularly interested in why she had come.

'Campion?' he said, when she had explained. 'No one's interested in Campion these days.'

When she said she had been asked to write an authorised biography he suggested it might be hard to find a publisher. She explained that it had been the publisher who had first approached her. He seemed disgruntled.

'They'll publish anything these days,' he said, refilling his glass.

'I suppose so,' she said humbly.

'So you want the dirt?' he said, more amiably.

'Not specially. I didn't know there was any. If there is I suppose I'd better have it.'

'There isn't,' he said, swallowing his wine in three noisy gulps and filling his glass again. 'There isn't. He was a saint. A bloody angel, that man. Died too young. Never got his due.'

'I've been trying to make up my mind what his due was exactly. Do tell me about him. How did you first come across him?'

'He wrote to me. I'd started some kind of futile farming thing down here – well, not far away, over towards Bath – and I wrote an article about it and he wrote to me and I went over there, to the Durdans you know, and what with one thing and another I got involved. I liked what he was trying to do.'

'He was trying to change people's ideas? In various ways?'

'Within the system. He used to say to me, in England you work from within the system. He always said movements from without don't work in this country, it's a very conservative country and yet at the same time it's not inflexible. If you want change you work from within. That's why he was against Mosley. As soon as Mosley started his own party he knew it would come to nothing. Mosley was too impatient, he said.'

'But I thought he didn't approve of Mosley at all. He refers in some letters I've seen to going to a meeting and thinking it all wrong.'

'He did think it all wrong. He didn't want a mass movement. He said again it wasn't English. A change of heart, that was what we were after. It was to be a change of heart, starting with the intelligentsia and the young, spreading through the written word, capturing the people of influence, avoiding demagoguery, by-passing the cynicism of the party political machines. Europe, agriculture, peace.'

He moved his plate and glass from the red-spotted handker-chief, wiped his mouth with it and then stuffed it into his trouser pocket. 'Sure you won't have anything to drink?'

Catherine shook her head. 'Do you think people nowadays have come round to your way of thinking?'

'Nowadays? Ha!'

'I mean, about Europe for instance.'

'Money. It's all money nowadays. Butter mountains, fat cat Common Market officials.'

'But at least we're in it?'

'What about Eastern Europe? Eastern Europe's not in it. A strong Europe to stand up to Russia and America, oh yes, they've got the idea of that now, a bit late in the day and after a bloody war. But it's only half of Europe. Supposing Eastern Europe had been German, wouldn't that have been better than what's happened now? What?' He drained his glass again. 'Give the Germans a free hand in the East, that's what we said.'

Catherine, faintly alarmed at the speed with which the bottle of wine was emptying, said mildly, 'Yes, but it would have been the Nazis, wouldn't it, that you were giving a free hand to?'

'Better the Nazis than the Bolshies,' he said. He leant forward on his stool, both hands on the stone table, and repeated, 'Better the Nazis than the Bolshies.'

'Why have either?' said Catherine.

She immediately wished she had not spoken. A brief expression of disgust crossed his face, then he stood up abruptly and went into the house. Catherine sat without moving in the deckchair. After the walk refreshment of some kind would have been welcome; she wished the wine did not look so villainous. Birdsong filled the air. She waited, sitting in the sun.

He re-emerged, carrying another bottle of wine, which he had evidently just opened. He waved it vaguely in her direction; she shook her head and he filled his own glass.

'Well now,' he said, sitting down again on his stool and evidently restored to good humour. 'Where were we? Yes, well, the Durdans. The great days of the Durdans. I used to go there a lot you know. Met all sorts of interesting people. I was struggling along with the farming, hideously hard work of course. We did well in the War, digging for victory, oh yes, we were needed then. But they would quarrel, you know. We had quite a number of people working together there. Lord, how they quarrelled. My wives were the worst. Fought like cats they did, all of them.'

'Did you have a lot of wives?' asked Catherine, surprised.

'Oh lord, yes. In succession naturally. One after the other, oh yes. No polygamy. Nothing like that. All legal and above board. Which meant they took all my money of course.' He gave a loud laugh, though clearly unamused. 'Oh yes, every penny they got off me. That's why I'm reduced to this.' He flapped his hand at his little dwelling as if he were shooing it away like a cat. 'Oh yes, I'm reduced to a hovel.'

'A very charming one.'

'Charm. You have to learn to see through charm. That's what Campion had of course, charm. Buckets of it. Oodles of it. Not at first, mind you. It had to work on you. The eyes, the sincerity, seeming to be so interested in you, all that. Oh yes, it was winning. That was what it was, winning. Of course he wasn't interested.' He flapped his hand again, this time in the direction of Catherine. 'Don't tell me that. Don't tell me he was interested. Of course he wasn't. He was interested in himself.' He was silent, drinking his wine.

'Was he?' said Catherine after a pause.

'Politicians,' he said. 'They're all the same. Only interested in themselves.'

'Of course I don't know anything about ...' Catherine stopped. She had been going to say she knew nothing about politics, but then thought that might lead him to question her qualifications as a politician's biographer.

'Care for a fuck?' he said, gazing dreamily towards the trees.

Determinedly unabashed, Catherine said politely, 'No thanks.

Tell me, if he was so interested in himself, what was it about him that made you say he was a saint?'

'Saint. Did I say he was a saint?' His gaze returned to hers. 'A saint can be self-obsessed, you know,' he said rather sharply. 'In fact I'd say a saint's very likely to be self-obsessed. Oh yes. Show me a saint and I'll show you an egomaniac.' He seemed to be expecting her to argue.

'I don't know any saints so I don't know,' she said pacifically. 'I expect you're right.'

His expression changed to one of quizzical amusement.

'You didn't think I meant it, did you?' he said.

'Of course I did.'

'About the fucking. I meant it.'

'Oh, I see. Well, the thing is, it's not exactly what I came for. I really have to find out about Campion.'

'You think I'm past it. I know. You think I'm an old wreck, played out, past it.'

'Of course I don't. I mean I don't think anything, one way or the other. I just want . . .'

'I'm not. I can tell you. Come on, have a drink.' He stood up, filled his glass and held it out to her. 'Just a little one.'

He approached her, holding out the glass. She shook her head. He drank the wine himself and sank to his knees in front of her. 'I'm a past master at this game I tell you. I love it, you see. I simply love fucking. That's all there is to it.'

'Yes, well, but you see all I really want is for you to tell me what you really thought of Neil Campion.'

'And then we'll fuck?'

She smiled and shook her head. He sank onto his haunches in front of her and said, 'He was a traitor.'

There was a pause while Catherine tried to adjust her ideas. Then she said, 'Surely not?'

He moved himself so as to sit cross-legged, still at her feet. Seeing him from closer than before she realised that the air of military decorum she had at first observed had either dissipated under the influence of the wine or had anyway been only superficial. There was a wildness in the small red-rimmed eyes, and the great nose, so distinguished at a distance, revealed itself to a closer gaze as curiously pitted and criss-crossed with broken veins; the breath, unsurprisingly, was heavily alcoholic.

'Campion. Oh yes. Neil Campion. All the charm, all the sincerity, man of principle, all that. Traitor. Traitor to his own.'

'But how?'

'Because he was a coward. He didn't have the guts. If you ask me he drove into that wall on purpose. Couldn't face his responsibilities.'

He spoke with finality. At the same time he had begun to sway very slightly from side to side as he sat in the grass before her and she began to fear that he might have started drinking before she arrived and be now about to fall asleep.

'What exactly were his responsibilities?' she asked quietly.

'He could have made peace,' he said. 'He had the contacts. He was in the Government. He had the contacts on both sides. He knew it was the right thing to do.' The swaying continued, rhythmically; evidently it was not involuntary.

'So do you think he was in touch with his friend Peter Heinrich at the beginning of the War?'

'I don't know that he was in touch with anybody. I know that he should have been.'

He stopped swaying and fell silent, an expression of discontent on his face.

'So,' said Catherine carefully. 'You mean he was a traitor because he was not a traitor. I mean he was not what would generally and at that time have been called a traitor?'

There was a pause. Then he looked her in the eyes and said, 'What is treachery? You tell me that. What is treachery?'

'I don't know,' said Catherine.

He got rather clumsily to his feet, picked up his glass and went over to the stone table where he refilled it. Holding it in one hand he pointed at her accusingly with the index finger of the same hand and said, 'Now you're going to lecture me about the Jews. And I'm going to tell you there was no policy to exterminate the Jews until 1942 at the Wannsee Conference. And that if we'd made peace with Germany before that date it might never have happened. And you're going to say . . . what are you going to say?'

'That I think you underestimate Hitler.'

'Hitler.' He flapped his hand. 'Hitler.' He dismissed him. Holding up his glass in front of him he began to stamp up and down singing, 'Hitler . . . has only got one ball, Goebbels . . . has got no balls at all . . .'

He put down his glass on the stone table. 'Oh, come on. I'll get a rug. Out here, on the grass. Say yes.' He stood with his hands clasped and his head on one side, smiling.

'No, please don't get a rug. I must go now. I've got to get back.'

'Oh, don't say that. I'll get a rug.' He hurried into the house. Catherine got to her feet and wondered whether to make a run for it but he was back almost immediately, spreading the rug on to the grass.

Catherine gripped the back of the chair and said, 'Thank you for talking to me. I'm off now.'

'You think I'm too old.'

'No, no, it's just that . . . Anyway I'm too old myself.'

'An attractive woman like you? What are you, forty, forty-five? Nothing wrong with that. Age has never been a barrier with me, I can tell you that. Except Daphne Daley, of course.' He paused, looking thoughtful, and sat down on the stone table. 'There is the case of Daphne Daley. Remember her? Always in that pub, she was, the old Fitzroy. Yes, she was always there, Daphne Daley. A lot of people used to have a go with her. Game old girl she was. But I must admit. Yes, well, I must admit that was a bit more than I could take, Daphne Daley, yes.' He seemed to have gone into a sort of contemplative trance.

Catherine said, 'Anyway, thanks and goodbye. My husband's waiting in the car. I'll have to run.'

She was halfway across the grass towards the wood before he began to move but he covered the ground at speed and caught her by the arm. 'You want it, I know you do,' he gasped alcoholically into her face. 'I can tell, it's what you want.' His grip tightened on her arm.

'Oh look, there's my husband. He said he'd come if I was a long time. Oh dear, I think he's going the wrong way. Here we are, Bernard. Bernard! Here I am!'

Pulling her arm free, she ran; then dodging behind the bushes she set off in what she hoped was the direction of her car, but avoiding the path by which she had come. When she felt she had reached sufficient cover she sat down at the foot of an oak tree and listened.

'Come back!' she heard. He was below her, on the path she had not taken. 'Bring him in. Like to meet him. Come in. Have a drink. Where are you?' But he had stopped on the path, looking round with hope clearly diminishing. 'Where are you?' he called once more. Hearing no answer he turned and walked slowly back towards his house.

Catherine, relieved, put her hand over her mouth lest he should hear her slightly hysterical giggle. Crouched under the tree, she leant against its trunk. 'Here I am, Bernard. Bernard, here I am.' The giggling gave way to huge uncontrollable sobs. She had a feeling that something was happening which had been going to happen for a very long time.

*   *   *

Alfred Madden presented himself at the front door of the Durdans and said that he was interested in the history of progressive education and that he understood there were some books about the school's founder in the library. Young Mr Roberts of the English department, who had happened to be passing and had therefore opened the door, said that he believed that to be the case but had he an appointment. Alfred Madden apologised profusely but said he had understood the library was available for the use of researchers; he thought perhaps he might have heard about it from a Mrs Hillery. Mr Roberts thought Mr Manderson would know about it, and went to look for him, leaving Madden to wait in the dim entrance hall, where he could hear clattering cutlery as tables were laid for lunch, and a murmur of voices from a nearby classroom and in the distance a Handel flute sonata, played with plangent sweetness. Mr Roberts came back to say that Mr Manderson was teaching but that the Headmaster's secretary had said that if it was anything to do with Mrs Hillery she was sure it would be all right; he led the way upstairs.

Left alone in the Founder's Library, Madden quickly found that section of it which contained matter concerning educational theory, with particular reference to Karl Eberling. He scanned the shelf for something specifically about the founding of the Durdans. Failing to find what he was looking for, he searched the neighbouring shelves. He picked out a book at random and found it to be the recollections of a member of the Royal Flying Corps in the First World War, with ill-reproduced photographs of young men in flying kit standing beside the cumbersome machines of the time. Replacing it on the shelf, which he now saw was full of books of a similar sort, he noticed a thin volume which had slipped behind the others. He pulled it out and saw that it was an anthology of poetry from the First World War; on the fly leaf it was inscribed 'To Neil from Peter'; underneath was written in the same hand

'Oh Balan my brother I have slain thee
And thou me, wherefore all the wide world shall speak of us both.'

Morte d'Arthur XII–XIII

Madden took a single sheet of folded paper from his pocket and slipped it between the pages of the book, which he inserted into the shelf of books about education, between a life of Karl Eberling and a history of progressive schools. Then he quickly left the room.

He went downstairs and out to his car without seeing anyone, drove into the nearby village and parked his car by the pub. Inside the pub he found Etta, sitting by herself in a corner of the saloon bar, looking tense. When she saw him she smiled.

'How beautiful you are,' he said, sitting beside her.

'I wish you would tell me what you are doing.'

He shook his head. 'You're sure she said she was coming again.'

'Of course. She was going to see Tom and Susannah on the way back, that's why she told me. She said she was coming in the next day or two.'

He nodded. 'Good. What are you drinking? Tomato juice? Have a glass of wine.'

He walked over to order it. There was no one else in the bar except for a group of young people in the opposite corner. He glanced idly at them as he ordered a glass of wine and a pint of bitter. A young man in a dark pullover leant his head back against the black panelling, blowing smoke rings; he looked rather pale. Two girls with long hair were talking quietly to each other. The fourth member of the group, who was short and curly-haired and spotty, was no doubt older than he looked; he was drinking beer, with what looked like a brandy chaser.

Madden nodded in their direction and said, 'Good morning.'

The young man looked at him with an expressionless face, then pushing himself away from the wall on which he was leaning said, 'Oh,' and then politely, 'Good morning.' The girls did not interrupt their murmured conversation. The other boy, having waited for his companion's lead, said, 'Good morning to you,' with a surprisingly middle-aged heartiness.

Madden, returning to Etta with two glasses, said, 'I want to tell you that I have once been in love before.'

She raised her eyebrows.

'Once?'

'Once,' he said firmly. 'When I found she was betraying me I went to bed with every woman I could lay my hands on. But I was not in love with them.'

'Betraying you. This is very melodramatic.'

'We were going to get married. It was very serious. It was quite a long time ago. She was an upper-class English girl with fair curly hair and long legs. Her father was a general.'

'A general!' said Etta, pretending to be impressed.

'I once heard him say to someone at a party she's got involved with this fellow, clever fellow, four by two, you know, clever.'

'I don't understand.'

'Rhyming slang. Four by two Jew.'

'This I have never heard. You have invented it.'

'No, I promise you. It's an expression they use in the Army.'

'Impossible.'

'He never liked me. Her mother never liked me either. She was always very nice to me, but that was from a sense of justice and not because she liked me. She was a very good woman, Marian's mother.'

'Marian. And Marian loved you?'

'I don't know. I think so, for a time. We stimulated each other, we egged each other on to show off in public. We were probably rather silly.'

'But you loved her?'

'Madly. Although at the same time I was always on the defensive with her, it wasn't a calm sort of relationship. I don't know what would have happened if we had married.'

Etta said nothing. She had no intention of making any

confessions of her own. Madden, however, seemed determined to continue.

'She went off with my best friend. I didn't know she'd been having an affair with him.'

'So you feel bitter, even now?'

'Yes.'

She laid a hand on his knee. She had beautiful hands, smooth-skinned and long-fingered, with almond-shaped nails. She was proud of them and had been pleased when he had once, holding one of them, quoted Thomas Hood.

'When the least moon has silver on't no larger

Than the pure white of Hebe's pinkish nail.'

'When I was young everyone I fell in love with went off with my best friend,' she said. 'It didn't make me write nasty things about them in my gossip column.'

He frowned heavily.

'How did you know I did that?'

'Because I am beginning to know you. So did she marry this best friend?'

'No. She reverted to type and married some young sprig of the aristocracy. Her father was the nephew of Neil Campion's wife, she was Effie Campion's great-niece.'

'Is that why you are interested in Campion?'

'No, but it's how I first heard about him.'

'You are a brooding and remembering person. My mind is too light to remember so much.'

'What do you think about if not about the past?'

'I try not to think at all. I find it upsetting.'

He smiled at her, thinking she was joking, but seeing her sombre expression realized that she had started to think about the present, and about their own situation, and that it was indeed upsetting her.

Finishing his beer he said, 'Let's go. We'll stop somewhere nice on the way back for a walk in the woods, hand in hand, like a simple country couple.'

'I think we don't look like a simple country couple,' said Etta, following him out of the pub.

*   *   *

Effie Campion telephoned Catherine and asked her if she would take some things down to the Durdans for Sam next time she went.

'He says he's got no clothes. I can't think why. He had masses when he went back. Anyway they're a bit bulky to pack, so if you could?'

'Of course. The only thing is I wasn't going to go for a bit. I seem to have got rather behind.'

'He can wait. Anything rather than all that awful paper and string and queueing in the post office. Just ring me up when you're going. No hurry.'

But Catherine's intention was never to go to the Durdans again. She was only waiting for her courage to come back before writing to her publisher to explain that she was going to give up the book. She was going to tell him that after months of work she had simply no idea what sort of person Neil Campion had been.

The truth was she had lost her belief in biography. She used to think that if you read a book about someone you would have a pretty good idea of what they were like. It now seemed to her that that was not so at all. You would have an idea of what someone else thought they were like; and, though that someone else might be, say, three parts right, they might equally be three parts wrong. She had the facts of Neil Campion's life, more or less, and she had the opinions of various people who had known him. None of these opinions seemed to her completely convincing, nor did they necessarily square with each other; and yet, if she were to create — to invent in fact — a portrait which was a composite of these various opinions, it would presumably, by being printed, bound, sold in bookshops, stored in libraries, become the Neil Campion the world might think (if it cared to think about it at all), the 'real' Neil Campion; and, because owing to his early death or perhaps because of his failings he had not been a man of great note in the history of his times, it was possible that her biography might be the only one, her portrait that of the 'real' Neil Campion for ever. She would have fixed him, pinned like a butterfly in the collecting box of history, in perpetuity. How could she take it upon herself to do such a thing to a fellow human being? She who had so little idea of what might be the 'real' Catherine Hillery?

When she had returned, tired, from her visit to Henry Hawker in his Hermitage in the woods, she had walked down the stairs to the basement where her kitchen was, and had said aloud as she went, 'And on the third day she descended into Hell,' which, though blasphemous, expressed her feeling that she had lost control of her thoughts. Catherine Hillery, widow of a professional man, down to earth, competent, independent, amused, Catherine Hillery who wrote biographies, went to the theatre, had sons, grandchildren, friends, trenchant views on everything under the sun, seemed to have disappeared, dispersed upon the wind, scattered like ashes on the forest floor beneath the Wiltshire trees. On what errors, on what illusions had she constructed the ramshackle system of connections she thought of as herself? There seemed now to be only a kind of alarm system, functioning without a central control, pumping out signals of distress, confused messages about primeval dangers. At night she sat up in bed with a thumping heart. By day she made herself odd little meals to try to curb her indigestion or sat heavily in a chair, between sleeping and waking, always listening. In the evening she made lists of things to do for the next day, but when the next day came she did not do them.

Apart from Effie Campion, only her son Tom telephoned. He asked whether she would like him to bring her some eggs one day; the new hens were laying well. She put him off, saying she was busy for a few days and would not eat them; he said he would come later in the week. She returned to her chair and listened to the sound she thought was the sound of the blood circulating in her head. There seemed nothing to do except to sit it out. She told herself that everyone was subject to occasional loss of self-confidence and subsequent depression. Certainly it had happened to her before, though perhaps it had never been so hard to control. About six months after Bernard had died there had been a bad few weeks; immediately after his death, on the other hand, she had not felt particularly sad. Reasonably solemn, perhaps, but not sad. How could you feel sad about the death of someone who had so clearly wanted to die? And there was no point in speculating as to why he had wanted to die. That she had done to excess in the two years before his death, asking with insufficient sympathy, 'Why are you so cross all the time, Bernard?' He wouldn't say, he wouldn't think, he didn't himself believe in speculating, he disapproved of introspection; it was simply the fault of people at the office, or of Nicholas and his dishonesty, or of Catherine herself. She was too critical, he said, she should be more on his side. When they were driving along in the car and he swore at other drivers, which happened quite frequently, he would bang the driving wheel with his hand and shout, 'You should be on my side,' quite red in the face, and she would say, 'But I haven't said anything,' and he would say, 'But I know what you're thinking.'

'This is like other people,' she had said once. 'It's not like us.'

For they were happily married, they always had been; not ecstatically but calmly, not romantically but reasonably. This was their private achievement, the small triumph of which they were both proud; and it seemed that in the last few years of his life Bernard had set out to destroy it. Of course she had joined in the destruction; she was not a patient person, and when he seemed unreasonable she snapped at him, and when he was bad-tempered she was annoyed with him for being bad-tempered, which added a further element of contention over and above whatever the cause of the bad temper might be. Also being better with words than he was she sometimes when they quarrelled said more hurtful things. But it was his mood to which they were both responding, not hers. So when she had wept so uncontrollably in the wood it had been because having called for Bernard she realised how much she wished he had been there, but also because of what it still seemed to her that he had done before he died, that was to say spoilt everything. It was not exactly that she could not forgive him; it was more that she could not understand what it was that she was to forgive. It had not occurred to her that she could forgive without understanding.

During the last few months of Bernard's life, Catherine had sometimes thought about Kit, with whom she had been in love when she was very young. The thought of him had hardly crossed her mind for many years, and yet once summoned to consciousness by an idle thought one evening (would even he have turned into a crotchety old man?) everything about him had come back to her with complete clarity. She thought of him without sorrow, he having been dead for forty years or so, but with pleasurable nostalgia, dwelling on his looks, so instantly recallable, the light and teasing tone of his voice, his endless prankish humour. They had been very young and very indiscreet. He was recovering from a broken leg after a bad parachute drop and she had only just finished her VAD training. She had gone into his room to take his temperature and he had said, 'Oh, there you are,' sitting up on his pillow looking extraordinarily well and handsome. The next day he had kissed her. Their lives had so far been so short that they had not had much to tell each other. Desperate to be more completely known to one another they had been reduced to absurdities.

'Oh, and I don't like strawberry jam.' 'How utterly extraordinary, I adore it.' Miraculous differences, amazing similarities. They had behaved without any regard for the conventions of the time, or for their respective roles as patient and nurse. Shrieks of laughter came from his room when she tried to give him a bed bath; when she supported him as he began to walk again their progress was irregular, interrupted by surreptitious kisses; when he was able to get about more easily he limped to the rendezvous to which she ran at any time of day or night and at which they made unrestrained incautious love. Their scandalous behaviour not unnaturally came to the attention of Miss Campion the Commandant, who sent for Catherine and reprimanded her with brutal frankness. Catherine, much abashed, exchanged no more than whispers with Kit for three whole days. After that things went on much as before. Miss Campion told Catherine she was an immoral girl who should be ashamed; Catherine defended herself in the name of Love. Miss Campion, quite immune to the power of the sacred name, sent her home, pending another posting. Desperate letters, a snatched meeting in London, and Kit returned to his training, somewhere in Lincolnshire. He bogged it again, as he would have put it, and this time died, having failed to let down his undercarriage on his first solo flight. Miss Campion remained in Catherine's private mythology as the monster who had deprived her of some days of irrecoverable happiness, besides having thoroughly humiliated her in the process. The wound caused by Kit's death healed with time, and after the war Catherine married Bernard, who had just become a junior Civil Servant.

Thinking about Kit all those years after his death had restored Catherine's faith in happiness as being in some sense what nature intended. For she and Kit had been natural, if nothing else. But when as she sat in her chair after talking to Tom on the telephone her untrustworthy thoughts veered in their scattered searchings in the direction of Kit, it was only to shy away quickly. She could not bear to remember her folly and vulnerability, her exposure to Miss Campion's scorn, her lack of any kind of sophistication. What a fool she must have seemed; and would seem again, no doubt, when she announced her failure as a biographer.

What she had to do now was somehow to put that announcement down on paper, and ascribe to it some kind of reasoning, and find an envelope for the letter, and address it correctly to Hugh Brackenbury the publisher, and stamp it, and walk to the post-box in the King's Road, and post it. For the time being it seemed, as a programme, impossibly onerous.

* * *

Alfred Madden wrote in the notebook in which he jotted down possible lines of enquiry for his column. 'Rumours about the Bedford brothers. Currency deal may be being investigated by the Inland Revenue. What to do about this?'

As far as he knew, Etta's husband Nicholas was still working for Ronald Bedford. If there were rumours to the latter's discredit, should Madden report them, or stifle them? He had not been able so far to find out what if anything lay behind them. On the other hand Etta would never forgive him if he failed to warn her of even the slightest rumour. It would confirm her worst suspicions about the Bedford brothers but there seemed no great harm in that; Nicholas would probably do well to start looking for another job anyway. Madden reached out for the telephone, then stopped and looked at his watch. Nicholas would be at home by now. It would have to wait until the next day. He was overcome by a feeling of extreme discontent at being deprived of the anticipated pleasure of hearing Etta's voice. He wrote in his notebook, 'The situation is becoming impossible.'

He was lying on his back on the brown sofa beneath the flamingoes, his head on a bulky pink cushion and his notebook leaning up against his bent knees. His runners were out this evening; in the morning he would receive their reports and if necessary embroider them. This was his evening for working on his novel. This novel was the story of a boy who had always been attracted by the huge size and secretive aspect of the building in whose shadow he had grown up and who eventually went to work in the kitchens there and found the place to be a lunatic asylum. He gradually infiltrated himself into the hierarchy of its management, found that there seemed to be no sanctions applied to any kind of brutality in keeping the patients in order, and before long established himself as supreme head of a regime based on terror. Ministry of Health officials came to inspect, and congratulated him warmly on his success. Dissatisfied, he became increasingly extreme in his behaviour, pushing always at the boundaries of the permissible and finding no resistance, until he accidentally set the place on fire and it came crashing down on his head; he died in a triumphant ecstasy; at last he had fulfilled his dream. Madden had read a good deal about the various forms of madness before starting the book and, since it seemed to him that the symptoms of many of them were evinced in behaviour quite usual among so-called normal people and only disabling as a result of being pushed to an unusual extreme, he had found himself increasingly drawn into describing the characters and conversations of the lunatics. It was beginning to look as if the book might be very long, even though he had a useful character known as Vercingetorix who when the conversations seemed to be going on too long could be called out of the corner where he usually sat quietly weaving baskets to make violent unprovoked attacks, sometimes fatal, on any characters with whom the author was becoming bored.

Since the activities of Ronald and Jack Bedford happened to be on his mind this evening, Madden introduced them into his novel as two financiers who in the outside world had been given to signing cheques for enormous figures which they were quite unable to meet (a well-known symptom of hypermania), and who were now planning a complicated swindle in connection with the asylum's bread supply.

He had written himself into a good humour by the time he went into the little kitchen, which was extremely untidy. Under the remote gaze of a group of giraffes he boiled a kettle and made a cup of soup from a packet. He was a person who liked to talk and he found the solitary nature of the writer's calling a hardship, but this evening he went back to the sofa and, having put his cigarettes and a bottle of whisky and a glass within easy reach, he switched on his telephone answering machine and settled down to write until late.

* * *

What irritated Catherine about Tom was also what she found reassuring. He made himself comfortable in her small armchair, throwing the cushion on the floor, and said, 'Pity about the money.'

'I'd pay it back of course. I mean the bit I've already had.'

He nodded. 'Nicer not to have to. And there's that lump sum on delivery.'

'But, Tom, I can't do it.'

'I think you're asking too much of yourself. I read a lot of biographies. Only thing I do read. One in I don't know how many makes you feel you knew the chap. The others just give you the facts, often rather too many of them. There's a splendid chap, can't remember his name. He wrote about Shelley.'

'Tom! You've read a book about Shelley?'

'And there's a woman too, she's very good. Turns them out at quite a lick, mostly about other women. Apart from those two I can't think of any. Your trouble is you don't read enough of these books. You're overestimating what you're up against.'

'It's not a competitive sport, writing biographies.'

'No, but it's not a bad idea to know the running. What about just getting down a simple outline of all the ascertainable facts and seeing what that looks like before you finally decide?'

'You mean without any interpretation at all?'

'I wouldn't bother with interpretations. Let the reader do the interpreting.'

'I suppose I could do that. Just a chronological record, and see what it looks like.'

'I would. After all, you've done a lot of work, it would be a pity to waste it. Shall I give myself another whisky and soda before I go?'

'I wish you would. Tell me how things are. How's the office?'

'Rather good as a matter of fact. They've decided to pay me some more money for no very good reason. And I've got a perfectly splendid programme of cricket matches laid on for the office team, mostly through friends of mine. It should be good. They say they've never had a captain who organised so many outside matches. Rather nice, that, isn't it?'

'Wonderful,' said Catherine. 'How wonderful, Tom.'

She felt a great deal more cheerful after he had gone. She began to think that if she could get the book into some sort of shape quite soon perhaps she might find time to take a cottage by the sea for August or September. She could ask her sister over from Ireland, the one who was such a keen ornithologist, and perhaps Tom would come with the children, leaving Susannah to have a nice break from the family by going to stay with her mother in St Albans. In pursuit of this aim, though without having quite given up the thought that if this plan of Tom's did not leave her with an outline she could consider sufficiently convincing she had still the alternative of backing out altogether, she drove down to the Durdans the following day. She had some research to finish in the library there, so that she could correctly date the stages in the development of the place from private house to school and give a brief history of the school in its earliest days. Neil Campion had been a

Guardian, as the members of the governing body were called, and he had remained one until his death. The early history of the school was a legitimate part of his biography, and that at least was easily obtainable.

Arriving at the Durdans and seeing as she approached the house the usual scattering of young figures among the trees, she thought again how charmingly appropriate a setting the place always seemed for an experiment in communal idealism; but when she had parked her car and begun to walk towards the arch which led round to the front door this impression was somewhat modified by a group who seemed to be trying to help each other through one of the small doors which surrounded the courtyard. In the centre of the group was a girl who as she struggled to make her way through the doorway was being quite spectacularly sick.

Catherine had announced her arrival to Miss Dillinger the secretary and was already halfway up the stairs towards the library when Mr Manderson, his red cloak swinging, came bounding up the stairs behind her.

'I'm most awfully sorry I was teaching when you last came,' he said.

He smiled at her ingratiatingly, disclosing rather yellow teeth. She had not noticed the teeth before, having instead been favourably impressed by the fresh complexion and the lustrous brown curls, though she would have preferred the latter to have been either cut or restrained by something more appealing than an elastic band.

'I didn't know you were teaching, you should have told me. I could easily have looked through the library on my own.'

'But I'm afraid you did. Not the first time you came, I mean, but the other day, when Mr Roberts let you in. Oh no, wait a minute, it was your assistant, I think.'

'I haven't got an assistant.'

'Oh dear, it sounds like our Mr Roberts again, getting it wrong as usual. Never mind, I'm here this time. Now let's see, was it the early years of the school you were interested in, or was it the whole period of Karl Eberling's association with it?'

Catherine had hoped to look through the books by herself.

'I noticed a girl who didn't seem at all well as I came in,' she said. 'I wondered if it would be a good idea to tell Matron.'

'Were there others with her?'

'Yes, but they didn't look too good themselves.'

'They look after each other,' said Mr Manderson. 'It's the best way, we find.'

'I thought they looked – not exactly sober.'

'Could be,' said Mr Manderson lightly. 'Could be.'

'Don't you mind?' asked Catherine, surprised.

Mr Manderson took a little turn around the room, his hands behind his back. Then he stood still and looked at Catherine as if in consideration.

'Mrs Hillery,' he said finally. 'What do these children face when they leave here?'

She shook her head.

'I'll tell you what they face. Unemployment. Pollution. Lives poisoned by the nuclear threat.' He turned with a swirl of his cloak and walked over to one of the windows, where he sat down on the window seat and went on, 'All we can do for them, and I repeat all, is to help them to become a little bit streetwise. And convince them in the process that we are their friends. That's how these boys and girls see me, Mrs Hillery, as a friend.'

'Does that mean they know you won't mind if they drink?'

'Let's say they know that I know when to turn a blind eye.'

'Do they take drugs as well?'

'Nothing more than cannabis as a rule. Which in my opinion ought to be legalised anyway. Glue sniffing is much more of a menace.'

'Do they do much of that?'

'It sweeps through from time to time. It sweeps through.'

'I thought Eberling's idea was that young people would be

diverted from these things until they were old enough to cope with them by all the activities they could have in a place like this. Art, music, making things, games.'

'Games,' said Mr Manderson, pouncing on the word. 'Games. Team spirit. The team spirit that got these children's fathers slaughtered like cattle in the trenches of Flanders.'

'Grandfathers surely.'

'Grandfathers if you will. No, no, we've moved on a bit in the school since those days. You won't find much team spirit now.'

'Perhaps if you had it they could be against it. I mean it's sometimes rather nice having something to be against when you're young.'

'These young people don't need anything to be against,' said Mr Manderson with finality. 'The world is too much against them.'

'Does Mr Rumble the Headmaster think as you do?'

'Suffice it to say that Mr Trumble and I do not always see eye to eye.'

'Oh well,' said Catherine. 'I'd better get on.' She turned towards the shelf where she knew she would find the biography of Karl Eberling which she had come to consult. 'Please don't let me keep you. I'll just work my way peacefully through this section here.'

*   *   *

Effie Campion patted her face all over with skin tonic, then she did some facial exercises which the woman at the beauty treatment place where she went once a month had told her would prevent her from getting lines round her mouth. Then with the back of her hands she made forward-sweeping movements underneath her chin to improve muscle tone and prevent the development of a double chin. Then she scrutinised her face closely in the mirror. She saw that she already had lines round her mouth, as indeed she had on most of the rest of her face, and that her chin though not double was, not to put too find a point on it, scrawny. She took in these facts without self-deception, but she was certainly not going to brood on them. No one liked getting older, but one was still better than some of one's friends (poor old Evelyn Anderson for instance) and the great thing was not to give in (as poor old Evelyn had done) and after all one's life was still terribly full. She began to apply her make-up. She liked this part of the day; putting on her face, she called it. One couldn't face the world until one had put on one's face. But one could jolly well face it afterwards.

Today she was going to lunch with Pauline Callender to meet some American friends of hers. Pauline always gave such nice little lunches, mostly old friends but just the right admixture of unknowns. There would probably be George Crombie, who had recently retired from Parliament and been rewarded with a knighthood; and perhaps Charles Moffatt, who had a charming collection of English watercolours and was a first-rate bridge player, or Cara McCall, widow of a Scottish landowner who had treated her atrociously during his lifetime but left her an unexpectedly large sum of money on his death. There might be that dress-designer who was so amusing about his vulgar clients from show business; and then no doubt poor Evelyn would be there. After that there was a tea-time meeting of the committee for the Lily of the Valley Ball for the Distressed Deaf. Some of the younger committee members were so awfully pretty and smart; it was nice to keep up with the children of one's friends. And then there were cocktails with Maureen Sharp, whose husband was Head of Protocol at the Foreign Office so one always met interesting people. After that she would probably come home and have something to eat and watch the television in bed. Her appetite was small and when she was not eating out she subsisted mainly on toast.

She was applying the finishing touches to her maquillage when the telephone rang.

'Yes, you can come and see me,' she said to Catherine Hillery. 'But not for long because I've got a lunch.'

A nice woman, that, she thought, putting down the receiver, what a sensible choice of Potty's.

By the time Catherine arrived Effie was in full fig, ready for her lunch party.

'You do look smart,' said Catherine in admiration.

'Terrible old dress, I've had it for years. Such a bore to have to dress up but I'm lunching with Lady Callender and she's rather a stickler. Now let me give you some coffee and tell me how you're getting on.'

'I've been getting on quite well, in fact I thought I'd just about finished the research, but I've come across rather a problem and I'd like to put it to you quite frankly and see what you say.'

As Catherine accepted a cup of coffee Effie noticed that she was looking nervous; since they had for some time now been on quite easy terms she was surprised.

'Don't worry,' she said. 'Ask me anything you like. Fire away.'

'Could I just mention something completely different first? It's nothing to do with me but I was thinking about it on the way here and wondering whether to say anything and I thought perhaps I should. It's about Sam. I just wondered if you were quite happy about that school. It's very interfering of me but it did strike me the last time I was there that some of the teachers there might be, I don't know, just not quite the best thing for young people?'

'My dear, what is one to do? All my friends' grandchildren are in the same boat. Schools these days are simply too frightful for words.'

'I wonder if the Durdans is quite typical?'

'What's the alternative? I can't have him in London. Goodness knows what he'd get up to. And, you see, they say one can't change schools until they've done their O-levels. And they keep saying he doesn't work so he won't get any O-levels. What is one to do?'

'Perhaps after O-levels?'

'I don't know when he's doing them. I think he may have already done some and failed. Or was that Mocks? What are Mocks, I wonder? But I'll definitely talk to the frightful Trumble about it. You're quite right, it's a terrible place and now you've said it I can't pretend I don't know about it.'

She gave one of her sudden concentrated smiles, a quick projection of intimacy as quickly withdrawn but while it lasted disarming.

Catherine went on hurriedly, 'I've got to ask you one thing. I know we've touched on it before but I need to get it quite clear. Is there any possibility at all as far as you know that at any time between the outbreak of war and his death your husband could have been in touch with any German or Germans whether opposed to Hitler or not opposed to Hitler?'

Effie looked her straight in the eye and said, 'None whatever.'

'And this piece of paper which I found in one of the books in the library at the Durdans,' said Catherine, handing over the folded paper she had found in the anthology of First War poetry, 'does that mean anything to you at all?'

Effie read it carefully.

'Nothing. And that is not my husband's writing.'

'Could it be Peter Heinrich's?'

Effie consulted the paper again.

'I couldn't swear to it but I'm pretty sure it's not.'

'So you've no idea who could have written it or how it could have got into the book?'

'None.'

Effie held out the piece of paper. Catherine took it and returned it to her bag.

'Thank you so much. That clears it up completely. I'll be off now and not bother you any more. I hope you enjoy your lunch.'

'How sweet of you. I don't know that I shall, but one has to do these things, doesn't one?'

* * *

Summer had set in. The garden at the Durdans was full of roses. In the thirties Effie had fallen under the influence of William Robinson, the author of *The Wild Garden*, and had undertaken a great planting campaign among the shrubs and trees which grew between the lawns and the river. Over the years of the school's possession the garden had acquired a slightly more institutional look than it had had in her day; successive gardeners had increasingly favoured the bedding out policies of the public parks, with round beds where wallflowers and tulips succeeded daffodils, and salvias replaced geraniums, but by the river the roses still ran riot and when necessary had been replaced by new plants of the same species; so that Sam, collecting material to take up to that part of the roof which he had decided to decorate, was able to fill his arms with a rich variety of blooms as well as the leafy branches of lime and beech which he had already cut from the trees. As he went back into the house he met Miss Dillinger who, passing him with her customary nervousness, said, 'Oh, Sam. For the Art Room? How lovely.'

He went upstairs, pushed his bundle of vegetation through the skylight first, then pulled himself up by his arms. There were now two mattresses side by side where there used to be only one. They were covered by some Indian cotton bedspreads which Sam had found in his grandmother's linen cupboard. He began methodically to arrange all round them first the branches of leaves and then the flowers, the Souvenir de la Princess de Lamballe and the Madame Alfred Carrière, the New Dawn and the Rambling Rector, the deep-scented Etoile d'Hollande. He kept a large watering can up on the roof, and had earlier filled

137

it with water. When he had finished his arrangements he watered the flowers and leaves thoroughly so that the evening air was filled with their scent; then he rinsed out four glasses and dried them on a corner of one of the bedspreads. He set them out at the foot of the mattresses and put a bottle of vodka and a bottle of British sherry beside them. Then he went downstairs to supper.

He returned to the roof at dusk, wearing his pyjamas. With him came Pat and Prue, wearing nightdresses from Laura Ashley, and Howard Clayborne Pope whose pyjamas, like Sam's, came from Marks and Spencer. They filled the glasses with vodka, Clayborne Pope adding a dash of sherry to his, and sitting in a circle cross-legged on the mattresses they raised their glasses and said with solemnity and in unison, 'Self-indulgence for ever!'

As a consequence of the concern of the school authorities about the spread of Aids, a friend of the Headmaster's, Sister Felicity (she was a member of a small order of nuns), had addressed the school on the subject of sex. The decision to ask her to do so had been reached by the staff with some difficulty. Some had felt that she should be asked only to talk to the top two forms in the school. Some had felt that she was not the answer at all, and had suggested the installation of a slot machine selling condoms in the Sixth Form common room. Others had pointed out that the Sixth Formers might not be above making such a facility available to more junior members of the school, for a variety of selfish considerations of their own. Young Mr Roberts had suggested that the children should be told to confine any sexual activities they might have to the school holidays, but was told he was being unrealistic. In the end Sister Felicity, who came with warm recommendations from other schools, was given carte blanche to say anything she thought appropriate to the whole school. She had explained to a rapt audience exactly what activities were liable to expose them to the danger of Aids, and had gone on to touch lightly on

138

those activities which were not liable to expose them to such a danger. The second part of her lecture had attracted even more attention than the first, since most of the children had heard or read a good deal about Aids already, but not many had heard so much about the more ingenious manifestations of Safe Sex. Sister Felicity ended her talk with a heartfelt appeal for self-restraint. 'Self-indulgence,' she had said, 'is to be looked on as an absolute evil.' Most of the children left her lecture dedicated (for the time being at all events) to total celibacy; a few had other thoughts.

In so far as Sam had a philosophy it was a philosophy of lack of restraint. He believed in a life of pure sensation. Somewhere he had heard or read – he could not remember where – the sentence he had written in large letters on the first page of one of his stolen exercise books, ONLY BY LIVING A LIFE OF PURE SENSATION CAN WE ESCAPE THE SILENT WATCHER IN THE SKULL. Sam did not think very deeply. He picked up the flavour of an idea and hurried on without further investigation. Further investigation might even have seemed to him a dangerous activity. His thoughts skidded over the surface of things, keeping moving, avoiding their own reflections, mayflies on a fast-flowing river full of fish. Thus, although he half-knew that the watcher in the skull represented his own (or the writer's) self-consciousness, he at the same time thought of it as being quite outside himself. He imagined – he even dreamed sometimes – that there was a white skull in the corner of every room he went into and that he had to keep himself from looking at it because if he did he might see behind the dark empty eye sockets the just discernible movement of whatever was in there, watching. Whatever it was it was presumably not human, or not quite; it could be a very small entirely malevolent man, but was more probably a nameless intelligence or at very best some kind of rat. It was clearly desirable to avoid (or at least forget) this creature's surveillance, and to do so by as it were losing oneself in the extremes of sensation, whether of pleasure, pain, fear, speed, intoxication, hilarity or any other kind of frenzy or amazement, seemed to Sam a reasonable programme. It was one not easy to put into operation at school, where there were inevitably longish periods of boredom and inactivity, but Sam found that during these periods he could drift quite easily into vague daydreams, featuring mostly himself with wings, moving through the universe inviolate and when seen (which was rarely) acclaimed. He avoided all conscious thought of his night dreams, with which had he wanted to he could have frightened himself as much as he liked, for he had long been subject to nightmares. These nightmares, which often involved nothing more than vast swirling movements of some kind of circular matter through interminable space but which were always unspeakably terrifying, were never allowed to intrude into his daytime life; like the skull they had to be driven out of his consciousness.

Sister Felicity's remarks about self-restraint interested Sam immediately (he was already listening attentively to the lecture, though shocked that a nun should know anything about such matters let alone speak of them openly) and her solemn abjuration to the effect that self-indulgence was to be regarded as an absolute evil came to him as a clarion call to action. He beat his left palm with his right fist and said 'Yeah!' in the tone of a member of the congregation in a black American Evangelist church. It was Clayborne Pope, who having noticed this gesture and activated by nothing more complicated than having had since earliest childhood a perfectly filthy mind, suggested that some kind of joint exploration of the matters raised by Sister Felicity might be in order, particularly if the twins could be induced to co-operate. It was Clayborne Pope too who after the first such experiment had kept the thing going, periodically handing out to the other three small folded pieces of paper saying ORGEY TONIGHT.

Sam had been introduced to sex by an Iranian girl called Alma quite soon after his arrival at the Durdans. He had immediately recognised it as a prime means of self-forgetfulness; but he had also taken his relationship with Alma very seriously, and had asked her to marry him as soon as they left school. Indeed he had suggested they might get married during the first school holidays in which they were both sixteen but before that time she was expelled from the school for being found in possession of a large supply of cannabis, and though they corresponded for a time her letters became gradually less frequent and she finally wrote to tell him that she had met a boy she liked at the London Comprehensive she was now attending and would not be writing to Sam any more. 'London boys,' she wrote hurtfully, 'seem older for their age than people at the Durdans.' It was at this time that Sam began to spend more and more time on the roof; but it was only since Sister Felicity's lecture that he had taken to sharing it on such a regular basis. He was a little divided in his mind as to how happy he was about this loss of total autonomy.

When they had emptied their glasses of vodka, Sam produced four capsules of sodium amytal which he had procured from an acquaintance in London. They took their clothes off, broke the capsules under their noses, succumbed to the hilarity thus induced, and began their orgy.

'Oh Christ, fucking prickles,' said Clayborne Pope.

Seizing bundles of branches and roses in their thin bare arms, and with little shrieks of pain as they felt the thorns on their tender breasts, Pat and Prue piled them up on the roof at one end of the mattresses. It was a warm summer night, moonlit and sweet-scented. Any chill the four of them might have felt in their nakedness was soon dispelled by their vigorous activity. Their youthful capacities were such that they could be sustained for some time, procuring for them climax after climax in their separate though at times coincidental searches for satisfaction. Gradually their heats abated; the girls lay side by side, their hair spread round their pale faces on the rumpled bedspread, seeming to sleep. Sam lay beyond them with part of one of the bedspreads round his exhausted limbs. Rolling his head to one side to avoid a branch which was pressing into his neck, he caught a glimpse of Clayborne Pope still frantically ejaculating into another bedspread. There came into his tired brain two cold thoughts, that Clayborne Pope looked rather disgusting, and that he, Sam, would probably have to wash the bedspreads. Looking up towards the indifferent moon, and with some faint thought of wolves, he tried a quiet experimental howl. There came back to him a recollection of how long ago in those scarcely to be imagined times when his parents were alive and they had all lived together, they had had a dog, a fox terrier, who used to howl like that when the telephone rang, and he, the child Sam, had imitated him, so they would howl together, and whichever parent came to answer the telephone – and sometimes it was both – would expostulate, laughing and hurrying and saying oh do stop you two. He put his head back, and feeling the sound reverberate in his throat gave a series of long loud intensely melancholy howls.

'They'll hear, they'll hear, someone'll hear.' Clayborne Pope was struggling into his pyjamas.

Pat, as if sleep-walking, put on her nightdress, went silently over to the skylight and slipped down it out of sight. Clayborne Pope followed. Prue tried to cover Sam with his pyjamas but he had turned his face into the crook of his arm and shook her away saying, 'No, no,' in a distressed tone. Hesitating, she saw the now-faded flowers, and first quietly putting his pyjamas within his reach she picked up and scattered a few rose petals over him. Feeling this inadequate she still delayed, but, no other course of action suggesting itself to her, she turned and followed the others through the skylight.

*   *   *

'You've been putting your foot in it,' said Brackenbury the publisher to Catherine.

'What can you mean?' Catherine had been watering the geraniums in her window box when the telephone rang and now struggled with one hand to close the window. 'I haven't done anything.'

'Oh yes, you have. I don't know what, but you don't get Ernest Pottinger on the move for nothing.'

'On the move? What's he doing?'

'He says you're to stop poking around in unnecessary areas and get on with the book. He wants to see a first draft as soon as possible.'

'I don't understand. What exactly did he say?'

'Just that. The telephone was ringing as I came into the office. I asked what you'd been up to and he just repeated that he thought it was time they saw some results, and that he was keeping in very close touch. How is the book by the way?'

'It's all right. Quite well in fact.'

'Good. I thought you'd be amused to hear you'd got the great man worried. Carry on anyway. Keep in touch.'

Catherine put down the receiver and sat for some time looking out of the window, which she had failed to close. Then she lifted the receiver again and dialled Etta's number.

'This friend of yours, Madden. I need to meet him.'

'Oh.'

'Could you arrange it, do you think?'

'Well I . . . it's a bit difficult.'

'Couldn't you just ask him for a drink or something? It's about this book I'm doing.'

'I don't know exactly. I mean, he might not come.'

'But, Etta, just for a drink?'

'I think he doesn't go out much.'

'But I thought he wrote a gossip column. How can you write a gossip column if you don't go out much? Don't say he makes it up. I've always thought they did.'

'No, no, I'm sure he doesn't make it up. Or maybe he does make it up. I don't know.'

'Why don't you just give me his telephone number then? I'll be very polite to him, I promise.'

'I'll see if I can find it. I'll ring you back.'

'Don't bother if you haven't got it. I can get hold of him through his newspaper.'

'I think I can probably find it. Yes, I do have it after all. Of course he may have moved.'

Reading nothing particular into what she took to be Etta's habitual evasiveness, Catherine telephoned Madden's flat, found him in and asked if they could meet to talk about Neil Campion. He said he would come round to see her immediately.

She had for some reason expected someone younger, and was surprised on opening her front door to be confronted with that ferocious gaze and squat powerful frame, and to notice the grey hairs among the abundant black. With the idea of impressing her with his seriousness and weight as an adversary, he had put on his soberest dark suit and a discreet spotted tie. He struck her as looking more like a successful financier than a journalist. He, noticing her pleasant smile and attractive voice and the agreeable atmosphere of the room into which she showed him, felt himself fully armed against charm; there was to be no question of compromise.

She had heard he was interested in Campion, she said, and wondered, smiling still, if they were rivals. He was cagey, said he'd become interested in Campion in the course of general study of the pre-War period. She asked what his particular concern with that period had been. Attitudes, he said, and then agreed, yes, attitudes to Germany. Had he thought there was anything odd about Campion's attitude to Germany? He implied, without exactly saying so, that he had found Campion's attitude to Germany not so much odd as typical, and then she took him by surprise and went straight to the point.

'You mean you were working on the theory that Campion

was pro-Nazi? And when you say typical you mean a lot of other English people were too?'

'Look, you're doing the authorised biography . . .'

'And what I'm wondering is why. Why am I doing the authorised biography? I know nothing about that period, nothing about politics. My previous biographies have been about people not in the least like Neil Campion. Why me?'

'Because they knew about me,' answered Madden, beginning to be excited.

'How did they know?'

'I did an interview with Effie Campion. It was ostensibly about her charity work, but there was enough about her husband to put them on the alert. I shouldn't have done that. I should have waited. Then I made the even bigger mistake of writing to Pottinger. She'd said if I wanted to know anything about her husband I'd have to ask Pottinger because he had all the papers. Of course she was just stalling really. So I wrote to Pottinger and got a pretty stiff reply. I let it rest a bit and then when I contacted him again I was told there was an authorised biographer and all the papers were with her. I'd obviously scared them stiff. I even mentioned in my letter to Pottinger that I was in touch with a newspaper which was interested in serialisation.'

'And they chose me just because I didn't know about politics and didn't know about that period and didn't know anything about anything. They must have asked Brackenbury for exactly that.'

'So,' said Madden, still not sure of her. 'So what will you do?'

She went to her desk and, taking a sheet of paper, held it out to him saying, 'Look at this.'

It was a list of names, headed Provisional Cabinet After the Event. At the top of the list was written Prime Minister and the name opposite it was Neil Campion's. Madden read it through slowly and handed it back to Catherine in silence.

'I found it in a book at the Durdans,' she said. 'It was a book given to Neil Campion by Peter Heinrich.'

Madden merely nodded, looking thoughtful.

'The thing is,' said Catherine, 'I'm not really such a fool as they think. Of course I realised that all that was an area which needed investigating. I investigated it. But I couldn't find anything. I went through everything I could find about all those various pro-German associations there were before the War and I came across hardly anything about Campion. He belonged to the Anglo-German Fellowship but he never seemed to go to any of the meetings. He joined The Link but he resigned in 1937. He never belonged to the Right Club, which was the really sinister one. He went to Germany twice in the early thirties to stay with Peter Heinrich.'

'Ah,' said Madden. 'Heinrich.'

'Well, but as far as I can make out Heinrich's circle seems to come to nothing much in any political sense. Vaguely mystical, rather upper-class, going in for long talks about the decline of humanism and the virtue of the artist-craftsman, miles from any centre of power in Germany and pretty ineffectual. In the end Heinrich himself seems to have got drawn into the resistance to Hitler by Adam von Trott, but that was after Neil Campion's death. He sounds quite a nice man, Peter Heinrich, but I should have thought he was completely ineffectual. Does any of this tie in with what you've found out?'

'There are closed files. There are still two files which MI5 haven't released, even though the thirty years they're supposed to wait have passed and the other files have been released.'

'So what do you suppose is in them?'

'Enough to embarrass people still living.'

Catherine looked at the list in her hand.

'Who among this lot is still alive? This one's dead, that one's dead . . .'

'Lord Sturmer's still alive.'

'We'll go and see him. I'll write and say I'm doing the

authorised biography. He won't refuse. You're my research assistant. I'll write and then I'll ring up the very day he gets my letter. We don't want him running to Mr Pottinger.'

'You think that's what Effie Campion did?'

'She must have done. I showed her that list, you see. It's a pity because I was beginning to like her.'

* * *

Young Mr Roberts was walking along the terrace on the garden side of the house one evening towards dusk when a bundle of dead branches and flowers landed on his head. Stepping back quickly to look up he caught a glimpse of Sam Campion looking down from the roof. Mr Roberts continued on his way towards what was known as the Garden Theatre, a dip in the ground beyond the squash courts where the bushes planted in the early days of the school had grown up to provide an excellent arrangement of exits and entrances; he was going to collect the various props which he knew from experience would have been left behind after his earlier and very successful dress rehearsal of *Twelfth Night*. The next day, however, when Sam appeared at an English Language class, Mr Roberts asked him after the lesson whether, when he did not come to a class, he was usually on the roof. Sam replied that he supposed he quite often was.

'Who is your tutor?' asked Mr Roberts.

'Mr Manderson. He doesn't mind my being on the roof.'

'I was thinking you'd have made an awfully good Feste. You haven't seen Twelfth Night, I suppose? Do come on Saturday. He's an interesting character, Feste, because you can play him in all sorts of different ways. I wish you'd watch him and tell me afterwards what you think.'

'Oh,' said Sam. 'Okay.'

'I was rather bored when I was at school, I'm afraid,' said Mr

Roberts. 'I suppose I wasn't much good at anything. And then someone forced me into a walk-on part in *Macbeth* and I was hooked. It's too late for this term, I suppose, but you might like to try Drama next term?'

'Okay,' said Sam.

'I won't let you forget,' said Mr Roberts.

Sam went upstairs and out onto the roof. There was only one mattress there now. After the last orgy he had taken the other one back to the dormitory it had come from. He had explained to the others that he did not want any more orgies on the roof for the time being; he didn't know why, he just felt it wasn't cool any more. The others made no objections. Clayborne Pope said he was definitely going to concentrate on his O-level work anyway. Prue told Sam privately that she was glad he had decided as he had because she didn't think Pat really liked the orgies; she'd been crying a lot lately. Pat told him the same thing about Prue. Sam hated it when the twins cried, which they did not infrequently; he was glad to be able to escape to the roof. Restored to solitary possession (for though other children sometimes came up to sunbathe or smoke they respected his corner between the two slopes of tiles) Sam spent a good deal of time asleep up there even in the daytime, becoming sunburnt, biding his time; something had to happen soon.

*   *   *

Madden was aware that he had to treat Catherine Hillery, upon whom he had perpetrated a fraud, with caution. He had also to keep his wits about him as things developed. His expectation was that the fraud would turn out to have been necessary only as a spur to further action on Catherine's part. He believed that the list he had inserted in the book of war poetry was so near the truth in its implications that it would emerge as not so much a forgery as an inspired guess, and in that case he saw no reason to disclose its true authorship; he must therefore hold himself ready to cover his tracks. As it was things seemed to be going more easily than he had anticipated. He had expected more resistance on Catherine's part to his baldly stated theory about Campion's true purposes and their possible ramifications. Being himself intensely class-conscious, he had expected to find in her some kind of class solidarity with the Campion family; he had thought she would identify herself with the Establishment, and recognise that its interests were unlikely to be served by the inconvenient curiosity of a Jewish journalist. Being also fiercely competitive, he was puzzled by her apparent lack of possessiveness about what might fairly be considered her territory. Who was writing the authorised life, after all? And yet she had simply said, 'We'll go and see him, you'll be my research assistant,' meaning presumably that he could pass in that capacity if Lord Sturmer were to ask who he was. Whatever else she might have meant Madden was determined to wait to find out; the important thing was to pursue his quarry, and he could do this much more easily in partnership with Catherine than without her knowledge. It seemed unlikely that she was seriously offering him anything formal, or anything financial, in the way of partnership, but the question could wait. He was inclined to think that if the Campion family had indeed selected her as biographer on the grounds of her naïvety, as she had angrily supposed, then they might well have had a point. She seemed to offer him no defences at all, revealing merely a curiosity which was almost childish.

'It's all so intriguing,' she said, as they set off towards the M4 in her small car. 'Of course if one thinks of all those French collaborators, I suppose there were bound to have been a few English ones if the Germans had invaded, but it's awfully hard to imagine. You'd be too young to remember, but we were all so patriotic in the war, one never heard of anybody who dreamt of anything else. But of course the fact is that if you're an ordinary person you really never have the faintest idea what's going on, do you?'

'Perhaps not.'

'Reading the newspapers doesn't help either. Perhaps I shouldn't say that, you being a journalist.'

'In this country it's very difficult to find out what's going on, even for journalists.'

'I suppose so. Tell me how you found out about those unreleased files.'

'It's no secret. They can hold back anything if they say it's on the grounds of national security.'

'And you've seen the others?'

'I've got it all in my notes. I can't really remember it all without my notebook.'

Because it was not like that. It was not something to be tossed about in frivolous conversation with light-voiced ladies smelling faintly of rose-water. People thinking Hitler quite wonderful, how too amusing. He knew the English upper-class flippant tone; wasn't it just what he had learnt so well to imitate at Oxford? And didn't he sometimes despise himself for using it, for being untrue to his own European inheritance of deep seriousness? To joke about evil was not clever, to mock at genocide not funny. They would say he had no sense of humour, but what he had was a sense of reality, of what was appropriate. The Mozart of *Cosi fan Tutte* wrote also the *Requiem*. It was such an acknowledgement of terror he wanted, such solemnity in the face of man's wickedness, not the exchange of country house pleasantries.

Catherine was aware of having in some way struck the wrong note, but he was mistaken in thinking her without her own vulnerabilities. It was true that except during those periods of unaccountable depression which she preferred not to think about, and which, after each incidence, she minimised to herself before almost forgetting, Catherine was as open and friendly as she appeared. She found something to like or at least to be amused by in most people she met, and she dealt with people frankly because she found frankness saved time; insofar as she had ever been interested in the minor competitiveness current in social intercourse she had outgrown all that. She felt it as a compensation for being no longer young to be able to let people take her as they found her. She was interested in the world and not much interested in herself, being as a result not very knowledgeable about herself, which was why her occasional depressions so bewildered her. She had her prejudices, however, and one of them was against what she took to be the world of fashion. A gossip columnist being in her view a servant of this suspect world, her attitude to Alfred Madden was less open than it seemed. Her manner was her usual one but her heart was not quite – or not yet – in it. Hence perhaps the note to which Madden had taken exception, a slight falsity, as it were a tinniness in the echo, to which his raw nerves made him sensitive. She complained of the traffic, implying she needed all her concentration for driving, in order to free him from the need to make conversation. He looked out of the window in silence; he had as usual been up late the previous night. Catherine, who did not smoke, had a sensitive nose for those who did. Madden, more casually dressed than when she had last seen him (as befitted, he thought, his role as a research assistant), was nevertheless neat and clean, but the smell of toothpaste and Floris mouthwash could not quite extinguish the faint fumes of alcohol and tobacco clinging probably, Catherine thought, to his hair, even perhaps to his abundant eyebrows. Bernard used to smoke a pipe; she had not minded that. But then he seldom lit it until after lunch. When Madden asked after they had driven some distance whether she would mind if he smoked she hoped fresh smoke might be preferable to stale, but as they approached a service station she said, 'I could do with a cup of coffee. Would you mind? We're in very good time.'

They parked, went upstairs, collected cups of coffee, sat down opposite each other.

'Have you known Nicholas and Etta long?'

But he was not prepared to enlarge on that subject, and to avoid it apologised for being tired, blaming his nocturnal existence and explaining his intention soon to give it up and concentrate on his writing.

'Unfortunately one's got to live in the meantime. I didn't want to stay in the academic world. My college offered me a lectureship but it's an awful straitjacket the academic life, don't you agree?'

'Is it? I'd have thought it rather pleasant.'

He shook his head. 'An awfully small world. Were you at Oxford?'

'Good heavens no. I left school at sixteen. I'm the last uneducated woman.'

He allowed himself to respond to her smile. Feeling better, he set out to discover more, his sleeping sympathy beginning to awaken. For he could be sympathetic; it was his quick understanding which had won Etta's initial interest. Once he forgot his pride his naturally keen curiosity took over. The effort of imagination required in order to encompass another's existence occasionally made him feel almost as if he had created the character himself. Sometimes he had; his fancy running ahead of his knowledge, he had been known to endow a new acquaintance with a character, usually flattering, to which he or she had in reality no right. Etta, who liked his enthusiasms, had seen more than one swan turn into a goose in his estimation; herself more detached, she enjoyed the day of the swan and was indifferent to the fate of the goose.

Between the service station and the Chippenham turn-off, Catherine began to assume in his eyes certain swanlike characteristics, one of which was that she offered Madden himself no immediate challenge. She had no cards to play on the academic front, nor on the grounds of literary success, hers being only marginally superior to his own; nor had she more fashionable names to drop, such being the very last activity likely to concern her. Beyond the age (or so he considered) at which a sexual challenge was to be expected, she was all the same an attractive woman, so that mild flirtatiousness on his part was acceptable, if only formal. In putting her down as responsive to his charm he was failing to take into account her generation's deference to the male, thereby missing also the fact that she did not necessarily altogether mean it; it was a convention she expected him to understand. Not understanding it, he took it personally and was flattered. Feeling that she liked him he began to like her; his queries elicited a simplified version of her life story and he felt it morally superior to his own, chiefly because there seemed to be no place in it for personal ambition. But he was not able to return confidence for confidence; there was too much of which he felt ashamed. Instead he returned to what she had told him about her life in the War, and how she had once met Neil Campion.

'But you mustn't mention that if you ever meet Eleanor,' she said. 'I haven't told her. There's no point. We didn't get on. She more or less sacked me. Anyway I was transferred to another hospital. If I want her to trust me while I'm doing the book it hardly seems sensible to remind her.'

'Sacked you?' He was amused. 'What had you done?'

'I was eighteen and very silly and I broke all the rules. Out after hours, you know the sort of thing. She was a tremendous dragon. We were all terrified of her.'

'Would you have been terrified of him?'

'Probably. But he had charm. She didn't. It made him much more formidable.'

'So the people who reported him as a personality, a potential leader and so on, you'd say they were right?'

'Yes.'

'He was forty-two when he died. May the ninth, 1941. Somewhere near Doncaster.'

'His wife says she has no idea where he was going.'

'Do you believe her?'

'I'm not sure. She's capable of concealing things.'

'I knew her great niece, Marian,' said Madden after a slight pause. 'It was during my upper-class phase. I mean my phase for falling for upper-class girls.'

'What sort of girls do you fall for now?'

'Foreign ones. Unfortunately. Anyway Marian's father disapproved of me. He thought I was a Jewish upstart, quite rightly.'

'And Marian?'

'She didn't exactly disapprove of me. But I think her father's view of me affected hers because after a bit she began to like me less. They're very hard to escape, those class attitudes.'

'Did they talk about Neil Campion?'

'That was how I first heard of him. Not that they mentioned him much. Something Marian's father said just happened to intrigue me.'

'You don't think you're muddling the two of them up in your mind, I mean Marian's father and Neil Campion?'

'That is very acute of you. But no. This is not a fantasy of mine about Neil Campion. There's substance in it.'

'What do you think he was doing?'

'I think he was conspiring with his German friend to bring about some kind of peace with Germany, either with Hitler himself or with other Germans who were going to dispose of Hitler, and I think he had English associates who were going to make up a new government, probably after some kind of coup here. I think there's no doubt that as a Minister of the Crown he was acting treasonably.'

'Which is where Pottinger comes in. To defend the family honour.'

'And to prevent anything else coming out, about other people as well as about Campion.'

'To defend the honour of England then.'

154

'If you like.'

'We'll see,' said Catherine. 'The only hard evidence we have of an actual plot is one piece of paper with a list of names on it, and we don't know who wrote that list. There's a difference between thinking about something, or wishing it would happen, and actually doing something about it. It wasn't treason to have had German friends before the War, or even to have kept in touch with them for as long as it was possible. I've been surprised to find out how many peace proposals there were going around in the first year or so of the War, and if there was treason involved there it was on the German side. Except that is it treason, when the person you are betraying is Hitler?'

'We're talking about a pact with the Nazis,' said Madden firmly. 'Made by English people and in return for power. Why should they try to hide the kind of vague muddling about you're talking of?'

'Some people will try to hide anything. What I want to do now is simply to find out where Neil Campion was going in May 1941 when he drove into that wall. Perhaps Lord Sturmer can tell us. I wonder if he's anything to do with the pippin.'

'The pippin?'

'It's an apple. Sturmer's Pippin.'

Catherine turned off the motorway and drove north onto the Gloucestershire plain. They came to a village of stone houses, flowering gardens, a handsome church, a post office stores of friendly aspect; beyond it a low stone wall surrounding a park was interrupted by an entrance gate and a neat lodge. On the wall beside the gate, which was open, was a small notice which said International Institute for the Study of Astral Projection. Catherine turned onto the drive.

'What's astral projection?' asked Madden.

'Something to do with space, do you think? I suppose they've let it for offices. He said we were to go to the side entrance.'

The house presented an imposing Regency front; it was built of darker stone than the local Cotswold variety. Catherine parked the car on the expanse of gravel in front of the entrance portico and made for the tall wrought iron gate at the side of the house which led through a beech hedge into a formal garden. Following the garden path towards a side entrance to the house she took in the strictly institutional aspect of the beds of begonias and salvias; it seemed the offices had charge of the gardening. Madden followed her, carrying a notebook and looking as he supposed unassuming; in effect morose. Before Catherine could ring the bell the door was hurriedly opened.

'I saw you arrive,' said Lady Sturmer triumphantly, also mellifluously, laughingly and altogether disconcertingly. She was wearing a sort of dressing-gown, or house-coat, or – the word suddenly came into Catherine's mind – peignoir, a long belted flowery robe in shades of turquoise and pink. Her white hair was combed out round her head in a simulation of youthful casualness; in fact it was so heavily lacquered to keep it in place that it had the consistency of candy floss. Her hands were tiny and white, with vivid crimson fingernails matching the toenails which protruded from the turquoise high-heeled bedroom slippers, or mules; her face was heavily powdered, her lips scarlet; rouge and mascara played their part in making her look, in spite of the roundness of her cheeks and the relative absence of wrinkles, extraordinarily old.

Backing away from the door, she made use of a conveniently placed table at the side of the corridor to which she had admitted them in order to manoeuvre the necessary about-turn. This achieved, she set off stiffly towards the end of the passage, calling out as she went, 'They're here, Pips. I'm bringing them along.'

She opened a door and explained, 'This is where we live. Rather tiny.'

They followed her into a very small sitting-room; it was dominated by an immense television set encased in a mahogany frame; other than that there was room only for two large chintz-covered armchairs and a similar sofa; the walls were hung with framed coloured photographs of horses. A small bald-headed old man wearing a tweed suit rose from one of the armchairs. He looked startled but shook hands, politely murmuring, 'So nice of you to come.'

Lady Sturmer invited them to sit down and offered them a drink. Catherine refused; Madden felt he had to do the same. Catherine mentioned her biography of Neil Campion. Lord Sturmer's face brightened; he had clearly just remembered who they were.

'Of course, of course. We've looked out a few photographs. Where are those photograph books?'

He found them, several thick leather-covered albums piled on the floor beside one of the armchairs. Catherine sat on the sofa and slowly turned the pages, while Lord Sturmer, having found his glasses, read out the captions beneath the faded amateurish snapshots. Madden sat in silence beside Catherine; Lady Sturmer, beyond him, kept up a flow of interjection and additional commentary, mainly in a sense flattering to her husband. The photographs showed groups of people standing about in front of large houses, sometimes in shooting clothes or tennis outfits, sometimes in cars of pre-War model, sometimes in twos and threes in garden chairs and wearing hats. Lord Sturmer, memories aroused, became animated, shifting his small frame to the very edge of his capacious armchair, and from time to time leaning right over Catherine almost as if he were about to lay his small bald head in her lap, and bringing a red-spotted handkerchief out of his trouser pocket and passing it over his shiny forehead, rubbing his nose vigorously as a gesture of enjoyment rather than of practical necessity, then leaning over again to replace the handkerchief in the trouser pocket.

'I remember that. D'you remember that, Muffie? Croquet at Maggie Greville's. Ribbentrop couldn't stand losing – d'you remember? There's that left-wing journalist fellow, frightful fellow with the Sapphist wife. That's that art humbug who was in cahoots with the American crook. Darling old Frau Ribbentrop, d'you remember, Muffie, she took us to tea with Herr Hitler? Ha ha ha. King of Spain. One always met royalty with Maggie. Holmwood Park – remember those days, Muffie, eh? Racing. Newmarket.'

'No one knows how much Pips did for the Turf,' said Lady Sturmer. 'Before we gave everything to astralism. That's not Newmarket, Pips, that's Goodwood.'

'We thought we were going to win the Derby. Lovely creature that, an Irish horse. Cliveden, that was fun. That's Lothian, some people thought him good-looking. Nearly got Muffie hooked on Christian Science, eh Muffie? Oh, that German degenerate we never liked, used to make silly jokes about Herr Hitler.'

'Show them the Durdans ones, Pips, that's what they're interested in. They want to know about Neil Campion.'

'We only went there once. They dropped us. We weren't intellectual enough for them.'

'No one could have called Effie intellectual, Pips. Lovely creature she was, full of go.'

'So full of go she went, what? As far as we were concerned anyway. Never saw them again after that one weekend. Babs Wrootham took us. She thought we'd be interested because we were all friends of Germany. They weren't our cup of tea.'

'Who was your cup of tea?' interposed Catherine quickly.

'Oh, the Right Club. Ramsey, splendid chap, would have been behind an alliance with Herr Hitler against the Russians all the way. We used to think Mosley might be some good but this fellow Ramsey told us he wasn't serious. Frivolous fellow apparently, swanning off to the South of France all the time. Not that one wasn't swanning off oneself but one didn't expect a Great Leader to do it. You never saw Herr Hitler in the South of France.'

'Or carrying on with other people's wives,' added Lady Sturmer firmly. 'No one could have called Herr Hitler a ladykiller.'

'Did you ever think of Neil Campion as a possible Great Leader?'

'Campion? I don't think so, did we, Muffie?'

'People mentioned him. I do remember people mentioning him. But he was always rather a dark horse, Neil Campion.'

'A dark horse, yes. That was what he was, a dark horse. No one ever quite knew what he was up to.'

'But was he up to something, would you say?'

'Bound to be. Clever fellow like that. Bound to be up to something.'

'I wouldn't say he was quite accepted, you know,' said Lady Sturmer. 'Effie was, of course. She married beneath her. He was a bit of an outsider.'

'Chip on his shoulder,' said Lord Sturmer. 'Nothing worse.'

'I wouldn't say that exactly, Pips. I wouldn't say he had a chip exactly. And of course he was quite assimilated if you know what I mean. He didn't have an accent or anything. But he hadn't been to Eton.'

'Really?' Lord Sturmer looked more interested. 'I never came across him at Harrow. He'd have been younger, would he?'

'He went to Sherborne,' said Catherine.

'Oh,' said Lord Sturmer, losing interest. 'Bad luck. Anyway here we are. Here's the Durdans house-party.'

They were lined up on the familiar doorstep, a group in motoring clothes, arriving or leaving, dogs, smiles, cloche hats, tweed caps, Neil, Effie, one or two unexceptionable notabilities of the time, Pips and Muffie, a genial Karl Eberling, a handsome young man who was Peter Heinrich. But they could remember little of Peter Heinrich; he had been out most of the time, playing golf.

'Was Neil Campion as outspoken as you were in your admiration for Hitler?' asked Catherine.

'So many people were got at by Communist propaganda,' said Muffie, looking distressed.

'We got pretty unpopular at one time,' said Lord Sturmer.

'They threatened to send us to the Isle of Man.' He dipped his head over Catherine's knees again, extracted the red-spotted handkerchief and rubbed his nose vigorously. 'They thought we were a danger to the State.'

'Show them the letter, Pips.' Lord Sturmer heaved himself out of his chair and began to ruffle about behind it with a certain amount of grunting and muttering.

'He loves showing people the letter,' said Muffie indulgently. 'But it did frighten us off. We'd been going to write to Herr Hitler but they opened all our letters, you know. The most frightful things were done in that way in the War. So we didn't write. We decided to wait until he landed. We were hoping for an invasion, you see. We were going to go and see him the minute he arrived and offer him this house as his headquarters. I suppose it was lucky it didn't happen because it would have been blown up and then we'd never have been able to give it all to Simon.'

She smiled seraphically.

'Simon?' asked Catherine.

'He used to be Simon of Sloane Street,' said Lady Sturmer as if no further explanation were needed.

'Here we are,' Lord Sturmer held out a framed letter. It read,

> 'Dear Pips,
>   Enough is enough. If you don't stop charging round the country telling everyone what a splendid fellow Hitler is I'll have you interned under War Regulation 18B.
> Love to Muffie.
>   Yours'

followed by an enormously distinguished signature and a P.S. in capital letters I MEAN IT.

'I see,' said Catherine, handing back the letter. 'So you didn't have any contact with the Germans during the War?'

'What could we have done?' said Lord Sturmer. 'No one in England took a blind bit of notice of anything we said anyway.'

'And yet of course Pips was absolutely right,' said Lady Sturmer. 'Look what's happened now. Half of Germany under the Russian yoke and the other half our ally against the Bolshie threat which is what should have happened years ago.'

'You didn't feel the Nazi regime was something that had to be fought? Even after the War when it all came out about the concentration camps?'

'If you mean Belsen and so on . . .' said Lord Sturmer. 'They only got so bad because the Germans were losing the War. They were meant to be transit camps. The Jews were all to be sent to the East. And no doubt if they'd been winning the war they wouldn't have killed them when they got them there. They'd just have re-settled them. And why not? Far too many Jews in Germany. Why not send them somewhere else? We'd do better to do the same thing with the blacks here. No sense in quibbling over that sort of thing when there was Herr Hitler fighting our battles for us against the villain Stalin. Who incidentally killed far more innocent Russian peasants when he was collectivising the Russian farms than ever Herr Hitler did when he suggested to the Jews they might move a few hundred miles to the East.'

Alfred Madden, who had been sitting in complete silence, occasionally making a note but registering by his facial expression no reaction whatsoever to the conversation, suddenly jumped to his feet and in a strangled voice and a strong Indian accent said, 'It is necessary for me to visit the toilet facilities.'

Lord and Lady Sturmer both began the backwards and forwards rocking movements which were preparatory to any attempt to get out of their armchairs. Madden rushed from the room chattering Indian sounds to the effect that he would find his own way.

'He'll be quite all right,' said Catherine firmly. 'Do please just tell me – because then we must go, and not waste any more of your time – can you think of anyone who might have been a close associate of Neil Campion's whom I could go and see? Or anyone who might know where he was going on May the ninth, 1941 when he crashed into a wall somewhere near Doncaster and died? Or anyone who might have been involved with him in working out a possible alternative government which could have taken over and made peace with the Germans if they'd invaded?'

The two old people, giving up all attempts to raise themselves from their armchairs, sat upright like children, their feet not quite touching the ground, and stared at Catherine with expressions of dismay.

'Well!' said Lady Sturmer as if disgusted.

'You mean to say . . . ?' began Lord Sturmer.

'No one had done more for the cause than Pips.'

'I must say I would have thought . . .'

'He ought to have been the first person to have been approached.'

'One doesn't want to push oneself forward. But if nothing else I am a member of the House of Lords.'

'Do you mean,' said Catherine, 'that you were not aware of any such plan?'

'I simply can't believe they'd have done such a thing without Pips. I just can't believe it. You mean Neil Campion had some scheme of his own and wasn't going to involve Pips? I don't know when I've been so shocked.'

'I don't know that there was any scheme,' said Catherine. 'I just wondered who would have known about it if there had been one.'

'Pips would of course.'

'And you didn't?' Catherine asked him.

He shook his head slowly. 'They must have left me out.'

Catherine felt suddenly tired. 'I expect there's some quite different explanation. I don't seem to be very good at working things out, that's all.'

'Never mind, Pips,' said Lady Sturmer. 'That all belongs to

the past now. We've found a new way of looking at things. Would you be interested in seeing round the Institute at all?'

Madden, who had returned, still looking pale, and was hovering by the door, said, 'We better be going.' His accent now veered towards Jamaica, or possibly Wales. 'We got things to see to.'

'We've taken up so much of your time,' said Catherine, gathering up her notebook and handbag and making for the door.

'It's been delightful,' said Lady Sturmer graciously. 'We never see anyone nowadays. We're quite cut off. Astralism is our only interest. We've made everything over to them. Pips says it's all in return for a free hair-do once a week.' She laughed gaily and patted the enamelled candy floss with a modest hand.

'All part of the deal,' said Lord Sturmer. 'I get my weekly trim as well.' He repeated her gesture on his own few short grey hairs, with garish effect.

'Are they hairdressers then, the astralists?' asked Catherine, vaguely imagining some kind of training college.

'Only Simon himself,' said Lady Sturmer. 'He did my hair for years you see, when he was in Sloane Street. And then one day he started talking about astral projection and how you can control your psyche and disembody it and send it anywhere in the universe, and he told me all about the poet Yeats and wonderful wonderful Madame Blavatsky, and so it all started. We set up the Institute, funded it ourselves to begin with, and now we have associates all over the world.'

'But mainly in California,' added her husband.

'Mainly in California,' she agreed. Catherine could only say how interesting it was, how nice, how kind, until she had reached the car, shaken hands, accepted some leaflets, agreed (in the absence of any comment from Madden) that a course of astralism might be just the thing for his nerves ('Serenity,' Lady Sturmer almost sang the word. 'One achieves such serenity'), and at last driven away down the long drive. Madden asked her to drop him at the nearest railway station.

'I'd rather, if you don't mind,' he said. 'I'm afraid I can't take that sort of thing. I don't think it's funny.'

'I'm not laughing,' said Catherine mildly.

But she dropped him at Chippenham station, glad enough to drive home on her own.

*　*　*

Through the summer night, past the notice about the great trees being prayers, Sam moved silently in bare feet over the cool but scarcely damp grass towards the dell theatre. The moon was nearly at the full, and the night was cloudless, the stars unobscured. There was a nightingale in the distance, in the scrubby copse of elder, thorn and blackberry between the beech wood and the garden fence; Sam, no naturalist, took it as a portent, something unprecedented, a blackbird singing in the night. Skirting the squash courts, and taking the path which led him past the windows of the girls' house where sometimes a light in one of the rooms would disclose Mrs Green their house mistress in front of a blank television screen (the existence of this possibility being the reason for his choosing that path when he could just as well have gone the other side, by the kitchen garden) he turned down a path between high laurels (Mrs Green having this time disappointed him) and came to the open moonlit space of the theatre, bordered by the dark clumps of shrubs which provided its wings. He crossed the mown grass to stand centre stage, and facing an imaginary audience raised both arms above his head, hands open, fingers extended, and breathed deeply. Then he walked up and down a few times, taking possession. Then he spoke.

'Aye but to die . . .'

He had learnt the lines from his *Complete Shakespeare*, during a class when others were reading aloud from *A Midsummer Night's Dream* on other pages.

'. . . and go we know not where.'

He spoke slowly, absorbed in both sound and sense.

'To lie in cold obstruction and to rot
This sensible warm motion to become
A kneaded clod and the delighted spirit to reside
In thrilling regions of thick-ribbed ice
Or to be blown with something violence' (his memory failing him) 'round about
The something earth; or to be worse than worst of those
Whom lawless and uncertain thoughts
Imagine howling. 'Tis too horrible . . .
The weariest and most loathed human life
That age, ache, penury and imprisonment can lay on nature
is paradise
To what we fear of death.'

He did not know any more of the speech. When he had finished it he said it through again with only the slightest change of inflexion. Then he walked over to one side of the moonlit space, came forward and sat down with crossed legs so that he would have been close to the audience had one existed, and said it again very quietly. Then he sprang to his feet and walked up and down the front of the stage quite rapidly, gesticulating and haranguing the imaginary audience with the same speech. Then he went back to his original position in the centre of the space and stood absolutely still to say it once more, with the full weight of horror and fear in the fall of the first phrase, 'Aye but to die . . .' and of desolation in the second '. . . and go we know not where.' It was the only piece of poetry he knew by heart.

When he had finished he bowed several times very deeply, and gave one or two modestly disclaiming waves of the hand. Then he ran back over the grass to the foot of the drainpipe down which he had come, shinned up it and climbed through the open window into his dormitory. Richard Clayborne Pope was standing beside his bed and, apparently quite unsurprised at his materialisation, whispered loudly, 'Just leaving something in your locker. Poker winnings. Hakkim Sayeed. Huge bag of grass.'

'Thought it was bridge you played.'

'More money in poker.'

*   *   *

Madden liked to introduce a note of hysteria into his mornings at the office. He wore dark glasses and rapped out commands, speaking meanwhile on two telephones at the same time, as well as looking at the photographs which were being held out to him one by one by a bored-looking photographer. He insulted the photographer, complained of inaccuracies in one of his underlings' reports, sent another underling out to cover a fashion show, briefed a nervous girl on what to look out for at a wedding in the afternoon. 'I want to know who the young Royals talk to, whether both lots of parents and their present spouses are there – ex-wife and step-mother on the bride's side don't speak – watch for anything there. Randolph Best is said to have Aids – I want to know whether he's there or not – his daughter's a bridesmaid. Bob, you can drop that story about the Iranian diplomat, the *Mail*'s running it. Tell Downing Street we don't know who gave us the story about the secretary, it was an anonymous tip-off. I'll see the libel man at twelve. It can't be later. I'm lunching at the House of Commons. Get someone to follow up that lead on the City row will you? I'm not interested in the spy scandal, we've had enough of them.'

The five people who worked on the column with him were impressed by his apparently endless supply of inside information but they did not like him. He in turn despised them, just as he fundamentally despised his work, although he could put up a good case for it when challenged; someone has to sort out the rotten apples he would say. The atmosphere of urgency, the snapped commands, the chain-smoking, the dark glasses, were stratagems for getting through the day; it was himself he was trying to galvanise.

'I told you to tell Downing Street we don't know,' he shouted. 'Who's this? Mrs Who? No, of course I'm not busy.'

'You sound it,' said Catherine. 'I just wanted to ask you something. About that story in *Private Eye* about the Sturmers . . .'

'Yes, of course it was me.'

'I wish you hadn't done it. Pottinger asked them who'd been to see them lately. He rang up the publishers in a fury. Apparently he's writing to me. I'm going to have to finish the book without finding out any more, you know. I've still got nothing to go on except that one piece of paper and we don't even know who wrote it. And now Effie Campion's rung me up to say they're threatening to expel her grandson from school and will I go down with her to reason with them.'

'Why you?'

'I've no idea. But I can't possibly refuse.'

'Talk to her about those other names. Tell her about the Sturmers. It might start her talking. No need to mention me. I'll see what I can do in the meantime. I can see we'll have to hurry. Don't worry, I'll find something.'

'You can't find something if there isn't anything to find,' said Catherine.

*   *   *

Rain fell relentlessly on the water meadows. The crowd had thinned to a scattered group, holding umbrellas and waiting. The occasion was the annual Southern Counties inter-schools steeplechase. No runners were in sight. Catherine, whose shoes

167

were not water-tight, held her borrowed umbrella over the fragile and still furious Effie Campion, and wished she had not come. She had forgotten how depressing an experience the receiving of a rejected pupil from a school could be. Mr Trumble, determined but nervous, had said that Sam had the temperament of the addict. He had sat behind a large desk and told them that over the years he had come to recognise this temperament.

'The silent boy,' he had said. 'The withdrawn boy. The boy of whom his teachers say that he seems always to be in a dream. The boy who avoids games, takes no part in the life of the house, is pale, is, as I say, withdrawn.'

'Exactly what they used to say about masturbation,' said Effie briskly.

She sat very straight on the edge of her chair, trembling visibly with rage. She was wearing even more make-up than usual and the two round patches of rouge on her cheeks stood out hectically against the white powder which she had liberally applied to the rest of her face. Mr Trumble blushed at the mention of masturbation. He tried to cover up the blush with a cough, and patted himself rather hard on the chest. A single man, fairly new to a job he had had no idea would be so difficult – he had been a housemaster at a minor West Country public school and had impressed the governors of the Durdans by his youthful enthusiasm – he was terrified of Effie and looked forward keenly to seeing the last of her.

'One might say that in many ways one has replaced the other,' he said, still hoping to blind her with some sort of science. 'The search for self-forgetfulness goes on. There is more than one way of contemplating one's navel.'

'I thought masturbation meant contemplating something quite other than one's navel,' said Effie, who knew how to push home an advantage.

This time Mr Trumble's blush was impossible to conceal; it brought tears to his eyes.

'Perhaps you would like to talk to Mr Manderson,' he said desperately. 'Mr Manderson is the boy's tutor. He has taken a lot of trouble with him.'

'His attitude seemed rather defeatist when I spoke to him,' said Catherine.

'He's very popular with the students,' said Mr Trumble defensively. 'He speaks their language. But he's been able to get nothing out of Sam, nothing at all. He grilled him for three hours after the discovery was made.'

'Grilled him?' said Effie.

'There were other people involved in this thing. We're sure of it. We've told him we can't consider anything less than expulsion unless he gives us the other names. But we can't get a thing out of him.'

'I should think not. He's not a sneak.'

'But Mrs Campion, it's not sneaking. We don't think in those terms. They're old-fashioned terms if you'll forgive my saying so. We don't call it sneaking. We call it being a responsible member of the community.'

'I bet you do,' said Effie.

Catherine had not felt she had much to contribute to the conversation; she could see there was no hope of saving Sam. She had sat silent while he was sent for, remembering the interviews she and Bernard had had with Nicholas's headmaster, a man both of them had liked. She remembered Bernard's humiliation, her own bewilderment, the frightening pallor of Nicholas's handsome feeble face. Perhaps she could have done more for him, at just that time, after he had been expelled from school. Bernard had said they must be strict. She supposed they had always expected too much of him, the elder son; probably that was why Tom had been such a conformist, so as not to disappoint his parents all over again. At least Effie Campion was prepared to fight for Sam, who was only her grandson and whom she understood, as far as Catherine could tell, hardly at all.

Sam had explained, tired, patient, remote, that yes, he had had the cannabis and no, he was not prepared to say where he had got it. And then there had been the absurdity of the games master bursting in and saying what hope had they of winning the championship that afternoon if Sam were not allowed to run. Mr Trumble had protested, the games master had become indignant, Effie had berated them both, Sam had suddenly said, 'I don't mind running.'

'How can you possibly run for a school which has just expelled you?' Effie had said.

Sam had looked at Mr Trumble from the immense distance from which he sometimes seemed to speak and had said, 'I wouldn't be running for the school. I'd just be running.'

So they waited in the rain. The runners had been out of sight for some time. There had been about seventy of them and most of them had looked a good deal more promising than Sam, competent short-haired healthy boys among whom Sam stood out by virtue of his greater height, his longer hair, his pallor and the impression he gave of having his thoughts elsewhere. Nevertheless he had started somewhere about the middle of the group and the twins, Pat and Prue, who had come to stand beside Catherine and Effie, said he was noted for his endurance.

'We think it's terrible,' they said. 'We're definitely going to get our parents to take us away.'

'Perhaps Mr Trumble didn't have much alternative,' said Catherine mildly. 'Cannabis is illegal.'

They became incoherent. Mr Trumble didn't understand, they said, Mr Manderson had said he wouldn't tell Mr Trumble and then he had told him. Mr Trumble was a terrible headmaster, he was only headmaster because the other headmaster had thrown himself out of the window but it had all been hushed up and anyway they were definitely going to leave. But Catherine had noticed that the other Durdans children had not spoken to Sam before the race; expulsion had its stigma.

A boy appeared from the trees two hundred yards away, the first runner. It was not Sam. Catherine looked at her watch.

'They can't keep us waiting much longer,' said Effie.

The boy ran towards the finishing line, tired but moving well. Another boy emerged from the trees not far behind him. As they approached it became clear that the second boy was Sam and that he was very tired indeed. Pat and Prue ran towards him with high-pitched encouraging cries and were held back by a master from one of the other schools who was acting as a steward. Two or three other boys had now emerged from the wood but it was clear that the race for first place was between the leader and Sam.

'He's going to win,' said Effie.

But he was not going to win. He was exhausted. His long legs were not quite under control; he slipped on the wet grass but did not fall. He was gasping for breath. Catherine, forgetting she was taking the umbrella away from Effie, ran a few steps towards him, then stopped. He passed her, gasping, absorbed in his own agony; on his face as well as effort and exhaustion was wild aspiration. Catherine wept for him, unexpectedly shaken by sobs. He wanted to win. Through incapacity or lack of training he was not going to do so, but he had given himself away. The defensive fastidiousness, the pride, the remoteness, had fallen away, leaving nothing but hope, nothing but courage, nothing but desire. Catherine was overwhelmed by a kind of furious regret; she wanted to shout at the uncaring world until it crowned him with the laurel for which he longed. Turning away from the finishing line she walked about aimlessly in the rain in search of calm.

Effie meanwhile had decided to send Sam to the school whose representative had won the race. She had come to this decision very quickly on seeing how the master from this school had spoken to Sam immediately after congratulating the winner. She expatiated on his sportsmanlike attitude as Catherine drove her back to London, with Sam silent in the back of the car.

'I thought he set a jolly good example. That's what you need, Sam, masters you can look up to. All those people at the Durdans are so utterly dreary and middle-class. They weren't like that in Eberling's day. His staff were gents. Well, nearly gents, some of them. Obviously no schoolmaster's going to be a hundred per cent gent, otherwise he wouldn't be a school-master, would he? Anyway this man from Bellington Hall seemed quite excellent. He said all you needed was training, Sam. He was extremely nice about you. I had a word with him while you were changing. You can go a bit faster, Catherine, you know, there's no need to crawl. This car's very good on a wet road.'

Catherine, accelerating very slightly, glanced into the driving mirror and noticed that Sam appeared to be asleep. Relieved, she thought of old Hugh Campion the schoolmaster, Effie's brother-in-law; and then she thought perhaps she ought to go and see Hugh and Eleanor again. There might be something she had not thought to ask them, something Eleanor perhaps might know.

'By the way,' she said to Effie, 'I meant to ask you something. There was an envelope among the letters Eleanor gave me – the ones from Africa, you know, that I told you about – an envelope saying "for Eleanor in the event of my death". There wasn't a letter in it and she couldn't remember anything about it. You never saw a letter of that kind, I suppose?'

Effie did not answer. Catherine glanced at her and saw that from having been very upright and commanding in her attitude all day she had shrunk back into her seat, seeming suddenly much smaller. Her face looked yellowish through the make-up and her mouth was turned down at the corners.

'I think I've had enough for one day,' she said peevishly.

'Of course you have. I'm sorry. It just came into my mind.'

They drove in silence; it seemed that Effie, like Sam, was sleeping. Her eyes were closed and her head bent slightly to one side. After some time and without opening her eyes she said rather plaintively, speaking like a tired child, 'It wasn't my idea, you know, this book. Those two old fusspots started agitating after some stupid article about me appeared in the paper. That awful man Madden had written it. I said I didn't know what they were talking about. I sent them to see Potty. Potty said there must be an authorised biography. I always do what Potty says. Potty said the letter was forgery, at least I think he said it was a forgery, or an aberration or something. He said he hadn't seen it. Eleanor said she'd just shown it to him and he said no, she hadn't. She's awfully slow on the uptake Eleanor, it's something to do with having been a headmistress.'

Catherine said, 'Did you see the letter too?'

'I didn't want to. I knew it was all rubbish. I don't need to see letters. Goodness knows what he might have written. I never understood half of what he wrote anyway. That wasn't the point. The point was he was perfection. If anyone seriously tried to blacken his name I would kill them. As a man he was perfection. You can have no conception of what that means.'

'I have a sort of idea,' said Catherine.

*   *   *

As Alfred Madden began to walk up the stairs towards the door of the flat in which Etta and Nicholas Hillery lived he was startled to hear shouting, and the bursting open of the door, and feet running down the stairs towards him. A heavy saucepan hit the wall opposite him and clattered to the floor; as he turned the corner of the stairs he was almost knocked off his feet by Nicholas, who was holding his arms above his head as if to ward off blows.

'She's trying to kill me.'

He pushed Madden to one side, seized the banister to swing himself round the corner and ran on down the stairs, making an extraordinary sound between a shriek and a giggle. Etta appeared at the top of the stairs holding an earthenware milk jug.

'What's happening?' asked Madden.

Etta threw the jug at him, cutting his forehead and spattering his jacket with milk. Then she turned back into the flat. Holding a handkerchief to his bleeding forehead Madden continued up the stairs and, pushing open the door, which she had not closed behind her, walked into the sitting-room. Etta immediately appeared with a basin of water and, first telling him to sit down, carefully washed his cut. Then she gave him a pad of cotton wool soaked in cold water and told him to hold it to his forehead.

'It is not necessary that it should be stitched,' she said.

Obediently holding the pad to his forehead he saw that in spite of her apparent calm there were tears rolling down her cheeks.

'What's the matter?' he whispered, deeply distressed.

'Your jacket. Please take it off, it is covered with milk, it will smell.'

He stood up and she helped him to remove his jacket. He lowered his hand from his forehead and put his arms around her. She took the cold pad from his hand and herself held it to his forehead. He kissed her gently.

'You must tell me.'

She shook her head. He led her into the bedroom and made love to her with the utmost tenderness. Afterwards he said, 'My life can have no meaning at all unless I can spend it with you.'

Etta, sighing, left the bed and went to clean his jacket. Then she cooked them some scrambled eggs and told him that Nicholas had come home during his lunch hour to fetch some papers he had left behind that morning, and that she had already looked at the papers and had found among them a note from a girl called Amanda, it was for this reason that she was throwing a saucepan at Nicholas as he ran down the stairs just as Madden was coming up them. Amanda, it seemed, was the

174

fair-haired girl to whom Nicholas had been talking at the party given by Ronald Bedford at which Etta had kicked the well-known journalist and had been followed down the road by Madden, who now, disheartened, said, 'But, if you . . .'

'No. If I have you it does not mean he can have her. It is not the same thing at all.'

'You mean it is a more serious thing?'

'Of course not. I mean Nicholas does not know about you, and I do know about her.'

'Etta, is this reasonable?'

'No. But I mind. It hurts me. I wanted him to leave the criminal Bedford. I encouraged him when he said this Amanda knew of a job in her firm. I was delighted when it turned out he can work this terrible computer he sits before all day. Side by side they sit, doing this funny language till all hours of the night, spinning money, like hypnotised spiders. I was happy for him. I thought all he cared for was these numbers. He has always cared only for numbers. And money.'

'So that's good, surely?'

'No, because it seems he cares also for this yellow-haired Amanda and they make silly messages between the numbers games. I know what you say. I know, I know. But it is the humiliation.'

'What about his humiliation?'

'He doesn't have any humiliation. He doesn't know about you.'

'Tell him. Please tell him. We can get married. He can marry Amanda.'

'I don't want him to marry Amanda.'

'Ah.'

Etta lowered her head, letting her hair fall forward on either side of her face. Madden confronted her across the table at which they still sat, though they had eaten the scrambled eggs.

'So,' he continued with an effort, 'when you said you loved me you didn't mean it.'

175

She looked up, wounded.

'Of course I did.'

'But you also love Nicholas.'

She lowered her head again.

'Not exactly.'

'Not exactly,' he repeated in a deadened tone.

Suddenly he stood up. His chair fell over backwards.

'What are you doing to me, Etta? I want to marry you. I want to take you away from here. I want to take you to Italy. I want to live in a high room with you, being true to you. You don't understand, you think I don't mean it. I've lied for you. I've perjured myself. I've laid a false trail, to try to finish things, to get out. I wanted to make sure Neil Campion was exposed. And then I wanted to get out, forget all that, forget England, forget English hypocrisy, live in truth, Etta, with you, don't you see?'

'I like England,' said Etta.

Madden began to walk up and down rather quickly on the thin Kelim rug which covered the floor between the two brown sofas.

'England. I don't know anything about England. I was brought up here, that's all, I never felt English. I suppose you could say England was kind to me and that's why I resent it. One resents people who are kind to one. At least that means I'll never resent you, Antonietta.'

'Don't use that horrible name.'

'It's the name your parents gave you. We try to disinherit ourselves I suppose. We try to disown our past, but we can't kick ourselves free. It is the twentieth-century dilemma.'

'I love my parents. I just don't like to be called Antonietta. I wish you would not make these twentieth-century remarks. You don't try to disown your past. You are obsessed with it. That is why you are so boring about being Jewish.'

Madden sat down slowly on one of the brown sofas.

'I didn't know I was boring about being Jewish.'

'I don't mind.' Etta reached across the table for his empty

176

plate, put it on top of hers, and stood up, about to carry them into the kitchen. 'You know, though, it is all because of being Jewish you want to persecute this Campion who has been dead so long. It was not Campion who killed your mother.'

There was a pause.

'I had forgotten how completely I had put myself in your hands,' said Madden.

Etta went out of the room with the plates. Madden stared sombrely in front of him on the sofa. Etta returned with two mugs of coffee. She gave him one of them and sat down on the opposite sofa, putting her own coffee beside her on a table. It always gave Madden pleasure to see her sit down, because she settled herself like a child, making herself comfortable without fuss. The physical pleasure which she obviously derived from so many simple circumstances was something she would probably carry quite unconsciously into her old age; perhaps, if he still knew her then, it would still make him smile.

'You make me sound so mean,' he said. 'Seeking some silly sort of vicarious revenge for my mother's death in order to assuage my own guilt. I mean the immediate cause of her death was presumably my birth. In her weakened condition and so on.'

Etta merely nodded.

'But there is something about English smugness,' he said. 'And secrecy. There would have been an English Quisling. I want to show that, that's all.'

'Why?'

'Because it's true.'

'Oh, truth. Besides, how do you know?'

'I don't know, for sure. That's why I tried to lead Catherine in the right direction, to make her look where I might not be able to look without the authority they had given to her.'

'To do this you lied to her?'

'I planted some false evidence.'

'Then you had better plant some more false evidence. To

contradict the first false evidence. And then you can leave it to her to find out what really happened. It is of no importance. In Italy all public people have discreditable secrets.'

Madden sighed deeply, feeling suddenly that he might sleep.

'You undermine all my most fundamental beliefs. I don't know whether that is a good thing or a bad thing.'

'How could I know?' Etta looked at him sorrowfully. 'I know nothing.'

* * *

Hugh Campion, retired headmaster, walked along Holland Road at the shuffling uneven pace which was the best his increasingly arthritic limbs could do for him. He wore an old mackintosh, outside the collar of which he had draped a long scarf whose gaudy colours recalled the student camaraderie of more cheerful times; his neck protruded from the mackintosh collar like a tortoise's from its shell. The damp smell of autumn infiltrated the fumes of the traffic which thundered past him; yellow leaves fell intermittently onto the broad pavement. Autumn gave Hugh comfort, and a feeling of renewal. He liked the thought of the evenings coming earlier, the books to be read, the start of the Michaelmas term. He had been to the library, and carried in his canvas shopping bag two novels by Angela Thirkell and a biography of Lucius Cary, second Viscount Falkland. He planned to take the novels straight into his bedroom, where Eleanor seldom ventured; she was inclined to be scornful about his choice of fiction. He was not sure why Angela Thirkell's novels should be considered so very much inferior to the rattling tales of sea-faring men in Napoleonic times which Eleanor herself favoured, but he preferred to avoid confrontation. He had first read Angela Thirkell during the war and had found her attitudes reassuring. When Eleanor had said they were snobbish and sentimental it had distressed him, as if she had said those things about an old friend. Hugh's reading had always been to some extent a search for friends; his choice of the biography of the seventeenth-century Lord Falkland was part of the search. He liked the idea of a group of friends, to which in his imagination he could belong.

It was best of all of course if the friendships, like Horace Walpole's, had started at school; he loved the thought of Walpole and Gray, West and Ashton, the Quadruple Alliance, wandering by the banks of the Thames in their Eton days, precociously versifying, calling each other by the names of shepherds in pastoral romance. But he could not sympathise with the antiquarianism of the Strawberry Hill set. He disapproved of imitating mediaeval tombs to make drawing-room mantelpieces, preferring anyway the sober early Georgian proportions of the vicarage in which he had been brought up; also he found Walpole's gossip too cold-hearted. He had had a brief enthusiasm for the Holland House set but had been shocked by Lady Holland's infatuation with Napoleon, which seemed to him unpatriotic. At one time he had read a good deal about Garsington and the Bloomsbury Group, but as more and more books about them were published he lost his first enthusiasm; he did not care for so many irregular liaisons. He thought all sexual activity pretty horrible. Anything of that kind that might have taken place or almost taken place in his far-off youth was firmly forgotten, and lack of practice had long removed such inclinations as might have remained. Perhaps they lurked harmlessly at the back of his mind, for he occasionally gave a wheezing crow of laughter at some small piece of schoolboy smut he came across in his reading or heard on the wireless (he and Eleanor had once hired a television set but had returned it after a week's intensive and horrified viewing). He still cherished an affection for the Souls, though they too seemed to have been less than perfectly straightforward in their behaviour; in their case there was more excuse for giving them the benefit of the doubt. He considered himself more or less in a condition of amitié amoureuse with Lady Wemyss, and was quite certain in his own mind that Arthur Balfour had gone no further. This autumn, with the start of the new term – for he still thought of the year as divided into three terms and three holidays – he was beginning on the Great Tew set. He had always liked the age of Charles I. He liked the Caroline poets and the Van Dyke portraits and the fact that Charles I had such good taste; though he was sorry he had not been a better politician. The men who gathered round Lord Falkland at Great Tew seemed so particularly charming, brilliant, careless of worldly advancement, virtuous; if there was anything undesirable about their friendships he had yet to discover it. He was beginning to feel that he knew them a little, though of course being so long ago it was harder to imagine them; still, he felt he would have been at home at Great Tew. He was even thinking of making a little expedition there before the cold weather set in. He could take a train to Oxford; he was sure there would be a bus from Oxford to Great Tew. He knew the house was not the same but he had read that the village was not so very much changed. He would not tell Eleanor he was going because she would say he was too old, would fall off the train, or get the wrong bus. Of course he would tell her all about it when he got back.

On letting himself into the flat he found that Eleanor was making tea, and had some crumpets under the grill.

'Crumpets,' he said, hanging his mackintosh on his peg (they had one each in the dark passage just inside the door; Eleanor very much disliked finding his mackintosh on her peg). 'Makes you think it's really autumn.'

Eleanor spread the crumpets liberally with butter, piled them on a dish and covered them with the silver cover which had been their mother's. She put the dish on the trolley with the other tea things and wheeled the trolley along to the sitting-room, her slow-moving form seeming to fill the narrow passage with its bulk. Hugh shuffled after her contentedly, stopping only to leave his shopping bag on his bed. Eleanor, aware of the diversion the shuffling footsteps had taken, asked him what books he had brought from the library.

'Just some seventeenth-century stuff,' he said.

'What seventeenth-century stuff?'

'I'm reading about Lord Falkland at the moment, and his friends at Great Tew.'

'Ah.' Eleanor was not well up in seventeenth-century history.

'I used to find the Civil War so difficult to teach,' said Hugh, lowering himself into his customary chair and reaching out for a crumpet. 'I never liked to let the boys think that whatever happened in our history was anything other than for the best. And of course the Stuarts weren't much good as kings and a proper constitutional monarchy is much better, we all know that. But so many of the cavaliers do seem to have been such awfully nice people.'

'Chin,' said Eleanor, handing him a clean handkerchief.

'And democracy,' continued Hugh, wiping the melted butter off his chin with the handkerchief. 'Obviously democracy is a good thing. I mean one really can't blame democracy for television, can one?'

'Can't one?'

'Well no, Eleanor, I don't think one can really. But I must say I've always rather liked the idea of the cultured élite, setting the example, pointing the way.'

'I thought you voted Labour.'

'That's different. I was looking for idealism in politics. Besides, I voted SDP last time. The SDP woman was very well up in the rain forests.'

He ate his second crumpet in silence, feeling that Eleanor as usual despised his opinions, but after a few minutes she surprised him by saying, 'Neil liked that idea too, you know.'

He looked at her questioningly, his cup of tea halfway to his mouth, held in his trembling hand. 'Rain forests?'

'Élites. He believed in élites. He thought so many of the good people had died in the First World War that Europe could only survive if the ones who were left came together to work things out, but in private. I suppose he didn't have much faith in democracy. He was against all mass movements and dema- gogues – that was why he would have nothing to do with Fascism in England, Mosley and so on.'

'I should think not.' Hugh looked shocked.

'Yes, but he had quite a lot in common with them. It was mostly about methods that he disagreed.'

'Quite a lot in common with the Fascists?'

'Do drink your tea, Hugh. One has to try and see these things in their historical context. Fascism didn't seem so bad then.'

'Yes, it did.'

'All I mean is this. Neil wanted to save the European order, he had German friends, he felt he had more in common with Germans who had fought in the War than with English people who hadn't. Perhaps this made him too eager to see good in the Germans.'

'But he didn't see good in Hitler surely?'

'Supposing Neil had believed that he could make peace with the Germans, even if it meant making peace with Hitler and relying on other Germans to get rid of Hitler once it was done? Perhaps they couldn't get rid of him before because the German people wouldn't have stood for it when they thought he was winning the War. Just suppose something like that.'

'I can't,' said Hugh. 'Neil was a Minister of the Crown. He would never have done such a thing.'

'Do you think not?'

'Well of course not, Eleanor. It would have been very, very wrong of him.'

'Yes,' said Eleanor. 'I suppose it would.'

* * *

182

Mr Pottinger's ingratiating voice was misleading. His appearance was not ingratiating at all. He had a way of leaning forward and clasping his hands before him which could have been seen as a caricature of the deferential upper servant's attitude which he allowed the very great to expect of him, but Catherine found herself reminded more of a bird of prey. He had very little neck and when he leant forward in this attitude of deference which seemed to Catherine more ironical than sincere he reminded her of nothing so much as the peregrine falcon which used to sit on a sharp rock not far from the cottage which she and her ornithologist sister had taken one summer in Pembrokeshire. They had been able to see the bird clearly through their binoculars; it was a female, whose adult offspring would occasionally dash past her in the evening air so like a couple of miniature jet fighers that one almost waited for the following roar of sound. It was the hunched shoulders that chiefly impressed Catherine with a sense of the creature's power, the shoulders and the fact that they could tell from her reaction to their comings and goings about the cottage's tiny garden that she could see them a very great deal better than they could see her. Mr Pottinger gave Catherine a similar impression, except that what she found awe-inspiring in the peregrine she found in Mr Pottinger merely alarming. He had black hair, tinged with grey at the temples and sleekly combed back from his high white forehead. In keeping with the hawklike image Catherine had imposed on him, he had hooded eyes; she sat in his austere but commodious office searching her memory for the John Buchan character – was he hero or villain? – who had had eyes like that. She had noticed them on the only other occasion she had met Mr Pottinger. Brackenbury the publisher had brought her along to the same office to discuss the projected biography, and she had been distracted then by the same failure of memory. Was it Lord Lamancha or the villain of *The Thirty Nine Steps*? And then there was the sharp enquiring nose, less distinguished than

183

the forehead and the eyes, and the small mouth which seemed permanently set in a slight sneer, presumably at the thought of the inferior brains of the greater part of the rest of humanity. Mr Pottinger's brain was generally acknowledged to be razor sharp; those who had it in their service counted themselves lucky, those against whom it was employed trembled. Catherine wondered briefly what this great brain did when it was not extending itself in the intricacies of someone else's interest, but then thought that perhaps mercenaries were not expected to have private lives.

'Mrs Campion tells me you've been so helpful over her troubles with young Sam,' said the soothing voice, allowing itself a note of mild amusement.

'Only by going down to the school with her. I'm afraid there wasn't anything else I could do.'

'He's a shocker, isn't he? So many of them are these days. He'll probably be all right in a year or two as long as she doesn't give him any money.'

'It was a pity about the other schools.'

'None of them would have him. Don't blame them. He'll drive her mad in London, I'm afraid. But she's got him into the best crammer. Some of them are a menace. But tell me, how's the book going?'

Catherine looked across at the other person in the room, a quiet man who had been introduced to her as Major Hall and who after shaking her hand politely had retreated into a leather armchair some way behind and to one side of Mr Pottinger's desk, with his back to the window.

'Very well,' she answered firmly.

'Good,' said Mr Pottinger. 'Good. Nothing holding you up?'

'I'm not quite clear yet about what Neil Campion's German connections amounted to. I need to find out whether he was involved in anything to do with them when he crashed his car and died. He was driving north on the morning of the day Rudolf Hess landed in Scotland. It was probably just a coincidence.'

Mr Pottinger gave a short, cold laugh.

'This is not a detective story,' he said.

'I think any biography is to some extent a detective story.'

'In a sense, of course, I agree. But one doesn't want to stray into fiction, however tempting it may be. Campion had nothing to do with Hess.'

'I don't suppose he did. I'd just like to be certain.'

'Are you trying to suggest that there was some kind of link between Campion and his German friends, who I think I'm right in saying were anti-Nazi liberals, and Hess's flight to England?'

'I'm not trying to suggest anything. I'm simply trying to find out. I'm finding it difficult, partly because of mysterious messages which reach me through my publisher and which I must admit I rather resent, and partly because there are some files held by the Home Office which no one is allowed to see.'

'If I tell you that you're barking up the wrong tree, does that make no difference?'

'Is that what you're telling me? It wasn't clear. It might have been that you were telling me to stop barking up the right tree.'

Mr Pottinger leant back in his chair.

'In that case I'm delighted you're here,' he said briskly. 'I should have asked you to come and see me before, and I apologise for not having done so. It's the wrong tree all right.'

Catherine nodded slowly. 'Good,' she said.

'All right?' he said, as if to indicate that their business was at an end.

Catherine smiled. She too knew how to appear quite at ease.

'Of course. I suppose – does that mean that you've seen the files?'

There was no answering smile.

'I've no need to. I know how far Neil Campion's contacts with Peter Heinrich went, that is to say not very far. Plenty of people had contacts with Germany in the first years of the War, plenty of people had hopes of making peace with the anti-Hitler Germans, there was nothing odd about that. The plans didn't come to anything because the Germans couldn't get rid of Hitler, but there was nothing about anything Neil Campion was involved in which couldn't be reconciled with his service in Churchill's government. The truth is I'm afraid he wasn't always a faithful husband, it was most probably something of that sort which took him out in his car that day. None of his little liaisons were of the slightest importance to him and to bring anything out about them in the book would be enormously distressing to his widow. As you know she was devoted to him. She had no idea, naturally.'

'I see. But, if plenty of people had contacts in Nazi Germany, and if there was nothing odd about it, why have the files not all been opened?'

'Most of them have.'

'I know most of them have. Including the ones about the British Union of Fascists and all that. So why not the rest?'

Major Hall rose quietly from his armchair and came forward to lean casually, half-seated, on the corner of Mr Pottinger's desk. He folded his arms and looked down at Catherine seriously.

'Secrecy's a bore,' he said. 'It often makes people think there's more being concealed than there is, no smoke without fire and so on. But occasionally it's necessary, to protect people still living, to avoid embarrassment with a foreign country, or probably most often of all to protect our own methods. There are always one or two people or organisations we have to keep an eye on. There's no reason to let them know how we do it.'

Catherine nodded, looking at his brown herringbone tweed and noticing how well-polished his good brown shoes were. She was for some reason unwilling to look into his rather weather-beaten face.

'We've no reason to suppose that Campion was up to anything

funny. He said some rather wild things at times. He seems to have been an ambitious man who never quite found his place in his own generation. But he was loyal to the government he served in.'

'It had crossed my mind that it might have been your people who arranged for him to drive into a stone wall.'

He gave a shout of laughter. Looking now into his face she saw that his amusement was genuine and that he was looking at her with friendly admiration, as if he were liking her better than Mr Pottinger said he would. He held up a disclaiming hand.

'I wasn't there of course. But there's nothing I'm aware of that would indicate any such thing.' He slid off the edge of the desk. 'Well, I was passing and my old friend Pottinger asked me to look in to set your mind at rest so I'll be on my way now. I've told you all I know.'

Catherine rose too. She saw no need for further conversation with Mr Pottinger and, assuring him rather hurriedly that she would be getting on with the book now, she shook him by the hand and left with Major Hall. They parted on Mr Pottinger's doorstep. Major Hall had a hat, of soft brown felt, not too new; he held it ready to put on his head as he said mildly, 'I'm not sure that we totally convinced you there.'

'Oh, I'm convinced. Well, nine-tenths convinced. The one-tenth is because Mr Pottinger somehow gives me the impression it would be against his nature to tell one quite the whole truth.'

'Bit of a calculating machine, old Ernest. But he's a good man. Let's see, your husband was a Civil Servant, wasn't he?'

'Yes.'

'Wish I'd known him. Well, good luck with the book.'

He put the hat on his head, then lifted it slightly to say goodbye. It crossed her mind to tell him about the list of names she had found in the book at the Durdans, but she resisted the impulse. Walking away from him towards the carpark where she had left her car she was thankful she had done so; she had been tempted, because she had thought him so good-looking.

*   *   *

As he came out of Earls Court Underground station Sam tripped over the legs of a man who was sitting down with his back to the wall and his feet straight out in front of him. Sam recovered himself and apologised.

'Got the price of a cup of tea?' said the man, who had a well-trimmed red beard and glasses and looked like a youngish computer scientist, though his eyes were red-rimmed.

Sam asked him how much a cup of tea cost. The man said about thirty pence. Sam gave him a fifty pence coin and walked on down the Earls Court Road. He was wearing a dark overcoat several sizes too big for him which he had bought at consider-able expense from a second-hand clothes shop down the Fulham Road. It was a mild autumn day; he was walking slowly so as not to get too hot. As he walked he looked about him, at people's faces, at the buildings, at the traffic, into the shops. He was always expecting to see something extraordinary; as a result he often did. Small scenes from unaccountably strange lives seemed to enact themselves specially for him; violent quarrels or mysterious whisperings, weeping women, cats eating meat in butchers' windows, dogs lifting their legs on well-dressed men's trouser legs, barrows loaded with oranges overturned by men on motorbicycles shouting in a foreign tongue, car crashes succeeded by bizarre encounters between drivers of unvarying abnormality, Turks with no roofs to their mouths, exotic women in furs and stiletto heels, one-legged men with eye patches; such was Sam's vision of London. Turning into a quiet street of tall shabby houses and continuing his slow enquiring progress he was stopped by a muscular man with very short hair who waved something like a driving licence in his face and asked him if he was looking for something. When Sam answered in the negative the man told him to open the briefcase he was carrying, which was an old leather one which had belonged to his father. Sam protested, saying that it contained only books for the class to which he was on his way.

'Which school?'

'Challoners' Tutorial College.'

'It's in the next street.'

'I know.'

'This isn't the quickest way.'

'I know.'

'Most people go the quickest way to a place, don't they?'

'I don't know what most people do,' said Sam.

The man insisted on his opening the briefcase and turning out its few and harmless contents.

'There's been a lot of breaking and entering round here. There are empty houses, waiting to be pulled down. You want to look more as if you were going somewhere if you don't want to be stopped. Okay?'

'Okay.'

Sam walked on without looking behind him and turned the corner into the next street. Soon he turned again into the street in which Challoners' Tutorial College spread itself between three of the tall shabby houses. Before he reached its entrance he looked behind him to see whether the man had followed him; then he went quickly down the basement steps of one of the other houses. He went in through a door of which the lock had been broken, and feeling his way carefully along a dark passage went up some stairs and knocked at the door at the top. It was opened and a torch was shone in his face; then he was allowed to walk into the ground-floor staircase hall of what had once been a rather grand house.

'Straight up.'

The boy who had opened the door gesticulated with his head towards the stairs. He wore headphones and a thin squeak of rhythm mingled with the smell of marijuana from his stump of cigarette; he went back to his chair by the basement door. Sam went upstairs. The former drawing-room of the house had three tall windows. The shutters were now closed over them and the room was dimly lit by candles standing in jam jars and dispersed unsystematically about the room. There had evidently once been a chimneypiece, perhaps of marble; it had been roughly removed, leaving the wall scarred. Bare electric wires obtruded at various points where once there had been wall brackets. There was no furniture in the room though there were three large packing cases in one corner, on one of which a girl with spiky bleached hair was sitting, wearing a man's overcoat and black trousers and crying quietly into a sodden handkerchief. Ten or twelve people were sitting or crouching on the dusty floor round a piece of green baize, roughly rectangular though jagged round the edges as though cut from a larger piece of material by someone inexpert with scissors. There was one girl, rather fat, wearing a bright red dress and with a red carnation in her luxuriant black hair. She was wearing a great deal of make-up and a fixed ecstatic smile and was following the game intently. The others were boys, most of them wearing overcoats similar to Sam's. Two or three of them were evidently of Arab descent; one was a tall black boy in a well-tailored pale grey suit which he was careful not to soil by contact with the floor, another seemed to be American, another spoke only Greek; the rest were English. None was over eighteen. The room was warm and smelt of candle smoke, Miss Dior (from the fat girl), and marijuana. There were several cans of beer about the place. Sam approached the green baize and two boys immediately made room for him; several of the others greeted him. One of them, a thin feverish-looking boy who seemed to act as the host as well as the bank, offered him a can of beer. Sam refused, lighting a cigarette.

'Is it chemmy?'

'Vingt et un. How many chips? Hundred pounds? I'll take your cheque.'

Sam extracted a grubby and much-folded cheque book from his overcoat pocket, wrote out a cheque and handed it over.

'Don't you know how to do capital letters?' asked the feverish boy irritably, peering at the cheque in the candlelight.

'My bank doesn't like them.'

Two hours later Sam emerged from the basement and walked quickly past the tutorial college. Shortly afterwards groups of students began to come out of the building and walk towards the Earls Court Road. Sam, who had been waiting, followed one of the groups and came up beside a long-legged girl in a black leather mini-skirt who stopped in surprise at seeing him; the others walked on.

'Where have you been? Why didn't you come to the class?'

She was a Sri Lankan girl with beautiful narrow bones and a pale brown skin. She was hoping to go to Cambridge like her father and was very serious about her work.

'I was busy,' said Sam. 'They can't expect people to go to every class surely? Besides, I've got some money. I thought we ought to spend it on lunch.'

*　　*　　*

Eleanor Campion was reading about a sea battle in the Caribbean and at the same time half-listening to Choral Evensong on Radio Three. Hugh had gone out to a meeting of the West Kensington Historical Society. Eleanor thought he should not have gone, because he had a slight cough; his coughs often turned to bronchitis. She sat in her straight-backed chair between the window and the mahogany standard lamp which had been in their father's study, her heavy body at rest in the reliable framework of the familiar chair. The November mist outside the window almost obscured the sycamore tree. Who did Hugh think was going to look after him if he started to run a temperature? In her irritation she could not concentrate on crashing masts and splintering bulwarks; they mingled in her mind with psalms and thoughts of supper. She had scrubbed two large potatoes to go with the smoked haddock she was going to cook. The potatoes had to go into the oven before she started cooking the haddock; she wanted to put them in at half-past six and was afraid of forgetting. Her memory, which had always been good, had recently become capricious, bringing very clearly before her her mother's deathbed fifty years ago in the Somerset Vicarage and allowing her to forget things like potatoes and the name of the harmless man with whiskers who had been on her committee for the unmarried mothers' homes for at least five years. She thought often of her mother's death, but perhaps she had always done so. It had been long drawn out; she had had bone cancer and it had taken her two years to die. Eleanor's father the Vicar had allowed no one to mention the possibility of death. Eleanor had thought then as she did now that this had trapped them all in a parade of falsity; she believed in things being named. The psalm had given way to a sermon. Eleanor reached out to turn off the wireless; she did not expect a sermon with Choral Evensong. The wireless was out of her reach and the effort of getting to her feet was momentarily beyond her. 'To know as we are known,' the man was saying. Eleanor thought of her mother, whom she had never tremendously liked and about whom she consequently felt a slight but permanent guilt. Eleanor had stayed at home and seen her to her death without complaining, but she had been a critical and often brusque daughter, perhaps just for that reason, that she was the daughter, and not one of the sons. 'The boys', Mrs Campion called them. The boys would have liked this, the boys would have laughed at that, the boys would never have allowed their father to refuse to get another doctor when anyone could see this one was no good. The boys were Frederick and Leonard, who were dead, never Neil who was in

Africa or Sam the amiable young schoolmaster, so affectionate and so scorned. For she was a woman of steel, Mrs Campion. Her upright but ineffectual husband the Vicar feared and obeyed her; the boys had done the same. Neil, though never rebellious, had been elusive; what was worse in her eyes, he had been less of a success. Even his undoubted courage in the War had not quite satisfied his mother; the Royal Flying Corps was somehow too irregular. The boys had been in good regiments; what was more, they had been killed. Once when Neil was at school Eleanor had said of some recently reported exam success, 'How clever of Neil,' and her mother had said, 'What's cleverness if you can't get into the First Eleven? It's no use making faces, dear. He won't get into the First Eleven in life, you wait and see.'

Eleanor stirred in her chair, overcome by exasperation at the thought of her mother. The exasperation was followed by guilt, equally familiar. Those two years of agony and bitterness and on her own part lack of love would always be at the back of her mind, to be involuntarily recalled by so many small habitual acts, the pouring of a cup of tea, the opening of a medicine cupboard, some chance arrangement of objects on a bedside table. Eleanor turned back to her book, to the grappling irons and the shouts of the triumphant British seamen as they boarded the French frigate. The voice on the wireless said, 'To know the world as God knows it, we should have to be outside the space-time continuum.' Which would mean no more pain, Eleanor thought, not just from one's aching limbs but from the past. And then the telephone rang and she had to heave herself out of her chair and cross the room to the desk, pausing momentarily on the way to turn off the wireless.

'Eleanor?' Effie's sharp voice. 'Potty asked me to let you know. He's fixed everything. I knew he would. He's seen Catherine Hillery and told her she's barking up the wrong tree and she was perfectly reasonable as I knew she would be and everything's all right. We're in the clear.'

On the way back to her chair Eleanor turned the wireless on again. The sermon was over and they were singing one of the hymns most favoured by her father for Evensong, 'The day thou gavest Lord is ended'. She lowered herself into her chair. It was nearly dark. She ought to draw the curtains. But the mist seemed to have cleared; perhaps they were due for the first frost. She could see the leaves of the sycamore tree in the light from her own window. In the clear, she thought, like being outside the space-time continuum, which made everything unclear, everything a mist of past and present and things not meant, not understood. But she could not even imagine having no past. She was not just an old woman in a chair, now, this November evening, looking out of the window at the sycamore tree, her large face so deeply furrowed with wrinkles that it looked as though it needed washing, though she scrubbed it every day with a soapy flannel. She was also the plain capable resentful daughter who had watched her mother die, and the stolid child standing on the willow branch below the brother who from the top of the tree proclaimed his Kingship. She was the royal sister; they were sailing on the willow tree across the flat water meadows where a battle had been fought three hundred years ago. Three hundred years ago Monmouth's men had scattered in the marshes to be hunted by King James's soldiers and brought to brutal justice in the Bloody Assize of Judge Jeffreys; but that was all going to be reversed. King Monmouth had come again. All one summer they had been Monmouth and his faithful sister, the latter not known to history. Had he been nine, she six? Something like that; and they were setting England free from the yoke of the tyrant, Neil had said, and England had been the water meadows and the solitary men they saw from time to time there, calling up the cattle or clearing the ditches, and the woman in the sweet shop and the milkman with his fat horse and Mrs Fox Farmiloe saying to her daughter who was their friend, 'How can you go out like that, Margaret? What would the village think?' What would the village think, about Neil, about Potty, about barking up the wrong tree? Effie thought herself in the clear, dislikable, self-deceiving Effie. But Eleanor did not like deception, she did not like deception of any kind. Did she perhaps want Effie to suffer as she suffered, from a sense of having been betrayed? Was it for that reason she now contemplated some kind of betrayal of her own? Or was it because all her life she had been against mystification, in favour of naming things? She had her steeliness also, she was her mother's daughter. She had her fixed points, though they were not the same as her mother's. As to whether what she did now she did because she was a woman of principle or as some kind of revenge against the wife she felt had taken her favourite brother from her she could not have told. She heaved herself out of her chair again, and went back to the desk. Sitting down in front of it she reached for a piece of writing paper and began a letter to Catherine Hillery.

*   *   *

Vercingetorix the mad axeman had split the beautiful Belladonna in two as she lay in her bed; she had seen him coming but had been unable to make up her mind which side of the bed to get out of in order to run away. There were several descriptions of Belladonna earlier in Madden's novel; she lay in bed and looked at her dresses, which hung on a rail at the bottom of her bed; beside her, neatly laid out on a table, were her underclothes, of softest silk and lace. She never got up because she could never decide what to wear. Madden had lovingly and minutely described most of Etta's clothes, also her hair, her eyes, and her beautiful long neck. The morning after the axeman's attack he felt bereft, but told himself he felt free; he had come to believe that Etta would never leave Nicholas. He despatched a good deal of business on the telephone, was brisk, uncompromising, he hoped detestable, drinking coffee, smoking, talking on both lines (his newspaper paid his telephone bills), before he went out into the cold damp morning and walked towards the Underground with the intention of going to his office. He heard Etta calling him, turned to see her running after him, hair, coat, scarf, all flying in the misty now awakened air, but no, he thought, why should she say she has left him and come to me, why should that be given to me now, who has done nothing to deserve it?

'She knows,' she said urgently, when she was near enough to speak.

'Who? Who knows?'

'Catherine. She knows about the paper you put in the book.'

She stopped, breathless, leaning on his arm.

'I was coming to tell you. I went to take her a book, a catalogue for an exhibition I'd told her about. She goes to those things. It was so expensive, ten pounds, there was no point in her getting another. I went in and there was a boy there, very handsome. He said he'd seen us.'

'What boy? Where had he seen us?'

'There, at the school, in the pub. He was called Campion. She introduced us and he said, oh yes, I've seen you, very intensely, you know. I've seen you, in the pub, you were with a dark-haired man and we were the only people in the pub. What could I say? I said oh yes, of course, a friend, how clever of you, and I tried to change the subject, but of course Catherine was surprised I'd been there and asked about it and I couldn't think what to say. She suddenly said, you weren't with Madden, were you? What could I say? I said you had had something to do down there, I didn't know what, but of course I looked so guilty because I did know what, though I didn't then, so it was true at the time. I know she knows, she didn't say so but she's sure to have guessed. What could I do?'

'Nothing. We'll go there now. We were going to tell her anyway.'

'I have my car. It's outside your house.'

He sat beside her in silence as she drove, wondering why she was coming with him, why she had not dissociated herself, gone home, after her warning. By coming with him she was bringing into the open something that Catherine presumably either did not know or only suspected, her daughter-in-law's relationship with someone other than her son. It was unlike Etta, whose nature was so secretive.

He said, 'Don't look so worried.'

'She will be angry with you. She will think you have cheated her. She was angry with Nicholas when he did some dishonesties though he was her son, she is still in a way angry with him, she is like that.'

'People have been angry with me before. I've survived.'

She glanced at him, her expression fierce.

'She told me she liked you.'

He was silent, looking away from her, out of the window at the traffic. She was behaving in a way counter to her nature for his sake, to try to save Catherine's good opinion of him; all his hopes revived.

Catherine, opening her door to them, looked surprised and a little distant. When she led them into her sitting-room it was clear that she had been working at her desk; she had pushed back the chair when she went to answer the front-door bell but her notebook was open, her pen and reading glasses laid down beside it. The day was so dull that she had turned on the lamp on the desk. The quiet room full of books, and the light thrown onto the desk laid out with writing materials, filled Madden with nostalgia for the writer's life he was probably unlikely ever to achieve.

'I have to tell you that the list in the book of war poetry may not have been genuine,' he said.

'No. But it doesn't make much difference. I have had a letter from Eleanor Campion asking me to go and see her. Effie Campion is also going to be there. I think I shall probably get what I want, whatever that is.'

'Ah.'

'People are so possessive about their theories.' She had sat down in an armchair and now indicated by a gesture that Madden and Etta should do the same. 'As bad as scientists. Forging evidence about toads.'

'I was afraid you hadn't noticed that was what they were. Toads, I mean.'

'I don't know what they were,' said Catherine. 'Etta, what did you think of that boy who was here?'

Whether she was really more interested in Etta's opinion of the boy than in hearing his confession Madden did not know, but he recognised her right to be dismissive. He looked across at Etta, tense on the edge of her chair.

She answered Catherine cautiously. 'The boy? Oh. He seemed nice.'

'He's the grandson of Neil Campion. His parents were killed in an aeroplane crash some time ago. His grandmother has brought him up and he's just been expelled from that school. Well, you saw him in the pub. Of course he shouldn't have been there. The trouble is the grandmother can't cope with him in her smart little flat in Mayfair. He doesn't fit into her life at all. She went away for the weekend and he had a lot of people there and they left a terrible mess. You can imagine. Cigarette ends, broken glasses, bottles everywhere, it's not at all what she's used to. The cleaner threatened to give notice, all that. And then it turned out he's lost a lot of money by somehow or other finding a gambling club instead of going to his tutorial classes. He came to ask me to intercede with her, of all things. She's threatened to throw him out without any money. He thinks I should tell her that everyone's like that at his age. But of course they're not.'

'He looked so calm. Very calm, very well-behaved.'

'He has no sense, I suppose. No sense of survival, I some-times think. It flatters me that he trusts me, that's the trouble. I don't want to do something stupid. I have a room here, you see, that basement sitting room which both the boys had, one after the other. I suppose I could let him have that. But I don't want him to cause chaos. What should I do, do you think?'

'Could he be independent here? If he is not noisy you needn't know what he does. Is there a basement door?'

'Oh yes, he could have his own entrance.'

Madden watched their discussion in surprise; it was not at all what he had come for.

'I suppose I had better go,' he said eventually.

Catherine stood up at once and went towards the door to let him out. He looked at Etta. She shook her head, without smiling. As he went out he asked Catherine humbly if she would let him know the outcome of her meeting with Eleanor and Effie.

'I don't know. Perhaps.'

She seemed not so much angry as indifferent. He walked out into all the old afflictions.

*   *   *

As she turned the corner into the main road Catherine saw Effie's BMW draw up abruptly on the double yellow lines in front of the entrance to the block of flats where Eleanor and Hugh Campion lived. Catherine quickened her pace, prepared to offer to repark the car; it had been clamped more than once recently, each time to its owner's astonishment and fury. Perhaps Effie remembered this herself, for the car suddenly restarted and swung out into the traffic. By the time Catherine reached the entrance Effie was hurrying in her high heels down the pavement towards her, having presumably found a side-street in which to park. Catherine waited on the doorstep, noticing as she approached that Effie was wearing one of her smartest outfits, a bright red coat and skirt, adorned with her best diamond clips, and a small black fur hat. Her face was so perfectly made up that Catherine wondered if it had been done professionally; it seemed to lack the element of overstatement so often evident in Effie's own handiwork, presenting instead an enamelled surface so worked upon by delicate and softening brushwork as to approach the condition of a perfectly preserved Elizabethan miniature. The eyes gazed out of the mask as if there were an old Chinaman somewhere behind it.

Catherine complimented her on her appearance, knowing that this always gave pleasure. Effie nodded briskly. 'All the warpaint. I don't know what this is about and I don't like the sound of it. I tried to get out of coming but the creature insisted.'

She led the way into the building but had obviously no idea where to go once inside. Catherine guided her to the lift and along the dark passage to the door of the flat.

'What a ghastly place,' said Effie just as Eleanor opened the door.

Hugh appeared from his bedroom, shuffling about anxiously, trying to take coats and making too many people in the tiny entrance hall. Eleanor led the way into the sitting-room, asked them all to sit down and said heavily that she was glad they had come.

Hugh fussed. 'Will you be comfortable there? A cushion for you, Effie? So nice. Is it too early for a glass of sherry? A glass of sherry, Eleanor, don't you think? Later then. Later perhaps. Yes, I'll sit down.'

'I have a letter to read you,' said Eleanor. She sat at her desk, the chair half-turned towards the room so that she faced her audience. She put on her glasses and held the letter in both her hands; they were quite steady. 'The letter is addressed to me. It is dated May 9th, 1941.'

'I don't want to hear it,' said Effie sharply. 'I've heard quite enough about this wretched letter. I don't think it's of the slightest importance and I don't want to hear it. If it had been of any importance at all he'd have written it to me.'

'He explains in the letter why he didn't,' said Eleanor calmly.

'I shan't listen to a word of it. I shall simply sit here with my hands over my ears. Have you told Potty what you're doing?'

'I have decided his advice was wrong.'

Effie gave a little jump of annoyance in her chair, then ostentatiously clapped her hands over her ears. She held them there all the time that Eleanor was reading, gradually leaning back until her head was supported by the cushion behind her.

'It is dated May 9th, 1941,' said Eleanor again. 'It begins, dear Eleanor.' She read in a calm slow voice, almost devoid of expression. 'Dear Eleanor, I am setting off on a journey and I am writing to you before I go in case it does not end as I mean that it should. I have something to ask you to do for me, and something to explain to you. If I die, I should like you to see that my son Hector is educated at the Durdans. Effie has supported me over the school as she has over everything else but she does not feel about it as I do and she might be tempted to send Hector to Eton where her brothers went. I do not want him turned into a conventional Englishman. Conventional Englishmen have led this country into decline. It is because I believe all our policies since the end of the Victorian age have been mistaken that I am setting off tonight on what may well be a wild goose chase. Yes, I set it as far back as that – 1904 – the Entente Cordiale – that fat ass Edward VII thinking he was being a great statesman. But Germany is our natural ally in Europe, not France. Oh, but the Nazis, you say in your patriotic way, we are fighting the Nazis, the Nazis can't possibly be a good thing. The Nazis are not a good thing. But that does not mean Germany is not a good thing. If the Germans could get rid of Hitler . . . Now, I am setting off very early tomorrow to meet a friend of mine called Peter Heinrich, with whom I have kept in contact ever since the War began. I won't bore you with the various schemes and possibilities we have discussed. What has happened now is that I have had an urgent message from him to say that one of the Nazi leaders, possibly under orders but more probably not, is flying to Scotland tomorrow. Peter has only just discovered this plan and has had to move fast. He is being landed by submarine on the east coast of Scotland. I am to meet him. We are to follow Hess's moves (it is Rudolf Hess, the Deputy Führer) without disclosing ourselves and if there is any sign of his being successful in getting talks going with anyone in authority we will support him, openly or covertly depending on the course of events. The most likely thing seems to be that Hess will get only so far and no further in his attempts to negotiate. At that point we should declare ourselves and try to rally support for a pact. There might be German military landings in the south at the same time. I have said that I would be prepared to lead an alternative British Government. Peter and his associates think they can more easily depose Hitler once the war is over. You will say I am being foolhardy. One must take risks for things one believes in. You may say, how could I have gone on being a Government Minister, thinking as I do? But I have done my job efficiently. And as a Minister one has useful contacts. You may say, have I been fair to my colleagues? As I said just now, I believe all the Governments of the last fifty years have been leading us in the wrong direction. As to being fair to them, to our Governments, to our ruling classes, to . . . Eleanor, how fair have they been to me? How did they welcome me, when I appeared, so hopeful, wanting to be one of them? Do you remember how Mrs Fox Farmiloe despised us because our mother said pardon? Perhaps you never knew how the boys at school laughed at me because we were poor. When I was still only a child they sent me to fight in a filthy war, and I gave it all my heart and soul. What loyalty do I owe to the people who killed my only true friend? You don't know how boys of eighteen love each other. I don't mean sex though indeed at times I've wished we could have been as close even as that. Oliver Brooks was a perfect friend, a perfect young man. He was tired. He asked for leave. And they said no. After all he had done, all the plain heroism no one could deny (and they didn't deny it, they loaded him with medals) after all that, when he asked for a rest – a few days, a week – they said no. They sent him back to die. Don't talk to me of loyalty. I tell you I hugged to myself my feeling of being an outsider. Always. But I wanted them to acknowledge me. That's why I came back from Africa. And now they will. Or else I will fail completely. If I am honest I must say I think the latter's more likely. But such a failure has its own sort of grandeur – I mean *such* a failure . . . and I shan't have let down Peter, my good friend who was once my enemy. He sent me a book of poetry once in which he'd written something from the *Morte d'Arthur.* "Oh Balan my brother I have killed thee, and thou me, Therefore the wide world shall speak of us both." Dear old Eleanor, I wish you were coming with me.' Eleanor put the letter down on her desk, carefully. She took off her glasses and placed them beside the letter, moving them slightly so that they were precisely aligned. Then she turned back towards the room and sat expressionless, looking towards the window, meeting no one's eye. Hugh cleared his throat, looked apprehensively at Eleanor, and then down at his own clasped hands; he did not move. Effie was still leaning back against the cushions, her hands over her ears and her elbows forward; her eyes were tightly shut and her whole face was screwed up with the effort to keep them so; in spite of the make-up she looked like a tiny furious monkey. Catherine, who was in a state of some excitement, was the first to speak.

'Exactly. It's exactly what I thought. I mean I had no idea of the details but I was beginning to get the character. Effie do listen, the letter's finished now.'

Effie opened her eyes. 'What's that? Is someone else talking? I'm not listening, mind.'

'The letter's finished,' said Catherine.

Effie took her hands away from her ears.

'I didn't hear a thing. Not a thing. But if it's over I can go now.' She gathered up her bag and gloves and stood up.

Pausing only to say, almost jauntily, 'Goodbye, Eleanor,' she made briskly for the door, without another glance at Catherine.

Struggling to his feet as if through some invisible encumbrance, Hugh followed her. 'So sorry. Dreadful thing. No time for a glass of sherry? Another time. So sorry.'

Eleanor picked up the letter from the desk and held it out to Catherine who did not move.

'Take it.'

Catherine took it. 'I feel . . . for some reason I feel I ought to tell you that we have met before, a long time ago. I was a VAD in the War. I worked in your convalescent home and you sacked me because I was in love with one of the patients. I didn't behave very well.'

Eleanor's eyes opened to their fullest extent, exposing Catherine to the fierce blue stare she so well remembered. Then the lids were lowered again, the gaze veiled.

'Even you were concealing something,' Eleanor said. She looked extraordinarily tired.

'I'll go now,' said Catherine. 'Perhaps we can talk later.'

On her way out Catherine met Hugh, shuffling along the passage still faintly murmuring, 'So sorry. Another time. Sorry.'

She took his hand and said, 'It was all a long time ago. It doesn't really matter now.'

'It matters to us,' he said.

*　　*　　*

Catherine's daughter-in-law Susannah had not been long in the room (it was Catherine's sitting-room; Susannah had telephoned to say she happened to be in London and would like to look in) before Catherine understood that she had come for no less portentous a purpose than to fight for her children's rights. Not being very cunning, Susannah had broached the subject of Catherine's plan to let her basement room to Sam

Campion, which plan Susannah had heard about from her sister-in-law Etta, almost as soon as she arrived; and, not being very subtle either, she had let it be seen by Catherine, to whom the idea had come as a complete surprise, that this could conceivably in the distant future constitute a threat to her children's inheritance.

'I mean of course I think it's a wonderful idea your taking on someone to look after, goodness knows I understand how empty your life must be, I just dread getting to that stage myself, the children grown up and Tom – I mean statistically an awful lot more women are left widows than the other way round, aren't they? I mean I think you're just wonderful the way you cope, we all do. But one has to think of one's own and of course Tom would never do a thing, you know what he's like.'

'Never do a thing about what, Susannah?'

'You know what London property is. It's so expensive in this area now, we could never think of getting anything for the children round here. But of course the time will come, it's bound to, when they'll want somewhere in London. I mean everyone does at some stage. Even if they go to University somewhere else they're most likely to start work in London. Most people do, don't they?'

'But, Susannah, by the time Mark and Annabel are old enough to want to live in London Sam will have left long ago. So will I probably. I might have gone to live in a cottage in the country. Or be dead even.'

'Yes. Well.' She was trying to push some of the wisps of hair back into the soft untidy topknot. With her long black skirt and multi-coloured jacket she looked more like the art student she had been when Tom had met her, less like the suburban housewife Catherine unfairly considered her to have become. The usual smile was in place but it seemed now to express, rather than compassion, guilt.

'You mean you're thinking of the children having the house when I'm dead?' said Catherine, seeking elucidation.

'You make it sound so awful.' For once the smile disappeared completely, to be replaced by a look of desperate sincerity. 'It's not that I'm looking forward to it, if you see what I mean. But Etta said you were going to adopt this boy. I mean I wouldn't have worried if she hadn't said adopt. So I thought legally you know you might want to make him your heir. She said he was very fascinating. A strange fascination, she said.'

'Oh dear, did she? I expect it's just that he's rather good-looking. Etta likes people to be good-looking.'

Susannah looked merely bewildered.

'He had a grandfather,' continued Catherine more slowly. 'Who did have some kind of fascination. Although he wasn't at all the same sort of person as Sam, he had two other character-istics which I suspect Sam also has, a vast unfocussed ambition and a hopelessly undisciplined ultra-romanticism. And Sam hasn't even any kind of education to help him to control these things.'

'Will you educate him?'

'I'd rather someone else did. But I don't mind giving him shelter while they do.'

'And you are not going to adopt him?'

'Of course not. That's Etta's English. I'm simply thinking of letting him a room for a month or two.'

The compassionate smile was back. 'I don't think Etta is very happy. She hasn't said anything but I think there are problems.'

Catherine waved a hand dismissively. 'I don't want to know any more than I already suspect. If Etta has decided not to decide no one will shake her. She's a very obstinate girl, though I like her extremely. Don't worry. I have no intention of going mad in my old age and I have all the proper feelings for my grandchildren.

'They are so fond of you,' said Susannah anxiously.

'Perhaps they might come and stay with me on their own sometimes,' suggested Catherine, pushing home an advantage. 'I'd vaguely thought of taking a cottage by the sea next summer, with my sister. They might enjoy that.'

'Oh yes, I know they would. It wouldn't be near cliffs, would it?'

'More like marshes. My sister likes watching birds. There might be quicksand of course.'

'I know you're teasing. Tom could come and fetch them and perhaps stay a little. He loves that sort of thing. He often talks about holidays you had when he was a child. He said that was what was so sad about the time before anyone knew his father was so ill, when he became so difficult. It changed him so much, Tom said.'

'Did Tom say that? That Bernard became so difficult?'

'It was blood pressure, wasn't it? People always get like that. It must have been terrible for you.'

Shying quickly away from Susannah's compassion, which was back in full possession and which Catherine was so used to finding irritating that she was not prepared to accept it even when she might have been able to see it as appropriate, Catherine asked for the dates of the children's summer holidays, and wrote them down in her diary, and with talk of plans and possibilities and due expressions of grandmotherly concern despatched Susannah, reassured, in the direction of Peter Jones to start her Christmas shopping in what seemed to Catherine quite unnecessarily good time.

When she had gone Catherine went back into her sitting-room, intending to sit down at her desk, but seeing the circle of light and the open notebook realised at once that Susannah's visit had left her too restless to concentrate. Instead she returned to the hall, put on some boots and a mackintosh and went out of the house. Her country childhood had left her with the habit of going for regular walks, a habit she had never lost. Sometimes she walked as far as Hyde Park, but since that was some distance away she often walked instead quite slowly through the streets and squares of Chelsea and South Kensington, pausing at a churchyard or to watch the leaves being swept from under the trees in the gardens of some quiet square.

Sometimes such a walk tired her physically without changing a mood of which she had hoped to rid herself, sometimes it took her through a steady progress towards some kind of sought-for resolution, sometimes it bored her. She had had in this familiar though variable townscape as many moments of unexpected vision as might have been looked for in more recognisably picturesque surroundings. Sunlight on rain-wet pavements, a figure seen through trees walking up steps into a white house across a square, patterns of branches against a sky yellow with winter evening, could strike home like memories; at other times they seemed to hold a brightness of expectation unjustifiable by reason but demanding acceptance rather than question. The world into which she walked was one she had made hers, its streets and squares to some extent streets and squares of her mind, like the landscapes of recurring dreams. Walking in this world she walked at the same time through her own consciousness, the movement around her seeming to make more natural, and less nervous, the movement of her own thoughts.

She was not as dispassionate about Sam's taking up residence in her basement room as she had pretended to Susannah, nor had she taken as calmly as she had seemed to the report of Tom's remarks about Bernard's illness. Sam had a quality she put down as dangerous; there was something about him which made other people feel involved in his destiny. It was a kind of hinted-at significance, as if he were a poem waiting to be written. Aware of its influence on herself, Catherine was even more afraid of the effect of this quality on others; Sam was ripe for exploitation. On the other hand what right had she herself to claim to know what was best for him? She would keep her distance, of course, encourage him to find his influences elsewhere. The trouble was there was so much she wanted to tell him.

It was quite possible, she thought, rounding a corner into Onslow Square, that she was becoming too certain of what it was she wanted to tell people. Earlier in her life she had been less sure. On the other hand and if it was the guidance of the young she was thinking of, no one could say she had done particularly well with poor Nicholas. But she smiled and shook her head, walking briskly along the pavement, attracting a surprised stare from the old man in blue dungarees who was slowly sweeping leaves out of the gutter; there were so many mistakes one could make. Thinking of Nicholas as for ever 'poor Nicholas' was probably one of them; another would be to hope she could redeem her errors in that direction by her wiser behaviour with Sam. That was a thought she had better put out of her mind straightaway. Should she perhaps re-tell herself the story of that part of her life which was most closely involved with Nicholas, allowing herself to come out of the story with more credit, or at any rate less shame? Lives were stories; there was no way out of that. Time and the innate human need to give shape to things, to select so as to find order, meant that any life was just a story, one's own or anyone else's. Like all stories, the story of a life could only be an approximation to the truth, or perhaps a parallel. The story she told herself about her life was among other things the story of a long and happy marriage; she had thought it was going to be necessary to readjust it – indeed, in her mind, she had already done so – and now Tom, kind and useful as ever, though this time unwittingly, had given her back the original version, or something like it. For of course if Bernard had been so changed simply by illness, that explained those last bad years. It was stupid of her not to have noticed for herself, but she had always been stupid about illness, having no sympathy for it. The story could not be quite the same as it had been once, for the bad time was still there, but by being made explicable it had become also acceptable. The fact that one had acknowledged that life stories were no more than approximations to true stories did not mean that one should stop testing them against such discoverable truths as one could lay one's hands on. For if everyone was to be thought of as more or less an artist by virtue of the construction of these long and sometimes touching tales, redemption for the transient seemed to Catherine, if there were such a thing, to be not so much in the art as in the continuity of the effort to understand. Of course the end of the story about Neil Campion cast its light backwards over all the rest of his life, that being a story that had ended and could therefore be seen as a whole. The approximation to the truth about Campion which she now felt able to make might well be tested by some fact of which she was ignorant or some different view of the facts which someone else might have, but her conception of him was, to her way of thinking, coherent. She no longer sought to be definitive, any more than she did about herself. She paused on the patch of rough grass in front of the abandoned church of St Paul Onslow Square and said aloud 'Most people are wrong about most things most of the time.'

Why that conclusion should make her feel so cheerful she could not imagine, but she continued her walk, trying as she went to make her interior monologue into a dialogue, imagining an interlocutor, Bernard perhaps, although she never did have that sort of conversation with Bernard. What was the point of bothering about anything then, he seemed to say, in the face of all this wrongness. Her answer was that the possibility of being right, even if only for a moment, was always there; it was a question of seeing things in the right light. What light then, he asked, filling his pipe in that way he had. But she could not say. It was something that had always been known, had been called – well – all sorts of different names. But the thought was already slipping away from her. She only knew there was something in it, and that whatever it was it would be a long time, years perhaps, before that foolish Sam had any idea of it.

She paused to look down the length of the square garden, its trees touched with yellow November sunlight and its grass patterned with shadows which were already the long shadows of winter. If one found oneself inclined to look on life as being reasonably pleasant it was probably better not to look for particular causes.

There remained the question of what to do about the book.

*   *   *

Sam found it difficult to sit in a chair; he said it gave him a pain in his knees. When he was alone or with people of his own age he nearly always lay on his back on the floor. In public places where this was not possible he would stand up, or walk up and down, or perch on the edge of a table. Where this was inconvenient, which it often was, he would respond politely to requests to sit down but even then would sprawl across a table or tip his chair so far backwards as sometimes to fall over. When Catherine began to tell him the story of his grandfather and of her commission to write the biography, and the whole sequence of events which had followed it, he sat at first attentively on the edge of an armchair, both hands cupped round the mug of instant coffee he had made himself when she had told him she had a long story to tell him; but he soon put the mug down on the floor and lowered himself to sit beside it, leaning against the chair, which then slid backwards until it rested against the wall. He picked up his mug and followed the chair, pushing himself backwards on his bottom and spilling a little of the coffee on the rug, which he then rubbed ineffectually with his foot. Catherine did not notice; she was launched on her story and anxious to keep to her resolve to lay before him all the facts.

Sam had been made uneasy by the move to Catherine's basement room. He understood, indeed sympathised with, his grandmother's anger over the chaos he had wrought in her flat and in his own finances; he recognised that the move offered a solution to the problem which always arose after some error of his own had led to a justifiable expression of outrage on her part, the problem of how to signalise forgiveness and a new start. Obviously one had to hope for these things if for no other reason than that life had to go on, but the difficulty was in combining due acknowledgement of the seriousness of the offence with an excuse for Sam to move on from an attitude of apology which was neither dignified nor long sustainable. The decision having been made, Effie had been helpful. 'Take anything you like,' she had said, waving her hand to indicate that the entire contents of the flat were at his disposal. 'It's only a bare little basement. You need to make something of it.'

But the things in the flat had their places in the flat. It was enough that he was being thrown out; it was too much that he was required also to change the familiar framework of things as they were. This slightly panicky conservatism could co-exist in his mind with his picture of himself as a footloose adventurer acknowledging no limits and no rules, but it was not a comfortable co-existence. He took some cushions and his favourite mug. After his first night in the new room, he moved the mattress of his bed onto the floor, re-arranged the lighting and wired up his record player and speakers. His understanding of electricity was intuitive; he fused the lights twice but mended them without Catherine's having been aware of the event. In the murky light of red and green bulbs, and with a background of a solid rock beat, panic subsided, to be succeeded by something closer to euphoria. He wrote to his friends, the twins Pat and Prue, asking them to come and stay whenever they liked. They were leaving the Durdans at the end of term; they had persuaded their parents to send them to a comprehensive school in Bristol, where they lived. 'I'm sure it will be all right for you to come here,' he wrote optimistically. 'I'm going to do all my own cooking.'

Upstairs, reasonable and alert, Sam listened to Catherine's story; it surprised and interested him. When she had finished it, Catherine said, 'Now about the book. I am supposed to deliver it before very long and there's no doubt Brackenbury will be pleased with the story. I don't suppose he had any idea it was going to be so sensational. Because I think it will be sensational. I can imagine journalists having a fine time digging around for traitors among the whole Establishment of the time. I don't myself think they'll find any, but I'm sure they'll have a try. I'm absolutely against hushing things up. I've always thought everything in every way ought to be brought out and submitted to the light of reasonable enquiry. It's an article of faith if you like. It goes with believing in trusting ordinary people. But there's another thing. Are you listening, Sam?'

From seeming so attentive Sam was now smiling dreamily, his thoughts evidently elsewhere.

'I could have been King,' he said.

'What can you be talking about?'

'If he'd succeeded. I'd have been his heir.'

'He was hardly likely to have been made King. Whatever had happened he was far more likely to have been shot, by one side or the other. Probably both. It was a tremendous miscalculation of everything and everyone involved.'

'What makes you think he wasn't? Shot, I mean. Disposed of.'

'What do you mean?'

'Your friend Major Hall,' said Sam, animated. 'What makes you think the car crash wasn't arranged? You can't believe what they say, you know. Were there any witnesses?'

'Not that I know of.'

'I think we should find out. Where did he last fill up with petrol? Oh yes, I think we should investigate further. Why do you think those files are still closed? Oh yes.'

'Do stop saying oh yes. I don't know. I can't take in any more mysteries. I want you to tell me what to do about this book. You should decide. It's your family. If it comes out it's going to cause a great deal of distress to your grandmother and to Eleanor and Sam Campion. If it doesn't come out we shall have connived at a concealment, which I don't like. We shall also, to be practical, have failed to fulfil the contract for the book, so I suppose I'd have to pay back the advance. Whereas if it's published it might make some money. I've even thought that because it's your family perhaps you ought to have some of the money.'

Sam smiled brilliantly, all his so often wandering understanding focused. Catherine wondered for a moment whether she had made a mistake, but he was smiling at the thought that she might think him so stupid as not to recognise a test when he saw one.

'Ah,' he said. 'But we must let the old birds fall off their perches first.'

'So Brackenbury must wait?'

'Brackenbury must wait.'

* * *

Effie had written that Mona would have the keys, and as Catherine emerged from the lift onto the warm, thickly-carpeted landing outside the flat there she was, fitting a key into a mortice lock and turning, surprised, as Catherine approached.

'Mrs Campion's expecting me,' said Catherine. 'She wrote to me and told me to come at ten because if she didn't answer the door you'd be there with the key. I don't know whether she's got flu or something?'

'She's been looking a bit peaky. But then she often does, first thing, you know.'

Mona was a pretty young woman in a sky-blue track suit. When she had unlocked the mortice, she fitted another key into the yale lock and led the way into the flat. The sitting-room door was open and sunlight filled the little entrance hall.

'I'll carry on,' said Mona, going into the kitchen. A few moments later the subdued sound of Capital Radio came from behind the kitchen door.

There was no one in the sitting-room. Catherine walked through it, calling 'Anyone in?', and knocked gently at the bedroom door. Hearing no answer, she quietly opened it. Sunlight fell through the partly-drawn curtains; there was no sound except the distant undertone of traffic. The room was tidy, only the bed-clothes disturbed. They had been so arranged as to form a sort of nest, in the midst of which, like an abandoned bird, lay Effie. Over her nightdress she wore two rows of pearls and on her bony hands a number of diamond rings; her make-up was in place, and the angle at which she lay on the pillows was only a little unnatural. Catherine, shutting the door quietly behind her and slowly approaching the bed, thought she looked as though she might have been dead a thousand years. There was an envelope propped up on the bedside table. It had Catherine's name on it, but feeling the solemnity of the occasion she did not take it, but stood in silence for some time beside the bed. At last the sound of Mona beginning to hoover in the sitting-room made her move; she picked up the letter and went towards the window.

'It seemed the best thing to do,' she read. 'Putting one's hands over one's ears doesn't keep out the sound of a voice. I got your letter saying you weren't going to publish the book but the trouble is I know. I didn't want to, which was why I wouldn't listen when they talked about it before, but after I'd heard the letter I couldn't pretend. He was thinking about all that all the time and not telling me. I suppose he thought I was too stupid. Which I am. Half the time I've no idea what's going on. But I'm not so stupid as not to know that a pact with Hitler would have been a pact with the Devil. If Peter had been going to arrange a revolution in Germany at the same time, that might have been different. But he couldn't. Peter couldn't even meet the right train, all his efficiency was a fraud, that was what was so nice about him. Neil knew that really, he must have done. So I don't know what game he was playing. Whatever it was he didn't tell me. Which cancels out everything really. The only thing I ever thought I knew was Neil. Even though I didn't understand half of what he said I thought I understood *him*. But I didn't. Which means I don't understand anything, and never did. I'm going to swallow all my sleeping pills and unless that fool of a doctor has given me the wrong ones that ought to do the trick. I hope you don't think it's a sin. I know some people do but I'm not religious myself. I used to be. I thought one should, as if God was the next one up after the Queen and rather the same sort of thing. But really the Church has become so impossible these days what with dropping the Prayer Book and being so unpleasant about women. I don't in the least want women vicars, but if we did have them they could hardly be more idiotic than men vicars and now that the subject's been raised it seems to have brought out some very unfortunate attitudes. Do you know I turned on the television the other day and there was some perfectly frightful clergyman, obviously my inferior in every possible way, telling me I was a member of the secondary sex and appointed by God to tend his needs (whatever they may be, I dread to think). And the interviewer was nodding away encouragingly all the time. I ask you. How could anyone expect me to go to Church after that? You will look after Sam far better than I can, I wouldn't dream of leaving him otherwise and I absolutely count on you to see that he understands that. It's high time I died, I'm tremendously old and quite useless. The fact that I'm doing it myself doesn't make much difference. Anyway, Catherine, you'll hush that up for me, now won't you?'